THE HISTORY OF MR. POLLY

HERBERT GEORGE WELLS
1866-1946

THE HISTORY OF
MR. POLLY

H. G. WELLS

With an Introduction by
FRANK WELLS

COLLINS
LONDON AND GLASGOW

GENERAL EDITOR: G. F. MAINE

First published, *1910*
This edition, *1953*
Reprinted, *1959*
Latest reprint, *1966*

Printed in Great Britain
COLLINS CLEAR-TYPE PRESS

HERBERT GEORGE WELLS

HERBERT GEORGE WELLS was born on 21st September 1866 at Bromley, Kent. Destined for the profession of a draper, he became instead one of the great intellectual lights of his age.

His father, Joseph Wells, kept a small hardware shop and was an enthusiastic professional cricketer. His mother, whose maiden name was Neal, had been in domestic service before her marriage. The shop in Bromley High Street never prospered; its income was barely sufficient to keep the family above the poverty line.

From his father, young Herbert George (' Bertie ' as he was called) had inherited a taste for reading which he was able to indulge freely at the local Literary Institute and lending library. He was sent to school locally, first to some cottage school and later to an establishment called Morley's Academy. In 1880, when the family found itself in great financial difficulties, Mrs. Wells was offered and accepted a post as housekeeper to her former employers at Uppark, Sussex, and Herbert George was apprenticed to a firm of drapers in Windsor. However, he did not satisfy his employers and had to leave after one month. For a very brief spell he acted as pupil teacher at a school in Somerset, and after that he was a chemist's assistant at Midhurst for one month (January 1881). In April of the same year he found himself once more a draper's apprentice, this time at Southsea. After two years in this soul-destroying occupation he could bear it no longer and left.

He next obtained a post as assistant master at Midhurst Grammar School, and in 1884 was awarded

a scholarship (of one guinea a week) at the Normal
School of Science (now the Imperial College of Science)
South Kensington, London. For three years he studied
physics, chemistry, geology, astronomy and biology—
the latter under Professor Thomas H. Huxley. On
termination of his studies he became assistant master
in a school at Holt, North Wales. There he had a
severe football accident from the effects of which he
suffered for many years. He returned to London in
July 1888, and early in 1889 joined the staff of Henley
House School at Kilburn. In October 1890 he took a
B.Sc. degree with first-class honours in zoology at
London University. His next appointment (from
1891-93) was that of a biology tutor for the University
Correspondence College.

In the summer of 1893 a serious hæmorrhage of the
lungs forced him to take a long rest and to adopt a
completely sedentary occupation. Around 1891-92 he
had contributed essays to various educational and
other journals and in 1893 while he was recuperating
from his illness he began to write short stories, essays
and reviews for periodicals and magazines, among
them *The Pall Mall Gazette*, *St. James's Gazette*, *Black
and White*, the *New Review* and *The Saturday Review*.
In 1893 his first major work *A Textbook of Biology* was
published. The year 1895 saw the publication of a
volume of short stories *The Stolen Bacillus*, a volume
of collected essays, and of two novels, *The Time
Machine* and *The Wonderful Visit*. The former established his reputation as a writer of extraordinary
power and imagination.

In 1895 also he married Miss Amy Catherine
Robbins, a former pupil of his—his first marriage
(1891) to a cousin having meanwhile been dissolved.
Two sons were subsequently born of his second
marriage (George Philip, 1901, and Frank, 1903).
The next few years brought his series of great scientific

romances: *The Island of Dr. Moreau* (1896), *The Invisible Man* (1897), *The War of the Worlds* (1898), *The First Men in the Moon* (1901) as well as many short stories, articles and novels, among them *Love and Mr. Lewisham* (1901).

In 1900 Wells built himself a house at Sandgate near Folkstone, which remained his home for nearly a decade, in the course of which he rose to a position of world-wide literary fame. There, at Sandgate, he wrote some of his most celebrated works, e.g. *Anticipations*, a volume of essays on sociological problems (1901), *The Sea Lady* (1902), *The Food of the Gods* (1904), *Kipps*, *A Modern Utopia* (both in 1905), *In the Days of the Comet* (1906), *The War in the Air* (1908), *Tono Bungay*, *Anne Veronica* (both in 1909), and *The History of Mr. Polly* (1910).

At the turn of the century, his health having greatly improved, Wells began to make frequent trips to the European Continent and in 1906 he went on his first tour to the United States. In 1903 he joined the Fabian Society, with which he remained actively (though not always harmoniously) connected for a number of years. In 1909 he moved to London, and in 1912 bought a house at Easton Park near Dunmow, Essex, which remained his home until his wife's death in 1927.

The New Machiavelli (1911) marks a new departure in Wells' creative work; the novel of ideas and of problems in which the (fictional) story becomes subordinate to the sociological and ideological message. The works *Marriage* (1912), *The Passionate Friends* (1913), *The Wife of Sir Isaac Harman* (1914), *The Research Magnificent* (1915), belong to this category.

Wells supported the first World War as the " War to end War " and in 1918 became for a short time director of Propaganda Policy against Germany on Lord Northcliffe's Enemy Propaganda Committee.

His most important work, written and published during the war was *Mr. Britling sees it Through* (1916) which achieved tremendous popularity.

Shortly after the war (1920) he visited Soviet Russia and in 1921 he attended the Washington Conference. In the years to follow he travelled much, and spent many winters away from the rigours of the English climate. Though he continued writing novels—his most important novel of the inter-war years was *The World of William Clissold* (1926)—he concentrated more and more on the propagating of ideas. The main thesis which he expounded during the last two decades of his life was that the human race must adapt itself to the material forces it has created, or perish. The three great works *Outline of History* (1920), *Science of Life* (1929), and *The Work, Wealth and Happiness of Mankind* (1932), were all designed to popularise the ideology appropriate to the task of creating a World State—in his view the only alternative to a return to barbarism and to final annihilation. In 1934 he published two volumes of autobiography, *Experiment in Living*.

The second World War was to him the confirmation that mankind had indeed lost the mastery over the forces of its own making and was heading inexorably towards doom. His last work *Mind at the End of its Tether* (1945) gave expression to his final mood of despair.

Having been ailing for some considerable time, he died in his London home on 13th August 1946.

H. d. R.

INTRODUCTION

REACHING the age of forty is a natural process that causes us much mental pain and gives us the opportunity to disturb our minds. Forty seems to be the ridge; behind us is prehistory and youth; before us is nothing but old age and death. This thought, which should have, in fact, no particular attachment to forty any more than to any other moment of our lives, is nevertheless a fortyish thought and it disturbs many of us sufficiently to make us review what we imagine to be our past lives and decide what we will do with the rest. Few of us, having made a decision, act upon it and forty passes by as forgotten as New Year's days and other feasts of momentary promises; nevertheless, having done nothing, we never deny that life begins at forty.

There are many characters that men would like to be, and they have from time to time been Tarzan, Len Hutton, Peary and the man in the Big Top with a blonde in his teeth. Women too could wish-imagine themselves as Mata-Hari, Eileen Joyce, Florence Nightingale and the blonde in the teeth of the man in the Big Top. We have some envy of such characters and would like occasionally to have been them, or our personal selection of things like them; so too as we look forward with trepidation to forty we envy and hope to be one of those people who do something about it, or as we look back on forty with some wonder, we can still envy those that did.

So it is that we find Alfred Polly to be a man of our own hearts, even though we would not, in similar circumstances, have made the same decisions. He is a real person, although his author rated him less highly. H. G. had, in his own words, " to admit that the larger part of my fiction was written lightly and with a certain haste. Only one or two of my novels deal primarily with personality. . . ." He classified Mr. Polly as a caricature-individuality, that he doubted could have the vitality to endure into new social phases.

The History of Mr. Polly was published in 1910 and the social phase of that time is past. Alfred Polly still lives and is understood because he is primarily a personality that will exist everywhere in any social phase. He is the man who reaches early middle age and wonders how it is that he has come to his present destination, apparently a long unending terminus. He is a universal forty. To him his life has been a long grey passage with only occasionally a window looking out to a bright escape, such a window as he looked through and saw himself and Christabel, a window that, like others, was suddenly shut.

All the time, as we watch him we laugh at him, without cruelty because there is enough of Polly in us to be laughing at ourselves. There is enough of H. G. in Polly to excuse the writer for making us laugh. The reader may ask how much? How much of Polly and Kipps, of Trafford, Benham, Hoopdriver, Gemini and Theodore Bulpington is autobiographically himself? It is a question to all writers and all writers to themselves: how much identity is there between a man and his creature or is the character just John Smith No. 618?

When H. G. Wells submitted his thesis, that gained for him the D.Sc., he argued that each person, each " I," is an illusion made up of innumerable individual systems. There is no consolidated John Smith, there are a great many variations of the theme recognized as John Smith; sometimes one dominates the body, sometimes another, and all these John Smiths have one thing in common and that is their belief that they are John Smith. We say that an author is able to identify himself closely with the character he has created; it may be that no such thing occurs but that author No. 247 is the character. The fallacy in the argument and in the thesis itself, is in its infinite divisibility. It is nevertheless inescapable that, in plain language, there is much of Polly in H. G., and much of H. G., in Polly. There is also much of Polly in all men, because they too must, at some age or other, be forty; and the story, for all its stormy passage through the forties, like so many similar journeys, starts with indigestion and ends with ". . . not so much thinking, as lost in a smooth, still quiet of the mind."

That passing phase of discontent, anxiety and the realisation that youth is spent and cannot be regained, will continue to occur to human beings sometime, for scientists can never make us mortally immortal. For as long as that is so, Polly will be understood and loved, and people will be glad for him, and for themselves, that the phase is followed by contentment and tranquility.

This book was first published when its author was forty-four, so that, while his observation of the social scene in which Mr. Polly played his part was a matter of memory, his observation of the state of mind was fresh and it is, I think, for this reason that the state of mind is more real in the novel than are the characters themselves. They are all comedians, playing light-heartedly, with no tragedy in death or desertion, but only in the single struggle of one man trying to under-stand his own mind. At the time that this novel was published, novels were preferred to be without depth, " to illuminate life but not to penetrate it," while the author himself was passing through a phase of change and his novels were becoming more critical, more of ideas and less of character and events. This one with two other " character-caricature " novels can be taken to illustrate this transition. *Kipps* (1905) is a novel entirely of situation. We never see into the soul of Kipps; he is a character out of place, bounced like a ball by the events that made up his life. *Polly* (1910) lets us into a mind, the events and the comedy are very like those in *Kipps*, but at times, Polly reasons; he is puzzled because he is a philosopher, he criticises his own actions and is the master of his own soul. *The Bulpington of Blup* (1932) is still a comedy, and the principal character a caricature, but the book is really a very detailed analysis of a mind and its working. Kipps never seemed to have much mind at all; he makes us laugh at a puppet. Theodore Bulpington could do no more than carry around a mind for his author, and he makes us faintly uncomfortable. But Alfred Polly had a mind of his own and while the author can examine it, it is still Polly's.

Long after *The History of Mr. Polly*, H. G. Wells complained of the way in which his later works were reviewed: " People are simply warned that there are ideas in my books and advised not to read them . . ." but in 1910, Mr. H. G. Wells's new book, *The History of Mr. Polly* (Nelson, 2s. net) could be regarded " as an interlude, a piece of work airily thrown off for the amusement and recreation of the author, it is enough to say that it is a highly spirited and delightful tale, in Mr. Wells's most sympathetic vein, full of the familiar charm of his careless felicity and rapidity and ease." Readers who abhorred ideas would, if they had read that review at all, probably not have read it all. The review which has been quoted was in the " Times Literary Supplement " on the 22nd of April, 1910. After its light-hearted opening it became more serious—nasty thinking stuff—not the sort of jolly story that a chap likes to read—without a lot of *thoughts.* It is this " quite deceptive appearance of recklessness " that is the very strength of writing like *Polly.* The wary people can safely steer clear of *The Open Conspiracy, The Work, Wealth and Happiness of Mankind,* and all those serious books—but they are caught every time with a story " that streams forward with gay relish which appears to be solely concerned with the matter in hand." You laugh and forget the world in the performance of a clown, but it leaves you with the tears in you because he touches you with the depth and the sincerity of his trials and he calls on your pity for his mis-fit. So, too, to quote *The Times* again, is Polly, " though pictured for his own sake, has always an inherent reference to the strange wasteful organisation which lavishly produces him and yet seems to provide no place for him. He wedges himself into it only to be ruthlessly squeezed out; and though he finds his place at last, it is by virtue of his own small spark of originality which nothing quite succeeds in quenching. The bright side of Mr. Wells's drama is the challenge to originality offered by the very stupidity of life; the dark side is the huge and pitiless waste which it involves."

Alfred Polly is in no way a tragic clown. His is not the ending, so common of clowns, that leaves the audience embarrassed with tears in the last moments of darkness. Polly is a conqueror. In the beginning the world has battered him and is keeping him in his place; in the end he has made his own world, populated with only those people that he will let into it.

This then, is *The History of Mr. Polly.* The book has stood up to a long youth in a changing world. It has been made into a film and not a bad one. It has been broadcast, translated and published from sevenpence to half a guinea. But it has survived that strange passage through middle age and stands well to be established now in comfort as a classic: that is a work that has something in it for humanity for all time.

H. G. himself thought *The History of Mr. Polly* was certainly his happiest book and the one he cared for most, it " is warm with a pervading affection and even Miriam is left in peace and contentment at last to distribute eggs beyond refreshment to her unwary customers." That is dismissing this book too lightly. The Polly that will always live is the Polly that experienced " that God and Heaven watched over him, and all the earth was expectation "; the Polly that broke through the barrier of forty and found on the other side, both life and his sufficient beauty.

FRANK WELLS

CONTENTS

CHAPTER ONE

Beginnings, and the Bazaar

I

" Hole! " said Mr. Polly, and then for a change, and with greatly increased emphasis: " *'Ole!* " He paused, and then broke out with one of his private and peculiar idioms. " Oh! *Beastly* Silly Wheeze of a hole! "

He was sitting on a stile between two threadbare-looking fields, and suffering acutely from indigestion.

He suffered from indigestion now nearly every afternoon in his life, but as he lacked introspection he projected the associated discomfort upon the world. Every afternoon he discovered afresh that life as a whole, and every aspect of life that presented itself, was " beastly." And this afternoon, lured by the delusive blueness of a sky that was blue because the March wind was in the east, he had come out in the hope of snatching something of the joyousness of spring. The mysterious alchemy of mind and body refused, however, to permit any joyousness in the spring.

He had had a little difficulty in finding his cap before he came out. He wanted his cap—the new golf cap—and Mrs. Polly must needs fish out his old soft brown felt hat. " *'Ere's* your 'at," she said, in a tone of insincere encouragement.

He had been routing among the piled newspapers under the kitchen dresser, and had turned quite hopefully and had taken the thing. He put it on. But it didn't feel right. Nothing felt right. He put a trembling hand upon the crown and pressed it on his head, and tried it askew to the right, and then askew to the left.

Then the full sense of the offered indignity came home to him. The hat masked the upper sinister quarter of his face, and he spoke with a wrathful eye regarding his wife from under the brim. In a voice thick with fury he said, " I s'pose you'd like me to wear that silly Mud Pie for ever, eh? I tell you I won't. I'm sick of it. I'm pretty near sick of every-thing, comes to that. . . . Hat! "

He clutched it with quivering fingers. " Hat! " he repeated. Then he flung it to the ground, and kicked it with extraordinary fury across the kitchen. It flew up against the door and dropped to the ground with its ribbon band half off.

" Shan't go out! " he said, and sticking his hands into his jacket pockets, discovered the missing cap in the right one.

There was nothing for it but to go straight upstairs without a word, and out, slamming the shop door hard.

" Beauty! " said Mrs. Polly at last to a tremendous silence, picking up and dusting the rejected head-dress. " Tantrums," she added. " I 'aven't patience." And moving with the slow reluctance of a deeply offended woman, she began to pile together the simple apparatus of their recent meal, for transportation to the scullery sink.

The repast she had prepared for him did not seem to her to justify his ingratitude. There had been the cold pork from Sunday, and some nice cold potatoes, and Rashdall's Mixed Pickles, of which he was in-ordinately fond. He had eaten three gherkins, two onions, a small cauliflower head, and several capers with every appearance of appetite, and indeed with avidity; and then there had been cold suet pudding to follow, with treacle, and then a nice bit of cheese. It was the pale, hard sort of cheese he liked; red cheese he declared was indigestible. He had also had three big slices of grayish baker's bread, and had drunk the best part of a jugful of beer. . . . But there seems to be no pleasing some people.

"Tantrums!" said Mrs. Polly at the sink, struggling with the mustard on his plate, and expressing the only solution of the problem that occurred to her.

And Mr. Polly sat on the stile and he hated the whole scheme of life—which was at once excessive and inadequate of him. He hated Fishbourne, he hated Fishbourne High Street, he hated his shop and his wife and his neighbours—every blessed neighbour—and with indescribable bitterness he hated himself.

"Why did I ever get in this silly Hole?" he said. "Why did I ever?"

He sat on the stile and looked with eyes that seemed blurred with impalpable flaws at a world in which even the spring buds were wilted, the sunlight metallic, and the shadows mixed with blue-black ink.

To the moralist I know he might have served as a figure of sinful discontent, but that is because it is the habit of moralists to ignore material circumstances—if, indeed, one may speak of a recent meal as a circumstance—seeing that Mr. Polly was circum. Drink, indeed, our teachers will criticise nowadays both as regards quantity and quality, but neither church nor state nor school will raise a warning finger between a man and his hunger and his wife's catering. So on nearly every day in his life Mr. Polly fell into a violent rage and hatred against the outer world in the afternoon, and never suspected that it was this inner world to which I am with such masterly delicacy alluding, that was thus reflecting its sinister disorder upon the things without. It is a pity that some human beings are not more transparent. If Mr. Polly, for example, had been transparent, or even passably translucent, then perhaps he might have realised, from the Laocoon struggle he would have glimpsed, that indeed he was not so much a human being as a civil war.

Wonderful things must have been going on inside Mr. Polly. Oh! wonderful things. It must have been like a badly managed industrial city during a period of depression; agitators, acts of violence, strikes, the forces of law and order doing their best, rushings to and fro, upheavals, the *Marseillaise*, tumbrils, the rumble and the thunder of the tumbrils. . . .

I do not know why the east wind aggravates life to unhealthy people. It made Mr. Polly's teeth seem loose in his head, and his skin feel like a misfit, and his hair a dry stringy exasperation. . . .

Why cannot doctors give us an antidote to the east wind?

"Never have the sense to get your hair cut till it's too long," said Mr. Polly, catching sight of his shadow, "you blighted, desgenerated Paintbrush! Ugh!" and he flattened down the projecting tails with an urgent hand.

2

Mr. Polly's age was exactly thirty-seven years and a half. He was a short, compact figure, and a little inclined to a localised embonpoint. His face was not unpleasing; the features fine, but a trifle too large about the lower half of his face, and a trifle too pointed about the nose to be classically perfect. The corners of his sensitive mouth were depressed. His eyes were ruddy brown and troubled, and the left one was round with more of wonder in it than its fellow. His complexion was dull and yellowish. That, as I have explained, on account of those civil disturbances. He was, in the technical sense of the word, clean shaved, with a small fallow patch under the right ear, and a cut on the chin. His brow had the little puckerings of a thoroughly discontented man, little wrinklings and lumps, particularly over his right eye, and he sat, with his hands in his pockets, a little askew on the stile, and swung one leg.

" Hole! " he repeated presently.

He broke into a quavering song: " Roöötten Beëëastly Silly Hole! "

His voice thickened with rage, and the rest of his discourse was marred by an unfortunate choice of epithets.

He was dressed in a shabby black morning coat and vest; the braid that bound these garments was a little loose in places. His collar was chosen from stock, and with projecting corners, technically a " wing-pole "; that and his tie, which was new and loose and rich in colouring, had been selected to encourage and stimulate customers—for he dealt in gentlemen's outfitting. His golf cap, which was also from stock and aslant over his eye, gave his misery a desperate touch. He wore brown leather boots—because he hated the smell of blacking.

Perhaps after all it was not simply indigestion that troubled him.

Behind the superficialities of Mr. Polly's being moved a larger and vaguer distress. The elementary education he had acquired had left him with the impression that arithmetic was a fluky science and best avoided in practical affairs, but even the absence of book-keeping, and a total inability to distinguish between capital and interest, could not blind him for ever to the fact that the little shop in the High Street was not paying. An absence of returns, a constriction of credit, a depleted till—the most valiant resolves to keep smiling could not prevail for ever against these insistent phenomena. One might bustle about in the morning before dinner and in the afternoon after tea and forget that huge dark cloud of insolvency that gathered and spread in the background, but it was part of the desolation of these afternoon periods, those gray spaces of time after meals when all one's courage had descended to the unseen battles of the pit that life seemed stripped to the bone, and one saw with a hopeless clearness.

Let me tell the history of Mr. Polly from the cradle to these present difficulties.

> " First the infant, mewling and puking in
>   its nurse's arms."

There had been a time when two people had thought Mr. Polly the most wonderful and adorable thing in the world, had kissed his toe-nails, saying, " myum, myum! " and marvelled at the exquisite softness and delicacy of his hair, had called to one another to remark the peculiar distinction with which he bubbled, had disputed whether the sound he had made was just da, da, or truly and intentionally dadda, had washed him in the utmost detail, and wrapped him up in soft warm blankets, and smothered him with kisses. A regal time that was, and four-and-thirty years ago; and a merciful forgetfulness barred Mr. Polly from ever bringing its careless luxury, its autocratic demands and instant obedience into contrast with his present condition of life. These two people had worshipped him from the crown of his head to the soles of his exquisite feet. And also they had fed him rather un-wisely, for no one had ever troubled to teach his mother anything about the mysteries of a child's up-bringing—though, of course, the monthly nurse and her charwoman gave some valuable hints—and by his fifth birthday the perfect rhythms of his nice new interior were already darkened with perplexity. . . .

His mother died when he was seven. He began only to have distinctive memories of himself in the time when his education had already begun.

I remember seeing a picture of Education—in some place. I think it was Education, but quite conceivably it represented the Empire teaching her Sons, and I have a strong impression that it was a wall-painting

upon some public building in Manchester or Birming-
ham or Glasgow, but very possibly I am mistaken
about that. It represented a glorious woman, with a
wise and fearless face, stooping over her children, and
pointing them to far horizons. The sky displayed the
pearly warmth of a summer dawn, and all the painting
was marvellously bright as if with the youth and hope
of the delicately beautiful children in the foreground.
She was telling them, one felt, of the great prospect of
life that opened before them, of the splendours of sea
and mountain they might travel and see, the joys of
skill they might acquire, of effort and the pride of
effort, and the devotions and nobilities it was theirs to
achieve. Perhaps even she whispered of the warm
triumphant mystery of love that comes at last to those
who have patience and unblemished hearts. . . . She
was reminding them of their great heritage as English
children, rulers of more than one-fifth of mankind, of
the obligation to do and the best that such a pride of
empire entails, of their essential nobility and knight-
hood, and of the restraints and charities and disciplined
strength that is becoming in knights and rulers. . . .

The education of Mr. Polly did not follow this picture
very closely. He went for some time to a National
School, which was run on severely economical lines to
keep down the rates, by a largely untrained staff; he
was set sums to do that he did not understand, and that
no one made him understand; he was made to read
the Catechism and Bible with the utmost industry and
an entire disregard of punctuation or significance;
caused to imitate writing copies and drawing copies;
given object lessons upon sealing-wax and silk-worms
and potato bugs and ginger and iron and such-like
things; taught various other subjects his mind refused
to entertain; and afterwards, when he was about
twelve, he was jerked by his parents to " finish off "
in a private school of dingy aspect and still dingier

pretensions, where there were no object lessons, and the studies of book-keeping and French were pursued (but never effectually overtaken) under the guidance of an elderly gentleman, who wore a nondescript gown and took snuff, wrote copperplate, explained nothing, and used a cane with remarkable dexterity and gusto.

Mr. Polly went into the National School at six, and he left the private school at fourteen, and by that time his mind was in much the same state that you would be in, dear reader, if you were operated upon for appendicitis by a well-meaning, boldly enterprising, but rather overworked and underpaid butcher boy, who was superseded towards the climax of the operation by a left-handed clerk of high principles but intemperate habits—that is to say, it was in a thorough mess. The nice little curiosities and willingness of a child were in a jumbled and thwarted condition, hacked and cut about—the operators had left, so to speak, all their sponges and ligatures in the mangled confusion—and Mr. Polly had lost much of his natural confidence, so far as figures and sciences and languages and the possibilities of learning things were concerned. He thought of the present world no longer as a wonderland of experiences, but as geography and history, as the repeating of names that were hard to pronounce, and lists of products and populations and heights and lengths, and as lists and dates—oh! and Boredom indescribable. He thought of religion as the recital of more or less incomprehensible words that were hard to remember, and of the Divinity as of a limitless Being having the nature of a schoolmaster and making infinite rules, known and unknown, rules that were always ruthlessly enforced, and with an infinite capacity for punishment, and, most horrible of all to think, of limitless powers of espial. (So to the best of his ability he did not think of that unrelenting eye.) He was uncertain about the spelling and pronunciation of most

of the words in our beautiful but abundant and perplexing tongue—that especially was a pity, because words
attracted him, and under happier conditions he might
have used them well—he was always doubtful whether
it was eight sevens or nine eights that was sixty-three
(he knew no method for settling the difficulty), and he
thought the merit of a drawing consisted in the care
with which it was "lined in." "Lining in" bored him
beyond measure.

But the indigestions of mind and body that were to
play so large a part in his subsequent career were still
only beginning. His liver and his gastric juice, his
wonder and imagination kept up a fight against the
things that threatened to overwhelm soul and body
together. Outside the regions devastated by the school
curriculum he was still intensely curious. He had
cheerful phases of enterprise, and about thirteen he
suddenly discovered reading and its joys. He began to
read stories voraciously, and books of travel, provided
they were also adventurous. He got these chiefly from
the local institute, and he also "took in" irregularly,
but thoroughly, one of those inspiring weeklies that
dull people used to call "penny dreadfuls," admirable
weeklies crammed with imagination that the cheap
boys' "comics" of to-day have replaced. At fourteen,
when he emerged from the valley of the shadow of
education, there survived something, indeed it survived
still, obscured and thwarted, at five-and-thirty, that
pointed—not with a visible and prevailing finger like
the finger of that beautiful woman in the picture, but
pointed nevertheless—to the idea that there was
interest and happiness in the world. Deep in the being
of Mr. Polly, deep in that darkness, like a creature
which has been beaten about the head and left for dead
but still lives, crawled a persuasion that over and above
the things that are jolly and "bits of all right," there
was beauty, there was delight; that somewhere—

magically inaccessible perhaps, but still somewhere—
were pure and easy and joyous states of body and mind.

He would sneak out on moonless winter nights and
stare up at the stars, and afterwards find it difficult to
tell his father where he had been.

He would read tales about hunters and explorers,
and imagine himself riding mustangs as fleet as the
wind across the prairies of Western America, or coming
as a conquering and adored white man into the
swarming villages of Central Africa. He shot bears
with a revolver—a cigarette in the other hand—and
made a necklace of their teeth and claws for the chief's
beautiful young daughter. Also, he killed a lion with
a pointed stake, stabbing through the beast's heart
as it stood over him.

He thought it would be splendid to be a diver and
go down into the dark green mysteries of the sea.

He led stormers against wellnigh impregnable forts,
and died on the ramparts at the moment of victory.
(His grave was watered by a nation's tears.)

He rammed and torpedoed ships, one against ten.

He was beloved by queens in barbaric lands, and
reconciled whole nations to the Christian faith.

He was martyred, and took it very calmly and
beautifully—but only once or twice after the Revivalist
week. It did not become a habit with him.

He explored the Amazon, and found, newly exposed
by the fall of a great tree, a rock of gold.

Engaged in these pursuits he would neglect the work
immediately in hand, sitting somewhere slackly on the
form and projecting himself in a manner tempting to
a schoolmaster with a cane. . . . And twice he had
books confiscated.

Recalled to the realities of life, he would rub himself
or sigh as the occasion required, and resume his
attempts to write as good as copperplate. He hated
writing; the ink always crept up his fingers, and the

smell of ink offended him. And he was filled with un-expressed doubts. *Why* should writing slope down from right to left? *Why* should downstrokes be thick and upstrokes thin? *Why* should the handle of one's pen point over one's right shoulder?

His copy books towards the end foreshadowed his destiny and took the form of commercial documents. " *Dear Sir,*" they ran, " *Referring to your esteemed order of the* 26*th ult., we beg to inform you,*" and so on.

The compression of Mr. Polly's mind and soul in the educational institutions of his time was terminated abruptly by his father, between his fourteenth and fifteenth birthday. His father—who had long since forgotten the time when his little son's limbs seemed to have come straight from God's hand, and when he had kissed five minute toe-nails in a rapture of loving tenderness—remarked,—

" It's time that dratted boy did something for a living."

And a month or so later Mr. Polly began that career in business that led him at last to the sole proprietorship of a bankrupt outfitter's shop—and to the stile on which he was sitting.

3

Mr. Polly was not naturally interested in hosiery and gentlemen's outfitting. At times, indeed, he urged himself to a spurious curiosity about that trade, but presently something more congenial came along and checked the effort. He was apprenticed in one of those large, rather low-class establishments which sell every-thing from pianos and furniture to books and millinery, a department store, in fact the Port Burdock Drapery Bazaar at Port Burdock, one of the three townships that are grouped round the Port Burdock naval dockyards. There he remained six years. He spent most of the time inattentive to business, in a sort of uncomfortable happiness, increasing his indigestion.

On the whole he preferred business to school; the hours were longer, but the tension was not nearly so great. The place was better aired, you were not kept in for no reason at all, and the cane was not employed. You watched the growth of your moustache with interest and impatience, and mastered the beginnings of social intercourse. You talked and found there were things amusing to say. Also, you had regular pocket-money, and a voice in the purchase of your clothes, and presently a small salary. And there were girls! And friendship! In the retrospect Port Burdock sparkled with the facets of quite a cluster of remembered jolly times.

("Didn't save much money, though," said Mr. Polly.)

The first apprentices' dormitory was a long bleak room with six beds, six chests of drawers and looking-glasses, and a number of boxes of wood or tin; it opened into a still longer and bleaker room of eight beds, and this into a third apartment with yellow-grained paper and American cloth tables, which was the dining-room by day, and the men's sitting and smoking room after nine. Here Mr. Polly, who had been an only child, first tasted the joys of social intercourse. At first there were attempts to bully him on account of his refusal to consider face-washing a diurnal duty, but two fights with the apprentices next above him established a useful reputation for choler, and the presence of girl apprentices in the shop somehow raised his standard of cleanliness to a more acceptable level. He didn't, of course, have very much to do with the feminine staff in his department, but he spoke to them casually as he traversed foreign parts of the Bazaar, or got out of their way politely, or helped them to lift down heavy boxes, and on such occasions he felt their scrutiny. Except in the course of business or at meal times the men and women of the establishment had very little opportunity of meeting; the men were in their rooms and the girls in theirs. Yet these feminine creatures, at once so near and so remote, affected him profoundly. He would watch them going to and fro, and marvel secretly at the beauty of their hair, or the roundness of their necks, or the warm softness of their cheeks, or the delicacy of their hands. He would fall into passions for them at dinner-time, and try to show devotions by his manner of passing the bread and margarine at tea. There was a very fair-haired, fair-skinned apprentice in the adjacent haberdashery to whom he said " good morning " every morning, and for a period it seemed to him the most significant event in his day. When she said, " I do hope it will be fine to-morrow," he felt it marked an epoch. He had had no sisters, and was innately disposed to worship woman-kind. But he did not betray as much to Platt and Parsons.

To Platt and Parsons he affected an attitude of seasoned depravity towards the creatures. Platt and Parsons were his contemporary apprentices in departments of the drapery shop, and the three were drawn together into a close friendship by the fact that all their names began with P. They decided they were the three P's, and went about together of an evening with the bearing of desperate dogs. Sometimes when they had money they went into public-houses and had drinks. Then they would become more desperate than ever, and walk along the pavement under the gas lamps arm in arm singing. Platt had a good tenor voice and had been in a church choir, and so he led the singing. Parsons had a serviceable bellow, which roared and faded and roared again very wonderfully. Mr. Polly's share was an extraordinary lowing noise, a sort of flat recitative which he called " singing seconds." They would have sung catches if they had known how to do it, but as it was they sang melancholy music-hall songs about dying soldiers and the old folks far away.

They would sometimes go into the quieter residential quarters of Port Burdock, where policemen and other obstacles were infrequent, and really let their voices soar like hawks, and feel very happy. The dogs of the district would be stirred to hopeless emulation and would keep it up for long after the three P's had been swallowed up by the night. One jealous brute of an Irish terrier made a gallant attempt to bite Parsons, but was beaten by numbers and solidarity.

The three P's took the utmost interest in each other, and found no other company so good. They talked about everything in the world; and would go on talking in their dormitory after the gas was out, until the other men were reduced to throwing boots. They skulked from their departments in the slack hours of the afternoon to gossip in the packing-room of the warehouse. On Sundays and Bank Holidays they went for long walks together, talking.

Platt was white-faced and dark, and disposed to undertones and mystery, and a curiosity about society and the *demi-monde*. He kept himself *au courant* by reading a penny paper of infinite suggestions called *Modern Society*. Parsons was of an ampler build, already promising fatness, with curly hair and a lot of rolling, rollicking, curly features, and a large, blob-shaped nose. He had a great memory, and a real interest in literature. He knew great portions of Shakespeare and Milton by heart, and would recite them at the slightest provocation. He read everything he could get hold of, and if he liked it he read it aloud; it did not matter who else liked it. At first Mr. Polly was disposed to be suspicious of this literature, but was carried away by Parsons' enthusiasm. The three P's went to a performance of *Romeo and Juliet* at the Port Burdock Theatre

Royal, and hung over the gallery fascinated. After that they made a sort of password of, "Do you bite your thumbs at Us, Sir?" To which the countersign was, "We bite our Thumbs."

For weeks the glory of Shakespeare's Verona lit Mr. Polly's life. He walked as though he carried a sword at his side and swung a mantle from his shoulders. He went through the grimy streets of Port Burdock with his eye on the first-floor windows—looking for balconies. A ladder in the yard flooded his mind with romantic ideas.

Then Parsons discovered an Italian writer, whose name Mr. Polly rendered as "Bocashieu," and after some excursions into that author's remains, the talk of Parsons became infested with the word "amours," and Mr. Polly would stand in front of his hosiery fixtures trifling with paper and string, and thinking of perennial picnics under dark olive trees in the everlasting sunshine of Italy.

And about that time it was that all three P's adopted turn-down collars and large, loose, artistic silk ties, which they tied very much on one side, and wore with an air of defiance; and a certain swashbuckling carriage.

And then came the glorious revelation of that great Frenchman whom Mr. Polly called "Rabooloose." The three P's thought the birth-feast of Gargantua the most glorious piece of writing in the world—and I am not certain they were wrong; and on wet Sunday evenings, when there was danger of hymn-singing, they would get Parsons to read it aloud.

Towards the several members of the Y.M.C.A. who shared the dormitory, the three P's always maintained a sarcastic and defiant attitude.

"We have got a perfect right to do what we like in our corner," Platt maintained. "You do what you like in yours."

"But the language," objected Morrison, the white-faced, earnest-eyed improver, who was leading a profoundly religious life under great difficulties.

"*Language*, man!" roared Parsons; "why, it's *LITERATURE*!"

"Sunday isn't the time for Literature."

"It's the only time we've got. And besides——"

The horrors of religious controversy would begin. . . .

Mr. Polly stuck loyally by the three P's, but in the secret places of his heart he was torn. A fire of conviction burned in Morrison's eyes and spoke in his urgent, persuasive voice. He lived the better life manifestly: chaste in word and deed, industrious, studiously kindly. When the junior apprentice had sore feet and homesickness, Morrison washed the feet and comforted the heart; and he helped other men to get through with their work when he might have gone early—a superhuman thing to do. No one who has not worked for endless days of interminable hours, with scarce a gleam of rest or liberty between the toil and the sleep can understand how superhuman. Polly was secretly a little afraid to be left alone with this man and the power of the spirit that was in him. He felt watched. Platt, also struggling with things his mind could not contrive to reconcile, said, "That confounded hypocrite."

"He's no hypocrite," said Parsons; "he's no hypocrite, O' Man. But he's got no blessed *Joy de Vive*—that's what's wrong with him. Let's go down to the Harbour Arms and see some of those blessed old captains getting drunk."

"Short of sugar, O' Man," said Mr. Polly, slapping his trouser-pocket.

"Oh, *carm* on," said Parsons; "always do it on tuppence for a bitter."

"Lemme get my Pipe on," said Platt, who had recently taken to smoking with great ferocity. "Then I'm with you."

(Pause and struggle.)

"Don't ram it down, O' Man," said Parsons, watching with knitted brows; "don't ram it down. Give it air. Seen my stick, O' Man? Right-o."

And, leaning on his cane, he composed himself in an attitude of sympathetic patience towards Platt's incendiary efforts.

4

Jolly days of companionship they were for the incipient bankrupt on the stile to look back upon.

The interminable working hours of the Bazaar had long since faded from his memory—except for one or two conspicuous rows and one or two larks—but the rare Sundays and holidays shone out like diamonds among pebbles. They shone with the mellow splendour of evening skies reflected in calm water, and athwart them all went old Parsons bellowing an interpretation of life, gesticulating, appreciating, and making appreciate, expounding books, talking of that mystery of his, the "Joy de Vive."

There were some particularly splendid walks on Bank Holidays. The three P's would start on Sunday morning early, and find a room in some modest inn and talk themselves asleep, and return singing through the night, or having an " argy bargy " about the stars on Monday evening. They would come over the hill out of the pleasant English country-side in which they had wandered and see Port Burdock spread out below, a network of interlacing street lamps and shifting tram-lights, against the black, beacon-gemmed immensity of the harbour waters.

"Back to the collar, O' Man," Parsons would say. There is no satisfactory plural to " O' Man," so he always used it in the singular.

"Don't mention it," said Platt.

And once they got a boat for the whole summer day, and rowed up past the moored ironclads and the black old hulks and the various shipping of the harbour, past a white troopship, and past the trim front and the slips and interesting vistas of the dockyard to the shallow channels and rocky, weedy wildernesses of the upper harbour. And Parsons and Mr. Polly had a great dispute and quarrel that day as to how far a big gun could shoot.

The country over the hills behind Port Burdock is all that an old-fashioned, scarcely disturbed English country-side should be. In those days the bicycle was still rare and costly, and the motor-car had yet to come and stir up rural serenities. The three P's would take footpaths haphazard across fields, and plunge into unknown winding lanes between high hedges of honeysuckle and dog-rose. Greatly daring, they would follow green bridle-paths through primrose-studded undergrowths, or wander waist-deep in the bracken of beech woods. About twenty miles from Port Burdock there came a region of hop-gardens and hoast-crowned farms; and farther on, to be reached only by cheap tickets on Bank Holiday times, was a sterile ridge of very clean roads and red sandpits and pines, and gorse and heather. The three P's could not afford to buy bicycles, and they found boots the greatest item of their skimpy expenditure. They threw appearances to the winds at last, and got ready-made working-men's hobnails. There was much discussion and strong feeling over this step in the dormitory, and the three P's were held to have derogated from the dignity of the emporium.

There is no country-side like the English country-side for those who have learned to love it; its firm yet gentle line of hill and dale, its ordered confusion of features, its deer parks and downland, its castles and stately houses, its hamlets and old churches, its farms and ricks and great barns and ancient trees, its pools and ponds and shining threads of rivers, its flower-starred hedgerows, its orchards and woodland patches, its village greens and kindly inns. Other country-sides have their pleasant aspects, but nonesuch variety, none that shine so steadfastly throughout the year. Picardy is pink and white and pleasant in the blossom time; Burgundy goes on with its sunshine and wide hill-sides and cramped vineyards, a beautiful tune repeated and repeated; Italy gives salitas and wayside chapels, and chestnuts and olive orchards; the Ardennes has its woods and gorges—Touraine and the Rhineland, the wide Campagna with its distant Apennines, and the neat prosperity and mountain backgrounds of South Germany all clamour their especial merits at one's memory. And there are the hills and fields of Virginia, like an England grown very big and slovenly, the woods and big rivers weeps of Pennsylvania, the trim New England landscape, a little bleak and rather fine, like the New England mind, and the wide, rough country roads and hills and woodland of New York State. But none of these change scene and character in three miles of walking, nor have so mellow a sunlight nor so diversified a cloudland nor confess the perpetual refreshment of the strong soft winds that blow from off the sea, as our mother England does.

It was good for the three P's to walk through such a land and forget for a time that indeed they had no footing in it all, that they were doomed to toil behind counters in such places as Port Burdock for the better part of their lives. They would forget the customers and shopwalkers and department buyers and everything, and become just happy wanderers in a world of pleasant breezes and songbirds and shady trees.

The arrival at the inn was a great affair. No one, they were convinced, would take them for drapers, and there might be a pretty serving-girl or a jolly old landlady, or what Parsons called a "bit of character" drinking in the bar.

There would always be weighty inquiries as to what they could have, and it would work out always at cold beef and pickles, or fried ham and eggs and shandygaff, two pints of beer and two bottles of ginger-beer foaming in a huge round-bellied jug.

The glorious moment of standing lordly in the inn doorway and staring out at the world, the swinging sign, the geese upon the green, the duck-pond, a waiting wagon, the church tower, a sleepy cat, the blue heavens, with the sizzle of the frying audible behind one! The keen smell of the bacon! The trotting of feet bearing the repast; the click and clatter as the table ware is finally arranged! A clean white cloth! "Ready, Sir!" or "Ready, Gentlemen!" Better hearing that than "Forward, Polly! Look sharp!"

The going in! The sitting down! The falling to!

"Bread, O' Man?"

"Right-o! Don't bag all the crust, O' Man."

Once a simple-mannered girl in a pink print dress stayed and talked with them as they ate; led by the gallant Parsons they professed to be all desperately in love with her, and courted her to say which she preferred of them, it was so manifest she did prefer one and so impossible to say which it was held her there, until a distant maternal voice called her away. Afterwards, as they left the inn, she waylaid them at the orchard corner and gave them, a little shyly, three yellow-green apples—and wished them to come again some day, and vanished, and reappeared looking after them as they turned the corner, waving a white handkerchief. All the rest of that day they disputed over the signs of her favour, and the next Sunday they went there again.

But she had vanished, and a mother of forbidding aspect afforded no explanations.

If Platt and Parsons and Mr. Polly live to be a hundred, they will none of them forget that girl as she stood with a pink flush upon her, faintly smiling and yet earnest, parting the branches of the hedgerows and reaching down, apple in hand. . . .

And once they went along the coast, following it as closely as possible, and so came at last to Fishbourne that easternmost suburb of Brayling and Hampstead-on-the-Sea.

Fishbourne, seemed a very jolly little place to Mr. Polly that afternoon. It has a clean sandy beach, instead of the mud and pebbles and coaly defilements of Port Burdock, a row of six bathing-machines, and a shelter on the parade in which the three P's sat after a satisfying but rather expensive lunch that had included celery. Rows of verandahed villas proffered apartments; they had feasted in a hotel with a porch painted white, and gay with geraniums above; and the High Street, with the old church at the head, had been full of an agreeable afternoon stillness.

" Nice little place for business," said Platt sagely from behind his big pipe.

It stuck in Mr. Polly's memory.

5

Mr. Polly was not so picturesque a youth as Parsons. He lacked richness in his voice, and went about in those days with his hands in his pockets looking quietly speculative.

He specialised in slang and the disuse of English, and he played the rôle of an appreciative stimulant to Parsons. Words attracted him curiously, words rich in suggestion, and he loved a novel and striking phrase. His school training had given him little or no mastery of the mysterious pronunciation of English, and no confidence in himself. His schoolmaster indeed had been both unsound and variable. New words had terror and fascination for him; he did not acquire them, he could not avoid them, and so he plunged into them. His only rule was not to be misled by the spelling. That was no guide anyhow. He avoided every recognised phrase in the language, and mispronounced everything in order that he shouldn't be suspected of ignorance but whim.

"Sesquippledan," he would say. "Sesquippledan verboojuice."

"Eh?" said Platt.

"Eloquent Rapsodooce."

"Where?" asked Platt.

"In the warehouse, O' Man. All among the tableclothes and blankets. Carlyle. He's reading aloud. Doing the High Froth. Spuming! Windmilling! Waw, waw! It's a sight worth seeing. He'll bark his blessed knuckles one of these days on the fixtures, O' Man."

He held an imaginary book in one hand and waved an eloquent gesture. "So too shall every Hero inasmuch as notwithstanding for evermore come back to Reality," he parodied the enthusiastic Parsons, "so that in fashion and thereby, upon things and not *under* things articulariously He stands."

"I should laugh if the Governor dropped on him," said Platt. "He'd never hear him coming."

"The O' Man's drunk with it—fair drunk," said Polly. "*I* never did. It's worse than when he got on to Raboloose."

CHAPTER TWO

The Dismissal of Parsons

I

SUDDENLY Parsons got himself dismissed.

He got himself dismissed under circumstances of peculiar violence, that left a deep impression on Mr. Polly's mind. He wondered about it for years afterwards, trying to get the rights of the case.

Parsons' apprenticeship was over; he had reached the status of an Improver, and he dressed the window of the Manchester department. By his own standards he dressed it wonderfully. "Well, O' Man," he used to say, "there's one thing about my position here— I *can* dress a window."

And when trouble was under discussion he would hold that "little Fluffums"—which was the apprentices' name for Mr. Garvace, the senior partner and managing director of the Bazaar—would think twice before he got rid of the only man in the place who could make a windowful of Manchester goods *tell*.

Then, like many a fellow-artist, he fell a prey to theories.

"The art of window dressing is in its infancy, O' Man—in its blooming Infancy. All balance and stiffness like a blessed Egyptian picture. No Joy in it, no blooming Joy! Conventional. A shop window ought to get hold of people, *grip* 'em as they go along. It stands to reason. Grip!"

His voice would sink to a kind of quiet bellow. "*Do* they grip?"

Then, after a pause, a savage roar: "*Naw!*"

"He's got a Heavy on," said Mr. Polly. "Go it, O' Man; let's have some more of it."

39

"Look at old Morrison's dress-stuff windows! Tidy, tasteful, correct, I grant you, but Bleak!" He let out the word reinforced to a shout: "Bleak!"

"Bleak!" echoed Mr. Polly.

"Just pieces of stuff in rows, rows of tidy little puffs, perhaps one bit just unrolled, quiet tickets."

"Might as well be in church, O' Man," said Mr. Polly.

"A window ought to be exciting," said Parsons; "it ought to make you say, ''El-*lo*!' when you see it."

He paused, and Platt watched him over a snorting pipe.

"Rockcockyo," said Mr. Polly.

"We want a new school of window dressing," said Parsons, regardless of the comment. "A New School! The Port Burdock school. Day after to-morrow I change the Fitzallan Street stuff. This time it's going to be a change. I mean to have a crowd or bust!"

And as a matter of fact he did both.

His voice dropped to a note of self-reproach. "I've been timid, O' Man. I've been holding myself in. I haven't done myself justice. I've kept down the simmering, seething, teeming ideas. . . . All that's over now."

"Over," gulped Polly.

"Over for good and all, O' Man."

2

Platt came to Polly, who was sorting up collar-boxes.

"O' Man's doing his Blooming Window."

"What window?"

"What he said."

Polly remembered.

He went on with his collar-boxes with his eye on his senior, Mansfield. Mansfield was presently called away to the counting-house, and instantly Polly shot out by the street door, and made a rapid transit along the street front past the Manchester window, and so into the silkroom door. He could not linger long, but he gathered joy, a swift and fearful joy, from his brief inspection of Parsons' unconscious back. Parsons had his tail-coat off, and was working with vigour; his habit of pulling his waistcoat straps to their utmost brought out all the agreeable promise of corpulence in his youthful frame. He was blowing excitedly and running his fingers through his hair, and then moving with all the swift eagerness of a man inspired. All about his feet and knees were scarlet blankets, not folded, not formally unfolded, but—the only phrase is—shied about. And a great bar sinister of roller towelling stretched across the front of the window on which was a ticket, and the ticket said in bold, black letters: "*LOOK!*"

So soon as Mr. Polly got into the silk department and met Platt he knew he had not lingered nearly long enough outside.

" Did you see the boards at the back? " said Platt.

Mr. Polly hadn't. "The High Egrugious is fairly On," he said, and dived down to return by devious subterranean routes to the outfitting department.

Presently the street door opened and Platt, with an air of intense devotion to business assumed to cover his adoption of that unusual route, came in and made for the staircase down to the warehouse. He rolled up his eyes at Polly. "Oh, *Lor!* " he said, and vanished.

Irresistible curiosity seized Polly. Should he go through the shop to the Manchester department, or risk a second transit outside?

He was impelled to make a dive at the street door.

" Where are you going? " asked Mansfield.

" Lill dog," said Polly, with an air of lucid explanation, and left him to get any meaning he could from it.

Parsons was worth the subsequent trouble. Parsons

really was extremely rich. This time Polly stopped to take it in.

Parsons had made a huge asymmetrical pile of thick white and red blankets twisted and rolled to accentuate their woolly richness heaped up in a warm disorder, with large window tickets inscribed in blazing red letters: " Cosy Comfort at Cut Prices," and " Curl up and Cuddle below Cost." Regardless of the daylight he had turned up the electric light on that side of the window to reflect a warm glow upon the head, and behind, in pursuit of contrasted bleakness, he was now hanging long strips of gray silesia and chilly-coloured linen dustering.

It was wonderful, but——

Mr. Polly decided that it was time he went in. He found Platt in the silk department, apparently on the verge of another plunge into the exterior world. " Cosy Comfort at Cut Prices," said Polly. " Allittritions Artful Aid."

He did not dare go into the street for the third time, and he was hovering feverishly near the window when he saw the governor, Mr. Garvace—that is to say, the managing director of the Bazaar—walking along the pavement after his manner, to assure himself all was well with the establishment he guided.

Mr. Garvace was a short, stout man, with that air of modest pride that so often goes with corpulence, choleric and decisive in manner, and with hands that looked like bunches of fingers. He was red haired and ruddy, and after the custom of such complexions, hairs sprang from the tip of his nose. When he wished to bring the power of the human eye to bear upon an assistant, he projected his chest, knitted one brow, and partially closed the left eyelid.

An expression of speculative wonder overspread the countenance of Mr. Polly. He felt he must *see*. Yes, whatever happened, he must *see*.

"Wanttospeak to Parsons, Sir," he said to Mr. Mansfield, and deserted his post hastily, dashed through the intervening departments, and was in position behind a pile of Bolton sheeting as the governor came in out of the street.

"What on earth do you think you are doing with that window, Parsons?" began Mr. Garvace.

Only the legs of Parsons and the lower part of his waistcoat and an intervening inch of shirt were visible. He was standing inside the window on the steps, hanging up the last strip of his background from the brass rail along the ceiling. Within, the Manchester shop window was cut off by a partition rather like the partition of an old-fashioned church pew from the general space of the shop. There was a panelled barrier, that is to say, with a little door like a pew door in it. Parsons' face appeared, staring with round eyes at his employer.

Mr. Garvace had to repeat his question.

"Dressing it, Sir—on new lines."

"Come out of it," said Mr. Garvace.

Parsons stared, and Mr. Garvace had to repeat his command.

Parsons, with a dazed expression, began to descend the steps slowly.

Mr. Garvace turned about. "Where's Morrison? Morrison!"

Morrison appeared.

"Take this window over," said Mr. Garvace, pointing his bunch of fingers at Parsons. "Take all this muddle out and dress it properly."

Morrison advanced and hesitated.

"I beg your pardon, Sir," said Parsons, with an immense politeness, "but this is *my* window."

"Take it all out," said Mr. Garvace, turning away.

Morrison advanced. Parsons shut the door with a click that arrested Mr. Garvace.

" Come out of that window," he said. " You can't dress it. If you want to play the fool with a window——"

" This window's All Right," said the genius in window dressing, and there was a little pause.

" Open the door and go right in," said Mr. Garvace to Morrison.

" You leave that door alone, Morrison," said Parsons.

Polly was no longer even trying to hide behind the stack of Bolton sheetings. He realised he was in the presence of forces too stupendous to heed him.

" Get him out," said Mr. Garvace.

Morrison seemed to be thinking out the ethics of his position. The idea of loyalty to his employer prevailed with him. He laid his hand on the door to open it; Parsons tried to disengage his hand. Mr. Garvace joined his effort to Morrison's. Then the heart of Polly leapt, and the world blazed up to wonder and splendour. Parsons disappeared behind the partition for a moment, and reappeared instantly, gripping a thin cylinder of rolled huckaback. With this he smote at Morrison's head. Morrison's head ducked under the resounding impact, but he clung on and so did Mr. Garvace. The door came wide open, and then Mr. Garvace was staggering back, hand to head, his autocratic, his sacred baldness, smitten. Parsons was beyond all control—a strangeness, a marvel. Heaven knows how the artistic struggle had strained that richly endowed temperament. " Say I can't dress a window, you thundering old Humbug," he said, and hurled the huckaback at his master. He followed this up by pitching first a blanket, then an armful of silesia, then a window support out of the window into the shop. It leapt into Polly's mind that Parsons hated his own effort and was glad to demolish it. For a crowded second his attention was concentrated upon Parsons, infuriated, active, like a figure of earthquake with its coat off, shying things headlong.

Then he perceived the back of Mr. Garvace and heard his gubernatorial voice crying to no one in particular and everybody in general, " Get him out of the window. He's mad. He's dangerous. Get him out of the window."

Then a crimson blanket was for a moment over the head of Mr. Garvace, and his voice, muffled for an instant, broke out into unwonted expletive.

Then people had arrived from all parts of the Bazaar. Luck, the ledger clerk, blundered against Polly and said, " Help him! " Somerville from the silks vaulted the counter, and seized a chair by the back. Polly lost his head. He clawed at the Bolton sheeting before him, and if he could have detached a piece he would certainly have hit somebody with it. As it was he simply upset the pile. It fell away from Polly, and he had an impression of somebody squeaking as it went down. It was the sort of impression one disregards. The collapse of the pile of goods just sufficed to end his subconscious efforts to get something to hit somebody with, and his whole attention focused itself upon the struggle in the window. For a splendid instant Parsons towered up over the active backs that clustered about the shop-window door, an active whirl of gesture, tearing things down and throwing them, and then he went under. There was an instant's furious struggle, a crash, a second crash, and the crack of broken plate glass. Then a stillness and heavy breathing.

Parsons was overpowered. . . .

Polly, stepping over scattered pieces of Bolton sheeting, saw his transfigured friend with a dark cut, that was not at present bleeding, on the forehead, one arm held by Somerville and the other by Morrison.

" You—you—you—you annoyed me," said Parsons, sobbing for breath.

3

There are events that detach themselves from the general stream of occurrences and seem to partake of the nature of revelations. Such was this Parsons affair. It began by seeming grotesque; it ended disconcertingly. The fabric of Mr. Polly's daily life was torn, and beneath it he discovered depths and terrors.

Life was not altogether a lark.

The calling in of a policeman seemed at the moment a pantomime touch. But when it became manifest that Mr. Garvace was in a fury of vindictiveness, the affair took on a different complexion. The way in which the policeman made a note of everything and aspirated nothing impressed the sensitive mind of Polly profoundly. Polly presently found himself straightening up ties to the refrain of "'E then 'It you on the 'Ead —'Ard."

In the dormitory that night Parsons became heroic. He sat on the edge of the bed with his head bandaged, packing very slowly and insisting over and over again, " He ought to have left my window alone, O' Man. He didn't ought to have touched my window."

Polly was to go to the police court in the morning as a witness. The terror of that ordeal almost overshadowed the tragic fact that Parsons was not only summoned for assault, but " swapped," and packing his box. Polly knew himself well enough to know he would make a bad witness. He felt sure of one fact only—namely, that "'E then 'It 'Im on the 'Ead— 'Ard." All the rest danced about in his mind now, and how it would dance about on the morrow Heaven only knew. Would there be a cross-examination? Is it perjoocery to make a slip? People did sometimes perjuice themselves. Serious offence.

Platt was doing his best to help Parsons and inciting public opinion against Morrison. But Parsons would not hear of anything against Morrison. " He was all right, O' Man—according to his lights," said Parsons. " It isn't him I complain of."

He speculated on the morrow. " I shall 'ave to pay a fine," he said. " No good trying to get out of it." It's true I hit him. I hit him "—he paused and seemed to be seeking an exquisite accuracy. His voice sank to a confidential note—" on the head—about here."

He answered the suggestion of a bright junior apprentice in a corner of the dormitory. " What's the Good of a Cross summons," he replied, " with old Corks the chemist and Mottishead the house agent and all that on the Bench? Humble Pie, that's my meal to-morrow, O' Man. Humble Pie."

Packing went on for a time.

" But, Lord! what a life it is! " said Parsons, giving his deep notes scope. " Ten-thirty-five a man trying to do his Duty, mistaken perhaps, but doing his best; ten-forty, Ruined. Ruined! " He lifted his voice to a shout: " Ruined! " and dropped it to " Like an earthquake."

" Heated altaclation," said Polly.

" Like a blooming earthquake," said Parsons, with the notes of a rising wind.

He meditated gloomily upon his future, and a colder chill invaded Polly's mind. " Likely to get another crib, ain't I?—with assaulted the guv'nor on my reference. . . . I suppose, though, he won't give me refs. Hard enough to get a crib at the best of times," said Parsons.

" You ought to go round with a show, O' Man," said Mr. Polly.

Things were not so dreadful in the police court as Mr. Polly had expected. He was given a seat with other witnesses against the wall of the court, and after an interesting larceny case Parsons appeared and stood, not in the dock, but at the table. By that time Mr.

Polly's legs, which had been tucked up at first under his chair out of respect to the court, were extended straight before him, and his hands were in his trousers pockets. He was inventing names for the four magistrates on the bench, and had got to " the Grave and Reverend Signor with the palatial Boko," when his thoughts were recalled to gravity by the sound of his name. He rose with alacrity, and was fielded by an expert policeman from a brisk attempt to get into the vacant dock. The clerk to the Justices repeated the oath with incredible rapidity.

" Right-o," said Mr. Polly, but quite respectfully, and kissed the book.

His evidence was simple and quite audible after one warning from the superintendent of police to " speak up." He tried to put in a good word for Parsons by saying he was " naturally of a choleraic disposition," but the start and the slow grin of enjoyment upon the face of " the Grave and Reverend Signor with the palatial Boko " suggested that the word was not so good as he had thought it. The rest of the bench was frankly puzzled, and there were hasty consultations.

" You mean 'E as a 'Ot temper," said the presiding magistrate.

" I mean 'E as a 'Ot temper," replied Polly, magically incapable of aspirates for the moment.

" You don't mean 'E ketches cholera ? "

" I mean—he's easily put out."

" Then why can't you say so? " said the presiding magistrate.

Parsons was bound over.

He came for his luggage while every one was in the shop, and Garvace would not let him invade the business to say good-bye. When Mr. Polly went upstairs for margarine and bread and tea, he slipped on into the dormitory at once to see what was happening further in the Parsons case. But Parsons had vanished.

There was no Parsons, no trace of Parsons. His cubicle was swept and garnished. For the first time in his life Polly had a sense of irreparable loss.

A minute or so after Platt dashed in.

"Ugh!" he said, and then discovered Polly. Polly was leaning out of the window, and did not look round. Platt went up to him.

"He's gone already," said Platt. "Might have stopped to say good-bye to a chap."

There was a little pause before Polly replied. He thrust his finger into his mouth and gulped.

"Bit on that beastly tooth of mine," he said, still not looking at Platt. "It's made my eyes water something chronic. Any one might think I'd been Piping my Eye, by the look of me."

CHAPTER THREE

Cribs

I

PORT BURDOCK was never the same place for Mr. Polly after Parsons had left it. There were no chest notes in his occasional letters, and little of the " Joy de Vive " got through by them. Parsons had gone, he said, to London, and found a place as a warehouseman in a cheap outfitting shop near St. Paul's Churchyard, where references were not required. It became apparent as time passed that new interests were absorbing him. He wrote of Socialism and the rights of man, things that had no appeal for Mr. Polly. He felt strangers had got hold of his Parsons, were at work upon him, making him into some one else, something less picturesque. . . . Port Burdock became a dreariness full of faded memories of Parsons, and work a bore. Platt revealed himself alone as a tiresome companion, obsessed by romantic ideas about intrigues and vices and " society women."

Mr. Polly's depression manifested itself in a general slackness. A certain impatience in the manner of Mr. Garvace presently got upon his nerves. Relations were becoming strained. He asked for a rise of salary to test his position, and gave notice to leave when it was refused. It took him two months to place himself in another situation, and during that time he had quite a disagreeable amount of loneliness, disappointment, anxiety, and humiliation.

He went first to stay with a married cousin who had a house at Easewood. His widowed father had recently given up the music and bicycle shop (with the post of organist at the parish church that had sustained his home), and was living upon a small annuity as a guest of his cousin, and growing a little tiresome on account of some mysterious internal discomfort that the local practitioner diagnosed as imagination. He had aged with mysterious rapidity and become excessively irritable, but the cousin's wife was a born manager, and contrived to get along with him. Our Mr. Polly's status was that of a guest pure and simple; but after a fortnight of congested hospitality, in which he wrote nearly a hundred letters beginning:—

" *Sir,—Reffering to your advt. in the ' Christian World ' for an Improver in Gents' outfitting, I beg to submit myself for the situation. Have had six years' experience. . . .*"

and upset a penny bottle of ink over a toilet cover and the bedroom carpet, his cousin took him for a walk and pointed out the superior advantages of apartments in London from which to swoop down upon the briefly yawning vacancy.

" Helpful," said Mr. Polly; " very helpful, O' Man, indeed. I might have gone on here for weeks," and packed.

He got a room in an institution that was partly a benevolent hostel for men in his circumstances, and partly a high-minded but forbidding coffee-house, and a centre for Pleasant Sunday Afternoons. Mr. Polly spent a critical but pleasant Sunday afternoon in a back seat inventing such phrases as:—

" Soulful Owner of the Exorbiant Largenial Development." An Adam's Apple being in question.

" Earnest Joy."

" Exultant, Urgent Loogoobuosity."

A manly young curate, marking and misunderstanding his preoccupied face and moving lips, came and sat by him and entered into conversation with the idea of making him feel more at home. The conversation was awkward, and disconnected for a minute or so, and

then suddenly a memory of the Port Burdock Bazaar
occurred to Mr. Polly, and with a baffling whisper of
" Lill dog," and a reassuring nod, he rose up and
escaped, to wander out relieved and observant into the
varied London streets.

He found the collection of men he met waiting about
in wholesale establishments in Wood Street and St.
Paul's Churchyard (where they interview the buyers
who have come up from the country) interesting and
stimulating, but far too strongly charged with the
suggestion of his own fate to be really joyful. There
were men in all degrees between confidence and
distress, and in every stage between extravagant smartness and the last stages of decay. There were sunny
young men full of an abounding and elbowing energy
before whom the soul of Polly sank into hate and
dismay. " Smart Juniors," said Polly to himself, " full
of Smart Juniosity. The Shoveacious Cult." There
were hungry-looking individuals of thirty-five or so,
that he decided must be " Proletelerians "—he had
often wanted to find some one who fitted that attractive
word. Middle-aged men, " too old at Forty," dis-
coursed in the waiting-rooms on the outlook in the
trade; it had never been so bad, they said, while Mr.
Polly wondered if " Dejuiced " was a permissible
epithet. There were men with an overweening sense
of their importance, manifestly annoyed and angry to
find themselves still disengaged, and inclined to suspect
a plot, and men so faint-hearted one was terrified to
imagine their behaviour when it came to an interview.
There was a fresh-faced young man with an unin-
telligent face who seemed to think himself equipped
against the world beyond all misadventure by a collar
of exceptional height, and another who introduced a
note of gaiety by wearing a flannel shirt and a check
suit of remarkable virulence. Every day Mr. Polly
looked round to mark how many of the familiar faces

had gone, and the deepening anxiety (reflecting his own) on the faces that remained, and every day some new type joined the drifting shoal. He realised how small a chance his poor letter from Easewood ran against this hungry cluster of competitors at the fountain head.

At the back of Mr. Polly's mind while he made his observations was a disagreeable flavour of a dentist's parlour. At any moment his name might be shouted, and he might have to haul himself into the presence of some fresh specimen of employer, and to repeat once more his passionate protestation of interest in the business, his possession of capacity for zeal—zeal on behalf of any one who would pay him a yearly salary of twenty-six pounds a year. The prospective employer would unfold his ideals of the employee. " I want a smart, willing young man, thoroughly willing, who won't object to take trouble. I don't want a slacker, the sort of fellow who has to be pushed up to his work and held there. I've got no use for him."

At the back of Mr. Polly's mind, and quite beyond his control, the insubordinate phrasemaker would be proffering such combinations as " Chubby Chops," or " Chubby Charmer," as suitable for the gentleman, very much as a hat salesman proffers hats.

" I don't think you'd find much slackness about *me*, Sir," said Mr. Polly brightly, trying to disregard his deeper self.

" I want a young man who means getting on."

" Exactly, Sir. Excelsior."

" I beg your pardon? "

" I said excelsior, Sir. It's a sort of motto of mine. From Longfellow. Would you want me to serve through? "

The chubby gentleman explained and reverted to his ideals, with a faint air of suspicion. " Do *you* mean getting on? " he asked.

" I hope so, Sir," said Mr. Polly.

" Get on or get out, eh? '

Mr. Polly made a rapturous noise, nodded apprecia-tion, and said indistinctly, " *Quite* my style."

" Some of my people have been with me twenty years," said the employer, " my Manchester buyer came to me as a boy of twelve. You're a Christian? "

" Church of England," said Mr. Polly.

" H'm," said the employer, a little checked. " For good all round business work, I should have preferred a Baptist. Still——"

He studied Mr. Polly's tie, which was severely neat and businesslike, as became an aspiring outfitter. Mr. Polly's conception of his own pose and expression was rendered by that uncontrollable phrasemonger at the back as " Obsequies Deference."

" I am inclined," said the prospective employer in a conclusive manner, " to look up your reference."

Mr. Polly stood up abruptly.

" Thank you," said the employer, and dismissed him.

" Chump chops! How about chump chops? " said the phrasemonger with an air of inspiration.

" I hope then to hear from you, Sir," said Mr. Polly in his best salesman manner.

" If everything is satisfactory," said the prospective employer.

2

A man whose brain devotes its hinterland to making odd phrases and nicknames out of ill-conceived words, whose conception of life is a lump of auriferous rock to which all the value is given by rare veins of un-businesslike joy, who reads Boccaccio and Rabelais and Shakespeare with gusto, and uses " Stertoraneous Shover " and " Smart Junior " as terms of bitterest opprobrium, is not likely to make a great success under modern business conditions. Mr. Polly dreamt always of picturesque and mellow things, and had an instinctive hatred of the strenuous life. He would have resisted the spell of ex-President Roosevelt, or General Baden Powell, or Mr. Peter Keary, or the late Dr. Samuel Smiles quite easily—I doubt if even Mr. St. Loe Strachey could have inspired him; and he loved Falstaff and Hudibras and coarse laughter, and the Old England of Washington Irving and the memory of Charles the Second's courtly days. His progress was necessarily slow. He did not get rises; he lost situations; there was something in his eye employers did not like; he would have lost his places oftener if he had not been at times an exceptionally brilliant salesman, rather carefully neat, and a slow but very fair window-dresser.

He went from situation to situation, he invented a great wealth of nicknames, he conceived enmities and made friends—but none so richly satisfying as Parsons. He was frequently, but mildly and discursively, in love; and sometimes he thought of that girl who had given him a yellow-green apple. He had an idea amounting to a flattering certainty whose youthful freshness it was had stirred her to self-forgetfulness. And sometimes he thought of Fishbourne sleeping prosperously in the sun. And he had moods of discomfort and lassitude and ill-temper, due to the beginnings of indigestion.

Various forces and suggestions came into his life and swayed him for longer and shorter periods.

He went to Canterbury and came under the influence of Gothic architecture. There was a blood affinity between Mr. Polly and the Gothic; in the Middle Ages he would, no doubt, have sat upon a scaffolding and carved out penetrating and none too flattering portraits of church dignitaries upon the capitals; and when he strolled, with his hands behind his back, along the cloisters behind the cathedral, and looked at the rich grass plot in the centre, he had the strangest sense of being at home—far more than he had ever been at home before. " Portly capons," he used to murmur to himself, under the impression that he was naming a characteristic type of mediæval churchman.

He liked to sit in the nave during the service, and look through the great gates at the candles and choristers, and listen to the organ-sustained voices, but the transepts he never penetrated because of the charge for admission. The music and the long vista of the fretted roof filled him with a vague and mystical happiness that he had no words, even mispronounceable words to express. But some of the smug monuments in the aisles got a wreath of epithets; " metrorious urnfuls," " funererial claims," " dejected angelosity," for example. He wandered about the precincts, and speculated about the people who lived in the ripe and cosy houses of gray stone that cluster there so comfortably. Through green doors in high stone walls he caught glimpses of level lawns and blazing flower-beds; mullioned windows revealed shaded reading lamps and disciplined shelves of brown bound books. Now and then a dignitary in gaiters would pass him (" Portly capon "), or a drift of white-robed choir boys cross a distant arcade and vanish in a doorway, or the pink and cream of some girlish dress flit like a butterfly across the cool still spaces of the place. Particularly he responded to the ruined arches of the Benedictine's Infirmary and the view of Bell Harry Tower from the school building. He was stirred to read the *Canterbury Tales*, but he could not get on with Chaucer's old-fashioned English, it fatigued his attention, and he would have given all the story-telling very readily for a few adventures on the road. He wanted these nice people to live more and yarn less. He appreciated the wife of Bath very keenly. He would have liked to have known that woman.

At Canterbury, too, he first, to his knowledge, saw

Americans. His shop did a good class trade in West-gate Street, and he would see them go by on the way to stare at Chaucer's " Chequers " and then turn down Mercery Lane to Prior Goldstone's gate. It impressed him that they were always in a kind of quiet hurry, and very determined and methodical people—much more so than any English he knew.

" Cultured Rapacacity," he tried.

" Vorocious Return to the Heritage."

He would expound them incidentally to his attendant apprentices. He had overheard a little lady putting her view to a friend near the Christchurch gate. The accent and intonation had hung in his memory, and he would reproduce them more or less accurately. " Now, does this Marlowe monument really and truly *matter*? " he had heard the little lady inquire. " We've no time for side shows and second-rate stunts, Mamie. We want just the Big Simple Things of the place, just the Broad Elemental Canterbury Praposition. What is it saying to us? I want to get right hold of that, and then have tea in the very room that Chaucer did, and hustle to get that four-eighteen train back to London. . . ."

He would go over these specious phrases, finding them full of an indescribable flavour. " Just the Broad Elemental Canterbury Praposition," he would repeat. . . .

He would try to imagine Parsons confronted with Americans. For his own part, he knew himself to be altogether inadequate. . . .

Canterbury was the most congenial situation Mr. Polly ever found during these wander years, albeit a very desert so far as companionship went.

3

It was after Canterbury that the universe became

really disagreeable to Mr. Polly. It was brought home to him not so much vividly as with a harsh ungainly insistence that he was a failure in his trade. It was not the trade he ought to have chosen, though what trade he ought to have chosen was by no means clear.

He made great but irregular efforts, and produced a forced smartness that, like a cheap dye, refused to stand sunshine. He acquired a sort of parsimony also, in which acquisition he was helped by one or two phases of absolute impecuniosity. But he was hopeless in competition against the naturally gifted, the born hustlers, the young men who meant to get on.

He left the Canterbury place very regretfully. He and another commercial gentleman took a boat one Sunday afternoon at Sturry-on-the-Stour, when the wind was in the west, and sailed it very happily eastward for an hour. They had never sailed a boat before, and it seemed a simple and wonderful thing to do. When they turned, they found the river too narrow for tacking, and the tide running out like a sluice. They battled back to Sturry in the course of six hours (at a shilling the first hour and sixpence for each hour afterwards), rowing a mile in an hour and a half or so, until the turn of the tide came to help them, and then they had a night walk to Canterbury, and found themselves remorselessly locked out.

The Canterbury employer was an amiable, religious-spirited man, and he would probably not have dismissed Mr. Polly if that unfortunate tendency to phrase things had not shocked him. "A Tide's a Tide, Sir," said Mr. Polly, feeling that things were not so bad. "I've no lune-attic power to alter *that*."

It proved impossible to explain to the Canterbury employer that this was not a highly disrespectful and blasphemous remark.

"And beside, what good are you to me this morning,

do you think? " said the Canterbury employer, " with your arms pulled out of their sockets? "

So Mr. Polly resumed his observations in the Wood Street warehouses once more, and had some dismal times. The shoal of fish waiting for the crumbs of employment seemed larger than ever.

He took counsel with himself. Should he " chuck " the outfitting? It wasn't any good for him now, and presently, when he was older and his youthful smartness had passed into the dullness of middle age, it would be worse. What else could he do?

He could think of nothing. He went one night to a music-hall and developed a vague idea of a comic performance; the comic men seemed violent rowdies, and not at all funny; but when he thought of the great pit of the audience yawning before him, he realised that his was an altogether too delicate talent for such a use. He was impressed by the charm of selling vegetables by auction in one of those open shops near London Bridge, but admitted upon reflection his general want of technical knowledge. He made some inquiries about emigration, but none of the colonies were in want of shop assistants without capital. He kept up his attendance in Wood Street.

He subdued his ideal of salary by the sum of five pounds a year, and was taken at that into a driving establishment in Clapham, which dealt chiefly in ready-made suits, fed its assistants in an underground dining-room, and kept open until twelve on Saturdays. He found it hard to be cheerful there. His fits of indigestion became worse, and he began to lie awake at night and think. Sunshine and laughter seemed things lost for ever; picnics, and shouting in the moonlight.

The chief shopwalker took a dislike to him and nagged him. " Nar, then, Polly! " " Look alive Polly! " became the burden of his days. " As Smart a chap as you could have," said the chief shopwalker,

" but no *Zest*. No *Zest*! No *Vim*! What's the matter with you? "

During his night vigils Mr. Polly had a feeling. . . . A young rabbit must have very much the feeling when, after a youth of gambolling in sunny woods and furtive jolly raids upon the growing wheat and exciting triumphant bolts before ineffectual casual dogs, it finds itself at last for a long night of floundering effort and perplexity in a net—for the rest of its life.

He could not grasp what was wrong with him. He made enormous efforts to diagnose his case. Was he really just a " lazy slacker " who ought to " buck up? " He couldn't find it in him to believe it. He blamed his father a good deal—it is what fathers are for—in putting him to a trade he wasn't happy to follow, but he found it impossible to say what he ought to have followed. He felt there had been something stupid about his school, but just where that came in he couldn't say. He made some perfectly sincere efforts to " buck up " and " shove " ruthlessly. But that was infernal—impossible. He had to admit himself miserable with all the misery of a social misfit, and with no clear prospect of more than the most incidental happiness ahead of him. And for all his attempts at self-reproach and self-discipline he felt at bottom that he wasn't at fault.

As a matter of fact all the elements of his troubles had been adequately diagnosed by a certain high-browed, spectacled gentleman living at Highbury, wearing a gold pince-nez, and writing for the most part in the beautiful library of the Climax Club. This gentleman did not know Mr. Polly personally, but he had dealt with him generally as " one of those ill-adjusted units that abound in a society that has failed to develop a collective intelligence and a collective will for order commensurate with its perplexities."

But phrases of that sort had no appeal for Mr. Polly.

CHAPTER FOUR

Mr. Polly an Orphan

I

THEN a great change was brought about in the life of Mr. Polly by the death of his father. His father died suddenly—the local practitioner still clung to his theory that it was imagination he suffered from, but compromised in the certificate with the appendicitis that was then so fashionable—and Mr. Polly found himself heir to a debatable number of pieces of furniture in the house of his cousin near Easewood Junction, a family Bible, an engraved portrait of Garibaldi, and a bust of Mr. Gladstone, an invalid gold watch, a gold locket formerly belonging to his mother, and some minor jewellery and bric-à-brac, a quantity of nearly valueless old clothes, and an insurance policy and money in the bank amounting altogether to the sum of three hundred and fifty-five pounds.

Mr. Polly had always regarded his father as an immortal, as an eternal fact; and his father, being of a reserved nature in his declining years, had said nothing about the insurance policy. Both wealth and bereavement therefore took Mr. Polly by surprise, and found him a little inadequate. His mother's death had been a childish grief and long forgotten, and the strongest affections in his life had been for Parsons. An only child of sociable tendencies turns his back a good deal upon home; and the aunt who had succeeded his mother was an economist and furniture polisher, a knuckle-rapper and a sharp silencer: no friend for a slovenly little boy. He had loved other little boys and girls transitorily; none had been frequent and familiar enough to strike deep roots in his heart; and

he had grown up with a tattered and dissipated
affectionateness that was becoming wildly shy. His
father had always been a stranger, an irritable stranger
with exceptional powers of intervention and comment,
and an air of being disappointed about his offspring.
It was shocking to lose him; it was like an unexpected
hole in the universe, and the writing " Death " upon
the sky; but it did not tear Mr. Polly's heartstrings at
first so much as rouse him to a pitch of vivid attention.

He came down to the cottage at Easewood in response
to an urgent telegram, and found his father already
dead. His cousin Johnson received him with much
solemnity, and ushered him upstairs to look at a stiff,
straight, shrouded form with a face unwontedly quiet,
and, it seemed, by reason of its pinched nostrils,
scornful.

" Looks peaceful," said Mr. Polly, disregarding the
scorn to the best of his ability.

" It was a merciful relief," said Mr. Johnson.

There was a pause.

" Second—second Departed I've ever seen—not
counting mummies," said Mr. Polly, feeling it necessary
to say something.

" We did all we could."

" No doubt of it, O' Man," said Mr. Polly.

A second long pause followed, and then, to Mr.
Polly's great relief, Johnson moved towards the door.

Afterwards Mr. Polly went for a solitary walk in the
evening light, and as he walked, suddenly his dead
father became real to him. He thought of things far
away down the perspective of memory—of jolly
moments when his father had skylarked with a wildly
excited little boy; of a certain annual visit to the
Crystal Palace pantomime, full of trivial glittering
incidents and wonders; of his father's dread back
while customers were in the old, minutely known shop.
It is curious that the memory which seemed to link

him nearest to the dead man was the memory of a fit of passion. His father had wanted to get a small sofa up the narrow winding staircase from the little room behind the shop to the bedroom above, and it had jammed. For a time his father had coaxed, and then groaned like a soul in torment, and given way to blind fury; had sworn, kicked, and struck at the offending piece of furniture, and finally, with an immense effort, wrenched it upstairs, with considerable incidental damage to lath and plaster and one of the casters. That moment when self-control was altogether torn aside, the shocked discovery of his father's perfect humanity, had left a singular impression on Mr. Polly's queer mind. It was as if something extravagantly vital had come out of his father and laid a warmly passionate hand upon his heart. He remembered that now very vividly, and it became a clue to endless other memories that had else been dispersed and confusing.

A weakly wilful being, struggling to get obdurate things round impossible corners—in that symbol Mr. Polly could recognise himself and all the trouble of humanity.

He hadn't had a particularly good time, poor old chap; and now it was all over—finished. . . .

Johnson was the sort of man who derives great satisfaction from a funeral; a melancholy, serious, practical minded man of five-and-thirty, with great powers of advice. He was the up-line ticket clerk at Easewood Junction, and felt the responsibilities of his position. He was naturally thoughtful and reserved, and greatly sustained in that by an innate rectitude of body and an overhanging and forward inclination of the upper part of his face and head. He was pale but freckled, and his dark gray eyes were deeply set. His lightest interest was cricket, but he did not take that lightly. His chief holiday was to go to a cricket match, which he did as if he was going to church; and he watched critically, applauded sparingly, and was darkly offended by any unorthodox play. His convictions upon all subjects were taciturnly inflexible. He was an obstinate player of draughts and chess, and an earnest and persistent reader of the *British Weekly*. His wife was a pink, short, wilfully smiling, managing, ingratiating, talkative woman, who was determined to be pleasant, and take a bright, hopeful view of everything, even when it was not really bright and hopeful. She had large, blue, expressive eyes and a round face, and she always spoke of her husband as Harold. She addressed sympathetic and considerate remarks about the deceased to Mr. Polly in notes of brisk encouragement. " He was really quite cheerful at the end," she said several times, with congratulatory gusto; " quite cheerful."

She made dying seem almost agreeable.

Both these people were resolved to treat Mr. Polly very well, and to help his exceptional incompetence in every possible way; and after a simple supper of ham and bread and cheese and pickles and cold apple tart and small beer had been cleared away, they put him into the arm-chair almost as though he was an invalid, and sat on chairs that made them look down upon him, and opened a directive discussion of the arrangements for the funeral. After all, a funeral is a distinct social opportunity, and rare when you have no family and few relations, and they did not want to see it spoiled and wasted.

" You'll have a hearse, of course," said Mrs. Johnson; " not one of them combinations, with the driver sitting on the coffin. Disrespectful, I think they are. I can't fancy how people can bring themselves to be buried in combinations." She flattened her voice in a manner she used to intimate æsthetic feeling. " I *do* like them glass hearses," she said. " So refined and nice they are."

"Podger's hearse you'll have," said Johnson conclusively; "it's the best in Easewood."

"Everything that's right and proper," said Mr. Polly.

"Podger's ready to come and measure at any time," said Johnson.

"Then you'll want a mourners' carriage or two, according to whom you're going to invite," said Mr. Johnson.

"Didn't think of inviting any one," said Mr. Polly.

"Oh, you'll *have* to ask a few friends," said Mr. Johnson. "You can't let your father go to his grave without asking a few friends."

"Funerial baked meats, like," said Mr. Polly.

"Not baked; but of course you'll have to give them something. Ham and chicken's very suitable. You don't want a lot of cooking, with the ceremony coming into the middle of it. I wonder who Alfred ought to invite, Harold? Just the immediate relations. One doesn't want a Great Crowd of People, and one doesn't want not to show respect."

"But he hated our relations—most of them."

"He's not hating them now," said Mr. Johnson; "you may be sure of that. It's just because of that I think they ought to come, all of them—even your Aunt Mildred."

"Bit vulturial, isn't it?" said Mr. Polly unheeded.

"Wouldn't be more than twelve or thirteen people if they *all* came," said Mr. Johnson.

"We could have everything put out ready in the back room, and the gloves and whisky in the front room; and while we were all at the—ceremony, Bessie could bring it all into the front room on a tray, and put it out nice and proper. There'd have to be whisky, and sherry-or-port for the ladies. . . ."

"Where'll you get your mourning?" asked Johnson abruptly.

Mr. Polly had not yet considered this by-product of sorrow. " Haven't thought of it yet, O' Man."

A disagreeable feeling spread over his body, as though he was blackening as he sat. He hated black garments.

" I suppose I must *have* mourning," he said.

" *Well!* " said Johnson, with a solemn smile.

" Got to see it through," said Mr. Polly indistinctly.

" If I were you," said Johnson, " I should get ready-made trousers. That's all you really want. And a black satin tie, and a top hat with a deep mourning band. And gloves."

" Jet cuff-links he ought to have—as chief mourner." said Mrs. Johnson.

" Not obligatory," said Johnson.

" It shows respect," said Mrs. Johnson.

" It shows respect, of course," said Johnson.

And then Mrs. Johnson went on with the utmost gusto to the details of the " casket," while Mr. Polly sat more and more deeply and droopingly into the armchair, assenting with a note of protest to all they said. After he had retired for the night he remained for a long time perched on the edge of the sofa, which was his bed, staring at the prospect before him. " Chasing the o' man about to the last," he said.

He hated the thought and elaboration of death as a healthy animal must hate it. His mind struggled with unwonted social problems.

" Got to put 'em away somehow, I suppose," said Mr. Polly. " Wish I'd looked him up a bit more while he was alive."

2

Bereavement came to Mr. Polly before the realisation of opulence and its anxieties and responsibilities. That only dawned upon him on the morrow—which chanced to be Sunday—as he walked with Johnson before church time about the tangle of struggling building enterprise that constituted the rising urban district of Easewood. Johnson was off duty that morning, and devoted the time very generously to the admonitory discussion of Mr. Polly's worldly outlook.

" Don't seem to get the hang of the business some-how," said Mr. Polly. " Too much blooming humbug in it for my way of thinking."

" If I were you," said Mr. Johnson, "I should push for a first-class place in London—take almost nothing and live on my reserves. That's what I should do."

" Come the Heavy," said Mr. Polly.

" Get a better-class reference."

There was a pause. " Think of investing your money? " asked Johnson.

" Hardly got used to the idea of having it yet, O' Man."

" You'll have to do something with it. Give you nearly twenty pounds a year if you invest it properly."

" Haven't seen it yet in that light," said Mr. Polly defensively.

" There's no end of things you could put it into."

" It's getting it out again I shouldn't feel sure of. I'm no sort of Fiancianier. Sooner back horses."

" I wouldn't do that if I were you."

" Not my style, O' Man."

" It's a nest egg," said Johnson.

Mr. Polly made an indeterminate noise.

" There's building societies," Johnson threw out in a speculative tone. Mr. Polly, with detached brevity, admitted there were.

" You might lend it on mortgage," said Johnson. " Very safe form of investment."

" Shan't think anything about it—not till the o' man's underground," said Mr. Polly, with an in-spiration.

They turned a corner that led towards the junction.

" Might do worse," said Johnson, " than put it into a small shop."

At the moment this remark made very little appeal to Mr. Polly. But afterwards it developed. It fell into his mind like some small obscure seed and germinated.

" These shops aren't in a bad position," said Johnson.

The row he referred to gaped in the late painful stage in building before the healing touch of the plasterer assuages the roughness of the brickwork. The space for the shop yawned an oblong gap below, framed above by an iron girder; " Windows and fittings to suit tenant," a board at the end of the row promised; and behind was the door space and a glimpse of stairs going up to the living-rooms above. " Not a bad position," said Johnson, and led the way into the establishment. " Room for fixtures there," he said, pointing to the blank wall.

The two men went upstairs to the little sitting-room (or best bedroom it would have to be) above the shop. Then they descended to the kitchen below.

" Rooms in a new house always look a bit small," said Johnson.

They came out of the house again by the prospective back door, and picked their way through builder's litter across the yard space to the road again. They drew nearer the junction to where a pavement and shops already open and active formed the commercial centre of Easewood. On the opposite side of the way the side door of a flourishing little establishment opened, and a man and his wife and a little boy in a sailor suit came into the street. The wife was a pretty woman in brown, with a floriferous straw hat, and the group was altogether very Sundayfied and shiny and spick and span. The shop itself had a large plate-glass window whose contents were now veiled by a buff blind on which was inscribed in scrolly letters "Rymer, Pork Butcher and Provision Merchant," and then with voluptuous elaboration, "The World Famed Easewood Sausage."

Greetings were exchanged between Mr. Johnson and this distinguished comestible.

"Off to church already?" said Johnson.

"Walking across the fields to Little Dorington," said Mr. Rymer.

"Very pleasant walk," said Johnson.

"Very," said Mr. Rymer.

"Hope you'll enjoy it," said Mr. Johnson.

"That chap's done well," said Johnson, *sotto voce* as they went on. "Came here with nothing—practically, four years ago. And as thin as a lath. Look at him now!"

"He's worked hard, of course," said Johnson, improving the occasion.

Thought fell between the cousins for a space.

"Some men can do one thing," said Johnson, "and some another. . . . For a man who sticks to it there's a lot to be done in a shop."

3

All the preparations for the funeral ran easily and happily under Mrs. Johnson's skilful hands. On the eve of the sad occasion she produced a reserve of black sateen, the kitchen steps, and a box of tintacks, and decorated the house with festoons and bows of black in the best possible taste. She tied up the knocker with black crêpe, and put a large bow over the corner of the steel engraving of Garibaldi, and swathed the bust of Mr. Gladstone that had belonged to the deceased with inky swathings. She turned the two vases that had views of Tivoli and the Bay of Naples round, so that these rather brilliant landscapes were hidden and only the plain blue enamel showed, and she anticipated the long contemplated purchase of a tablecloth for the front room, and substituted a violet purple cover for the now very worn and faded raptures and roses in plushette that had hitherto done duty there. Everything that loving consideration could do to impart a dignified solemnity to her little home was done.

She had released Mr. Polly from that irksome duty of issuing invitations, and as the moments of assembly drew near she sent him and Mr. Johnson out into the narrow, long strip of garden at the back of the house, to be free to put a finishing touch or so to her preparations. She sent them out together because she had a queer little persuasion at the back of her mind that Mr. Polly wanted to bolt from his sacred duties, and there was no way out of the garden except through the house.

Mr. Johnson was a steady, successful gardener, and particularly good with celery and peas. He walked slowly along the narrow path down the centre, pointing out to Mr. Polly a number of interesting points in the management of peas, wrinkles neatly applied and difficulties wisely overcome, and all that he did for the comfort and propitiation of that fitful but rewarding vegetable. Presently a sound of nervous laughter and raised voices from the house proclaimed the arrival of the earlier guests, and the worst of that anticipatory tension was over.

When Mr. Polly re-entered the house he found three entirely strange young women with pink faces, demonstrative manners, and emphatic mourning engaged in an incoherent conversation with Mrs. Johnson. All three kissed him with great gusto after the ancient English fashion. "These are your cousins Larkins," said Mrs. Johnson. "That's Annie" (unexpected hug and smack), "that's Miriam" (resolute hug and smack), " and that's Minnie " (prolonged hug and smack).

" Right-o," said Mr. Polly, emerging a little crumpled and breathless from the hearty introduction. " I see."

" Here's Aunt Larkins," said Mrs. Johnson, as an elderly and stouter edition of the three young women appeared in the doorway.

Mr. Polly backed rather faint-heartedly, but Aunt Larkins was not to be denied. Having hugged and kissed her nephew resoundingly, she gripped him by the wrist and scanned his features. She had a round, sentimental, freckled face. " I should 'ave known 'im anywhere," she said, with fervour.

" Hark at Mother! " said the cousin called Annie. " Why, she's never set eyes on him before."

" I should 'ave known 'im anywhere," said Mrs. Larkins, " for Lizzie's child. You've got her eyes! It's a Resemblance! And as for never seeing him—I've *dandled* him, Miss Imperence, I've dandled him."

" You couldn't dandle him now, Ma! " Miss Annie remarked, with a shriek of laughter.

All the sisters laughed at that. " The things you say, Annie! " said Miriam, and for a time the room was full of mirth.

Mr. Polly felt it incumbent upon him to say something. " *My* dandling days are over," he said.

The reception of this remark would have convinced a far more modest character than Mr. Polly that it was extremely witty.

Mr. Polly followed it up by another one almost equally good. " My turn to dandle," he said, with a sly look at his aunt, and convulsed every one.

" Not me," said Mrs. Larkins, taking his point, " *thank* you," and achieved a climax.

It was queer, but they seemed to be easy people to get on with anyhow. They were still picking little ripples and giggles of mirth from the idea of Mr. Polly dandling Aunt Larkins when Mr. Johnson, who had answered the door, ushered in a stooping figure, who was at once hailed by Mrs. Johnson as " Why! Uncle Pentstemon! " Uncle Pentstemon was rather a shock. His was an aged rather than venerable figure. Time had removed the hair from the top of his head and distributed a small dividend of the plunder in little bunches carelessly and impartially over the rest of his features; he was dressed in a very big, old frock-coat and a long, cylindrical top-hat, which he had kept on; he was very much bent, and he carried a rush basket, from which protruded coy intimations of the lettuces and onions he had brought to grace the occasion. He hobbled into the room, resisting the efforts of Johnson to divest him of the various encumbrances, halted, and surveyed the company with an expression of profound hostility, breathing hard. Recognition quickened in his eyes.

" *You* here? " he said to Aunt Larkins, and then, " You *would* be. . . . These your gals? "

" They are," said Aunt Larkins, " and better gals——"

" That Annie? " asked Uncle Pentstemon, pointing a horny thumb-nail.

" Fancy you remembering her name! "

" She mucked up my mushroom bed, the baggage! " said Uncle Pentstemon ungenially, " and I give it to her to rights. Trounced her I did—fairly. *I* remember her. Here's some green stuff for you, Grace. Fresh it is, and wholesome. I shall be wanting the basket back, and mind you let me have it. . . . Have you nailed him down yet? Ah! You always was a bit in front of what was needful."

His attention was drawn inward by a troublesome tooth, and he sucked at it spitefully. There was something potent about this old man that silenced every one for a moment or so. He seemed a fragment from the ruder agricultural past of our race, like a lump of soil among things of paper. He put his packet of earthy vegetables very deliberately on the new violet table-cloth, removed his hat carefully, and dabbled his brow, and wiped out his hat-brim with an abundant crimson and yellow pocket-handkerchief.

" I'm glad you were able to come, Uncle," said Mrs. Johnson.

" Oh, I *came*," said Uncle Pentstemon. " I *came*."

He turned on Mrs. Larkins. " Gals in service? " he asked.

" They aren't, and won't be," said Mrs. Larkins.

" No," he said, with infinite meaning, and turned his eye on Mr. Polly.

" You Lizzie's boy? " he said.

Mr. Polly was spared much self-exposition by the tumult occasioned by further arrivals.

" Ah! here's May Punt! " said Mrs. Johnson, and a small woman dressed in the borrowed mourning of a large woman, and leading a very small, fair-haired, sharp-nosed, observant little boy—it was his first funeral—appeared, closely followed by several friends of Mrs. Johnson who had come to swell the display of respect, and who left only vague, confused impressions upon Mr. Polly's mind. (Aunt Mildred, who was an unexplained family scandal, had declined Mrs. Johnson's hospitality, to the relief of every one who understood—as Mrs. Johnson intimated—though who understood, and what, as my head master used to say, Mr. Polly could form no idea.)

Everybody was in profound mourning, of course—mourning in the modern English style, with the dyer's handiwork only too apparent, and hats and jackets of the current cut. There was very little crêpe, and the costumes had none of the goodness and specialisation and genuine enjoyment of mourning for mourning's sake that a similar Continental gathering would have displayed. Still that congestion of strangers in black sufficed to stun and confuse Mr. Polly's impressionable mind. It seemed to him much more extraordinary than anything he had expected.

"Now, gals," said Mrs. Larkins, "see if you can help," and the three daughters became confusingly active between the front room and the back.

"I hope every one'll take a glass of sherry and a biscuit," said Mrs. Johnson. "We don't stand on ceremony," and a decanter appeared in the place of Uncle Pentstemon's vegetables.

Uncle Pentstemon had refused to be relieved of his hat; he sat stiffly down on a chair against the wall, with that venerable head-dress between his feet, watching the approach of any one jealously. "Don't you go squashing my hat," he said. Conversation became confused and general. Uncle Pentstemon addressed himself to Mr. Polly.

"You're a little chap," he said; "a puny little chap. I never did agree to Lizzie marrying him, but I suppose bygones must be bygones now. I suppose they made you a clerk or something."

"Outfitter," said Mr. Polly.

"I remember. Them girls pretend to be dressmakers."

"They *are* dressmakers," said Mrs. Larkins across the room.

"I *will* take a glass of sherry," he remarked; and then mildly to Mr. Polly, "They 'old to it, you see."

He took the glass Mrs. Johnson handed him and, poised it critically between a horny finger and thumb. "You'll be paying for this," he said to Mr. Polly. "Here's *to* you. . . . Don't you go treading on my hat, young woman. You brush your skirts against it and you take a shilling off its value. It ain't the sort of 'at you see nowadays."

He drank noisily.

The sherry presently loosened everybody's tongue, and the opening coldness passed.

"There ought to have been a *post mortem*," Polly heard Mrs. Punt remarking to one of Mrs. Johnson's friends, and Miriam and another were lost in admiration of Mrs. Johnson's decorations. "So very nice and refined," they were both repeating at intervals.

The sherry and biscuits were still being discussed when Mr. Podger, the undertaker, arrived, a broad, cheerfully sorrowful, clean-shaven, little man, accompanied by a melancholy faced assistant. He conversed for a time with Johnson in the passage outside. The sense of his business stilled the rising waves of chatter and carried off every one's attention in the wake of his heavy footsteps to the room above.

4

Things crowded upon Mr. Polly. Every one, he noticed, took sherry with a solemn avidity, and a small portion even was administered sacramentally to the Punt boy. There followed a distribution of black kid gloves, and much trying-on and humouring of fingers. "*Good* gloves," said one of Mrs. Johnson's friends. "There's a little pair there for Willie," said Mrs. Johnson triumphantly. Every one seemed gravely content with the amazing procedure of the occasion. Presently Mr. Podger was picking Mr. Polly out as Chief Mourner to go with Mrs. Johnson, Mrs. Larkins, and Annie in the first mourning carriage.

"Right-o," said Mr. Polly, and repented instantly of the alacrity of the phrase.

"There'll have to be a walking-party," said Mrs. Johnson cheerfully. "There's only two coaches. I dare say we can put six in each, but that leaves three over."

There was a generous struggle to be pedestrian, and the two other Larkin girls, confessing coyly to tight new boots, and displaying a certain eagerness, were added to the contents of the first carriage.

"It'll be a squeeze," said Annie.

"*I* don't mind a squeeze," said Mr. Polly.

He decided privately that the proper phrase for the result of that remark was "Hysterial catechunations."

Mr. Podger re-entered the room from a momentary supervision of the bumping business that was now proceeding down the staircase.

"Bearing up," he said cheerfully, rubbing his hands together. "Bearing up!"

That stuck very vividly in Mr. Polly's mind, and so did the close-wedged drive to the churchyard, bunched in between two young women in confused dull and shiny black, and the fact that the wind was bleak and that the officiating clergyman had a cold, and sniffed between his sentences. The wonder of life! The wonder of everything! What had he expected that this should all be so astoundingly different?

He found his attention converging more and more upon the Larkins cousins. The interest was reciprocal. They watched him with a kind of suppressed excitement and became risible with his every word and gesture. He was more and more aware of their personal quality. Annie had blue eyes, and a red, attractive mouth, a harsh voice, and a habit of extreme liveliness that even this occasion could not suppress; Minnie was fond, extremely free about the touching of hands and such-like endearments; Miriam was dark and quieter than her sisters and regarded him earnestly. Mrs. Larkins was very happy in her daughters, and they had the naïve affectionateness of those who see few people and find a strange cousin a wonderful outlet. Mr. Polly had never been very much kissed, and it made his mind swim. He did not know for the life of him whether he liked or disliked all or any of the Larkins cousins. It was rather attractive to make them laugh anyhow; they laughed at anything.

There they were tugging at his mind, and the funeral tugging at his mind too, and the sense of himself as Chief Mourner in a brand new silk hat with a broad mourning band. He watched the ceremony and missed his responses, and strange feelings twisted at his heartstrings.

5

Mr. Polly walked back to the house because he wanted to be alone. Miriam and Minnie would have accompanied him, but finding Uncle Pentstemon beside the Chief Mourner they went on in front.

" You're wise," said Uncle Pentstemon.

" Glad you think so," said Mr. Polly, rousing himself to talk.

" I likes a bit of a walk before a meal," said Uncle Pentstemon, and made a kind of large hiccup. " That sherry rises," he remarked. " Grocer's stuff, I expect."

He went on to ask how much the funeral might be costing, and seemed pleased to find Mr. Polly didn't know.

" In that case," he said impressively, " it's pretty certain to cost more'n you expect, my boy."

He meditated for a time. " I've seen a mort of undertakers," he declared; " a mort of undertakers."

The Larkins girls attracted his attention.

" Lets lodgin's and chars," he commented. " Leastways she goes out to cook dinners. And *look* at 'em! Dressed up to the nines. If it ain't borryd clothes, that is. And they goes out to work at a factory! "

" Did you know my father much, Uncle Pentstemon? " asked Mr. Polly.

" Couldn't stand Lizzie throwin' herself away like

that," said Uncle Pentstemon, and repeated his hiccup on a larger scale.

" That *weren't* good sherry," said Uncle Pentstemon, with the first note of pathos Mr. Polly had detected in his quavering voice.

The funeral in the rather cold wind had proved wonderfully appetising, and every eye brightened at the sight of the cold collation that was now spread in the front room. Mrs. Johnson was very brisk, and Mr. Polly, when he re-entered the house, found the party sitting down.

" Come along, Alfred," cried the hostess cheerfully. " We can't very well begin without you. Have you got the bottled beer ready to open, Betsy ? Uncle, you'll have a drop of whisky, I expect."

" Put it where I can mix for myself; I can't bear wimmin's mixing," said Uncle Pentstemon, placing his hat very carefully out of harm's way on the book-case.

There were two cold boiled chickens, which Johnson carved with great care and justice, and a nice piece of ham, some brawn, and a steak-and-kidney pie, a large bowl of salad and several sorts of pickles, and after-wards some cold apple tart, jam roll, and a good piece of Stilton cheese, lots of bottled beer, some lemonade for the ladies, and milk for Master Punt: a very bright and satisfying meal. Mr. Polly found himself seated between Mrs. Punt, who was much preoccupied with Master Punt's table manners, and one of Mrs. Johnson's school friends, who was exchanging reminiscences with Mrs. Johnson of schooldays and news of how various common friends had changed and married. Opposite him was Miriam and another of the early Johnson circle, and also he had brawn to carve, and there was hardly room for the helpful Bessie to pass behind his chair, so that altogether his mind would have been amply distracted from any mortuary broodings, even if a wordy warfare about the education of the modern young woman had not sprung up between Uncle Pentstemon and Mrs. Larkins, and threatened for a time, in spite of a word or so in season from Johnson, to wreck all the harmony of the sad occasion.

The general effect was after this fashion:—

First an impression of Mrs. Punt on the right, speaking in a refined undertone: "You didn't, I suppose, Mr. Polly, think to 'ave your poor dear father *post-mortemed*."

Lady on the left side, breaking in: "I was just reminding Grace of the dear dead days beyond recall."

Attempted reply to Mrs. Punt: "Didn't think of it for a moment. Can't give you a piece of this brawn, can I?"

Fragment from the left: "Grace and Beauty they used to call us, and we used to sit at the same desk."

Mrs. Punt, breaking out suddenly: "Don't *swaller* your fork, Willie—You see, Mr. Polly, I used to have a young gentleman, a medical student, lodging with me——"

Voice from down the table with a large softness: "'Am, Elfred? I didn't give you very much 'am."

Bessie became evident at the back of Mr. Polly's chair, struggling wildly to get past. Mr. Polly did his best to be helpful. "Can you get past? Lemme sit forward a bit. Urr-oo! Right-o!"

Lady to the left going on valiantly and speaking to every one who cared to listen, while Mrs. Johnson beamed beside her: "There she used to sit as bold as brass, and the fun she used to make of things no one *could* believe—knowing her now. She used to make faces at the mistress through the——"

Mrs. Punt, keeping steadily on: "The contents of the stummik at any rate *ought* to be examined."

Voice of Mrs. Johnson: "Elfrid, pass the mustid down."

Miriam, leaning across the table: "Elfrid!"

"Once she got us all kept in. The whole school!"

Miriam, more insistently: "Elfrid!"

Uncle Pentstemon, raising his voice defiantly: "Trounce 'er again I would if she did as much now. That I would. Dratted mischief!"

Miriam, catching Mr. Polly's eye: "Elfrid! This lady knows Canterbury. I been telling her you been there."

Mr. Polly: "Glad you know it."

The lady, shouting: "I like it."

Mrs. Larkins, raising her voice: "I won't 'ave my girls spoken of, not by nobody, old *or* young."

POP! imperfectly located.

Mr. Johnson at large: "*Ain't* the beer up! It's the 'eated room."

Bessie: "'Scuse me, Sir, passing so soon again, but——" Rest inaudible. Mr. Polly, accommodating himself: "Urr-oo! Right? Right-o!"

The knives and forks, probably by some secret common agreement, clash and clatter together, and drown every other sound.

"Nobody 'ad the least idea 'ow 'E died—nobody. . . . Willie, don't *golp* so. You ain't in a hurry, are you? You don't want to ketch a train, or anything —golping like that!"

"D'you remember, Grace, 'ow one day we 'ad writing lessons . . ."

"Nicer girls no one ever 'ad—though I say it who shouldn't."

Mrs. Johnson, in a shrill, clear, hospitable voice: "Harold, won't Mrs. Larkins 'ave a teeny bit more fowl?"

Mr. Polly was rising to the situation. "Or some brawn, Mrs. Larkins?" Catching Uncle Pentstemon's eye: "Can't send *you* some brawn, Sir?"

"Elfrid!"

Loud hiccup from Uncle Pentstemon, momentary consternation, followed by giggle from Annie.

The narration at Mr. Polly's elbow pursued a quiet but relentless course. " Directly the new doctor came in, he said, " Everything must be took out and put in spirits—everything."

Willie—audible ingurgitation.

The narration on the left was flourishing up to a climax. " Ladies, she sez, dip their pens *in* their ink and keep their noses out of it."

" Elfrid! " persuasively.

" Certain people may cast snacks at other people's daughters, never having had any of their own, though two poor souls of wives dead and buried through their goings on——"

Johnson ruling the storm: " We don't want old scores dug up on such a day as this——"

" Old scores you may call them, but worth a dozen of them that put them to their rest, poor dears."

" Elfrid! " with a note of remonstrance.

" If you choke yourself, my lord, not another mouthful do you 'ave. No nice puddin'! Nothing! "

" And kept us in, she did, every afternoon for a week! "

It seemed to be the end, and Mr. Polly replied, with an air of being profoundly impressed, " Really! "

" Elfrid! " a little disheartened.

" And then they 'ad it! They found he'd swallowed the very key to unlock the drawer——"

" Then don't let people go casting snacks! "

" *Who's* casting snacks? "

" Elfrid! This lady wants to know, 'ave the Prossers left Canterbury? "

" No wish to make myself disagreeable, not to God's 'umblest worm——"

" Alf, you aren't very busy with that brawn up there! "

And so on for the hour.

The general effect upon Mr. Polly at the time was at once confusing and exhilarating; but it led him to eat copiously and carelessly, and long before the end, when after an hour and a quarter a movement took the party, and it pushed away its cheese-plates and rose sighing and stretching from the remains of the repast, little streaks and bands of dyspeptic irritation and melancholy were darkening the serenity of his mind.

He stood between the mantelshelf and the window— the blinds were up now—and the Larkins sisters clustered about him. He battled with the oncoming depression, and forced himself to be extremely facetious about noticeable rings on Annie's hand. "They ain't real," said Annie coquettishly. "Got 'em out of a prize packet."

"Prize packet in trousers, I expect," said Mr. Polly, and awakened inextinguishable laughter.

"Oh, the Things you say!" said Minnie, slapping his shoulder.

Something he had quite extraordinarily forgotten came into his head.

"Bless my heart!" he cried, suddenly serious.

"What's the matter?" asked Johnson.

"Ought to have gone back to the shop three days ago. They'll make no end of a row!"

"Lor, you *are* a treat!" said Cousin Annie, and screamed with laughter at a delicious idea. "You'll get the Chuck," she said.

Mr. Polly made a convulsive grimace at her.

"I'll die!" she said. "I don't believe you care a bit."

Feeling a little disorganised by her hilarity and a shocked expression that had come to the face of Cousin Miriam, he made some indistinct excuse and went out through the back room and scullery into the little garden. The cool air and a very slight drizzle of rain was a relief—anyhow. But the black mood of the replete dyspeptic had come upon him. His soul darkened hopelessly. He walked with his hands in his pockets down the path between the rows of exceptionally cultured peas, and unreasonably, overwhelmingly, he was smitten by sorrow for his father. The heady noise and muddle and confused excitement of the feast passed from him like a curtain drawn away. He thought of that hot and angry and struggling creature who had tugged and sworn so foolishly at the sofa upon the twisted staircase, and who was now lying still and hidden at the bottom of a wall-sided, oblong pit, beside the heaped gravel that would presently cover him. The stillness of it! the wonder of it! the infinite reproach! Hatred for all these people—all of them—possessed Mr. Polly's soul.

" Hen-witted gigglers," said Mr. Polly.

He went down to the fence, and stood with his hands on it, staring away at nothing. He stayed there for what seemed a long time. From the house came a sound of raised voices that subsided, and then Mrs. Johnson calling for Betsy.

" Ghoulish gusto," said Mr. Polly. " Jumping it in. Funererial Games. Don't hurt him, of course. Doesn't matter to *him*. . . ."

Nobody missed Mr. Polly for a long time.

When at last he reappeared among them his eye was almost grim but nobody noticed his eye. They were looking at watches, and Johnson was being omniscient about trains. They seemed to discover Mr. Polly afresh just at the moment of parting, and said a number of more or less appropriate things. But Uncle Pentstemon was far too worried about his rush basket, which had been carelessly mislaid, he seemed to think with larcenous intentions, to remember Mr. Polly at all. Mrs. Johnson had tried to fob him off with a similar but inferior basket—his own had one handle mended with string according to a method of peculiar virtue and inimitable distinction known only to himself—and the old gentleman had taken her attempt as the gravest reflection upon his years and intelligence. Mr. Polly was left very largely to the Larkins trio. Cousin Minnie became shameless, and kept kissing him good-bye—and then finding out it wasn't time to go. Cousin Miriam seemed to think her silly, and caught Mr. Polly's eye sympathetically. Cousin Annie ceased to giggle, and lapsed into a nearly sentimental state. She said with real feeling that she had enjoyed the funeral more than words could tell.

CHAPTER FIVE

Romance

I

MR. POLLY returned to Clapham from the funeral celebrations prepared for trouble, and took his dismissal in a manly spirit.

" You've merely ante-separated me by a hair," he said politely.

And he told them in the dormitory that he meant to take a little holiday before his next crib, though a certain inherited reticence suppressed the fact of the legacy.

" You'll do that all right," said Ascough, the head of the boot shop. " It's quite the fashion just at present. Six Weeks in Wonderful Wood Street. They're running excursions. . . ."

" A little holiday "; that was the form his sense of wealth took first—it made a little holiday possible. Holidays were his life, and the rest merely adulterated living. And now he might take a little holiday and have money for railway fares and money for meals, and money for inns. But—— He wanted some one to take the holiday with.

For a time he cherished a design of hunting up Parsons, getting him to throw up his situation, and going with him to Stratford-on-Avon and Shrewsbury, and the Welsh mountains and the Wye, and a lot of places like that, for a really gorgeous, careless, illimitable old holiday of a month. But, alas! Parsons had gone from the St. Paul's Churchyard outfitter's long ago and left no address.

Polly tried to think he would be almost as happy wandering alone, but he knew better. He had dreamt of casual encounters with delightfully interesting people by the wayside—even romantic encounters. Such things happened in Chaucer and "Bocashiew"; they happened with extreme facility in Mr. Richard le Gallienne's very detrimental book, *The Quest of the Golden Girl*, which he had read at Canterbury; but he had no confidence they would happen in England— to him.

When, a month later, he came out of the Clapham side door at last into the bright sunshine of a fine London day, with a dazzling sense of limitless freedom upon him, he did nothing more adventurous than order the cabman to drive to Waterloo, and there take a ticket to Easewood.

He wanted—what *did* he want most in life? I think his distinctive craving is best expressed as fun—fun in companionship. He had already spent a pound or two upon three select feasts to his fellow-assistants, sprat suppers they were, and there had been a great and very successful Sunday pilgrimage to Richmond, by Wandsworth and Wimbledon's open common, a trailing garrulous company walking about a solemnly happy host, to wonderful cold meat and salad at the Roebuck, a bowl of punch, punch! and a bill to correspond; but now it was a week-day, and he went down to Easewood with his bag and portmanteau in a solitary compartment, and looked out of the window upon a world in which every possible congenial seemed either toiling in a situation or else looking for one with a gnawing and hopelessly preoccupying anxiety. He stared out of the window at the exploitation roads of suburbs and rows of houses all very much alike, either emphatically and impatiently *TO LET*, or full of rather busy unsocial people. Near Wimbledon he had a glimpse of golf links, and saw two elderly gentlemen, who, had they chosen, might have been gentlemen of grace and leisure, addressing themselves to smite hunted little white balls great distances with the utmost bitterness and dexterity. Mr. Polly could not understand them.

Every road, he remarked as freshly as though he had never observed it before, was bordered by inflexible palings or iron fences or severely disciplined hedges. He wondered if perhaps abroad there might be beautifully careless, unenclosed high roads. Perhaps after all the best way of taking a holiday is to go abroad.

He was haunted by the memory of what was either a half-forgotten picture or a dream; a carriage was drawn up by the wayside and four beautiful people, two men and two women graciously dressed, were dancing a formal ceremonious dance, full of bows and curtseys, to the music of a wandering fiddler they had encountered. They had been driving one way and he walking another—a happy encounter with this obvious result. They might have come straight out of happy Theleme, whose motto is: " Do what thou wilt." The driver had taken his two sleek horses out; they grazed unchallenged; and he sat on a stone clapping time with his hands while the fiddler played. The shade of the trees did not altogether shut out the sunshine, the grass in the wood was lush and full of still daffodils, the turf they danced on was starred with daisies.

Mr. Polly, dear heart! firmly believed that things like that could and did happen—somewhere. Only it puzzled him that morning that he never saw them happening. Perhaps they happened south of Guilford! Perhaps they happened in Italy. Perhaps they ceased to happen a hundred years ago. Perhaps they happened just round the corner—on week-days when all good Mr. Pollys are safely shut up in shops. And so dreaming of delightful impossibilities until his heart ached for them, he was rattled along in the suburban train to Johnson's discreet home and the briskly stimulating welcome of Mrs. Johnson.

2

Mr. Polly translated his restless craving for joy and leisure into Harold Johnsonese by saying that he meant to look about him for a bit before going into another situation. It was a decision Johnson very warmly approved. It was arranged that Mr. Polly should occupy his former room and board with the Johnsons in consideration of a weekly payment of eighteen shillings. And the next morning Mr. Polly went out early and reappeared with a purchase, a safety bicycle which he proposed to study and master in the sandy lane below the Johnsons' house. But over the struggle that preceded his mastery it is humane to draw a veil.

And also Mr. Polly bought a number of books; Rabelais for his own, and *The Arabian Nights*, the works of Sterne, a pile of *Tales from Blackwood*, cheap in a second-hand bookshop, the plays of William Shakespeare, a second-hand copy of Belloc's *Path to Rome*, an odd volume of *Purchas his Pilgrimes* and *The Life and Death of Jason*.

" Better get yourself a good book on bookkeeping," said Johnson, turning over perplexing pages.

A belated spring, to make up for lost time, was now advancing with great strides. Sunshine and a stirring wind were poured out over the land, fleets of towering clouds sailed upon urgent tremendous missions across the blue sea of heaven, and presently Mr. Polly was riding a little unstably along unfamiliar Surrey roads, wondering always what was round the next corner, and marking the blackthorn and looking out for the first white flowerbuds of the may. He was perplexed and distressed, as indeed are all right-thinking souls, that there is no may in early May.

He did not ride at the even pace sensible people use, who have marked out a journey from one place to another, and settled what time it will take them. He rode at variable speeds, and always as though he was looking for something that missing left life attractive still, but a little wanting in significance. And sometimes he was so unreasonably happy he had to whistle and sing, and sometimes he was incredibly, but not at all painfully, sad. His indigestion vanished with air and exercise, and it was quite pleasant in the evening to stroll about the garden with Johnson and discuss plans for the future. Johnson was full of ideas. Moreover, Mr. Polly had marked the road that led to Stamton, that rising populous suburb; and as his bicycle legs grew strong his wheel, with a sort of inevitableness, carried him towards a row of houses in a back street in which his Larkins cousins made their home together.

He was received with great enthusiasm.

The street was a little dingy street, a *cul-de-sac* of very small houses in a row, each with an almost flattened bow window and a blistered brown door with a black knocker. He poised his bright new bicycle against the window, and knocked and stood waiting, and felt himself in his straw hat and black serge suit a very pleasant and prosperous-looking figure. The door was opened by Cousin Miriam. She was wearing a bluish print dress that brought out a kind of sallow warmth in her skin, and although it was nearly four o'clock in the afternoon her sleeves were tucked up, as if for some domestic task, above her elbows, showing her rather slender but very shapely yellowish arms. The loosely-pinned bodice confessed a delicately rounded neck.

For a moment she regarded him with suspicion and a faint hostility, and then recognition dawned in her eyes.

" Why ! " she said, " it's Cousin Elfrid! "

" Thought I'd look you up," he said.

" Fancy you coming to see us like this! " she answered.

They stood confronting one another for a moment while Miriam collected herself for the unexpected emergency.

"Exploratious menanderings," said Mr. Polly, indicating the bicycle.

Miriam's face betrayed no appreciation of the remark.

"Wait a moment," she said, coming to a rapid decision, "and I'll tell Ma."

She closed the door on him abruptly, leaving him a little surprised in the street. "Ma!" he heard her calling, and a swift speech followed, the import of which he didn't catch. Then she reappeared. It seemed but an instant, but she was changed; the arms had vanished into sleeves, the apron had gone, a certain pleasing disorder of the hair had been at least reproved.

"I didn't mean to shut you out," she said, coming out upon the step. "I just told Ma. How are you, Elfrid? You *are* looking well. I didn't know you rode a bicycle. Is it a new one?"

She leaned upon his bicycle. "Bright it is!" she said. "What a trouble you must have to keep it clean!"

Mr. Polly was aware of a rustling transit along the passage, and of the house suddenly full of hushed but strenuous movement.

"It's plated mostly," said Mr. Polly.

"What d'you carry in that little bag thing?" she asked, and then branched off to: "We're all in a mess to-day, you know. It's my cleaning up day to-day, I'm not a bit tidy, I know, but I *do* like to 'ave a go in at things now and then. *They'd* leave everything, I believe. If I let 'em. . . . You got to take us as you find us, Elfrid. Mercy we wasn't all out." She paused. She was talking against time. "I *am* glad to see you again," she repeated.

"Couldn't keep away," said Mr. Polly gallantly. "Had to come over and see my pretty cousins again.',

Miriam did not answer for a moment. She coloured deeply. " You *do say* things! " she said.

She stared at Mr. Polly, and his unfortunate sense of fitness made him nod his head towards her, regard her firmly with a round brown eye, and add impressively: " I don't say *which* of them."

Her answering expression made him realise for an instant the terrible dangers he trifled with. Avidity flared up in her eyes. Minnie's voice came happily to dissolve the situation.

" 'Ello, Elfrid! " she said from the doorstep.

Her hair was just passably tidy, and she was a little effaced by a red blouse, but there was no mistaking the genuine brightness of her welcome.

He was to come in to tea, and Mrs. Larkins, exuberantly genial in a floriferous but dingy flannel dressing-gown, appeared to confirm that. He brought in his bicycle and put it in a narrow, empty, dingy passage, and every one crowded into a small, untidy kitchen, whose table had been hastily cleared of the debris of the midday repast.

" You must come in here," said Mrs. Larkins, " for Miriam's turning out the front room. I never did see such a girl for cleaning up. Miriam's 'Oliday's a scrub. You've caught us on the 'Op, as the sayin' is, but Welcome all the same. Pity Annie's at work to-day; she won't be 'ome till seven."

Miriam put chairs and attended to the fire; Minnie edged up to Mr. Polly and said, " I *am* glad to see you again, Elfrid," with a warm contiguous intimacy that betrayed a broken tooth. Mrs. Larkins got out tea-things, and descanted on the noble simplicity of their lives, and how he " mustn't mind our simple ways." They enveloped Mr. Polly with a geniality that intoxicated his amiable nature; he insisted upon helping to lay the things, and created enormous laughter by pretending not to know where plates and knives and cups ought to go. " Who'm I going to sit next? " he said, and developed voluminous amusement by attempts to arrange the plates so that he could rub elbows with all three. Mrs. Larkins had to sit down in the windsor chair by the grandfather clock (which was dark with dirt, and not going) to laugh at her ease at his well-acted perplexity.

They got seated at last, and Mr. Polly struck a vein of humour in telling them how he learnt to ride the bicycle. He found the mere repetition of the word " wabble " sufficient to produce almost inextinguishable mirth.

" No foreseeing little accidentulous misadventures," he said, " none whatever."

(Giggle from Minnie.)

" Stout elderly gentleman—shirt sleeves—large straw waste-paper basket sort of hat—starts to cross the road —going to the oil shop—prodic refreshment of oil can——"

" Don't say you run 'im down," said Mrs. Larkins, gasping. " Don't say you run 'im down, Elfrid! "

" Run 'im down! Not me, Madam; I never run anything down. Wabble. Ring the bell. Wabble, wabble——"

(Laughter and tears.)

" No one's going to run him down. Hears the bell! Wabble. Gust of wind. Off comes the hat smack into the wheel. Wabble. *Lord! what's* going to happen? Hat across the road, old gentleman after it, bell, shriek. He ran into me. Didn't ring his bell, hadn't *got* a bell —just ran into me. Over I went clinging to his venerable head. Down he went with me clinging to him. Oil can blump, blump into the road."

(Interlude while Minnie is attended to for crumb in the windpipe.)

" Well what happened to the old man with the oil can? " said Mrs. Larkins.

" We sat about among the debreece and had a bit of an argument. I told him he oughtn't to come out wearing such a dangerous hat—flying at things. Said if he couldn't control his hat, he ought to leave it at home. High old jawbacious argument we had, I tell you. ' I tell you, Sir——' ' I tell *you*, Sir.' Waw-waw-waw. Infuriacious. But that's the sort of thing that is constantly happening, you know—on a bicycle. People run into you, hens, and cats, and dogs, and things. Everything seems to have its mark on you; everything."

" *You* never run into anything."

" Never. Swelpme," said Mr. Polly very solemnly.

" Never, 'E say ! " squealed Minnie. " Hark at 'im! " and relapsed into a condition that urgently demanded back thumping. " Don't be so silly," said Miriam, thumping hard.

Mr. Polly had never been such a social success before. They hung upon his every word—and laughed. What a family they were for laughter! And he loved laughter. The background he apprehended dimly; it was very much the sort of background his life had always had. There was a threadbare tablecloth on the table, and the slop basin and teapot did not go with the cups and saucers, the plates were different again, the knives worn down, the butter lived in a greenish glass dish of its own. Behind was a dresser hung with spare and miscellaneous crockery, with a workbox and an untidy work-basket; there was an ailing musk plant in the window, and the tattered and blotched wallpaper was covered by bright-coloured grocers' almanacs. Feminine wrappings hung from pegs upon the door, and the floor was covered with a varied collection of fragments of oilcloth. The windsor chair he sat in was unstable—which presently afforded material for humour. "Steady, old nag," he said; " Whoa, my friskiacious palfrey! "

" The things he says ! You never know what he won't say next! "

3

" You ain't talkin' of goin'! " cried Mrs. Larkins.

" Supper at eight."

" Stay to supper with *us*, now you 'ave come over," said Mrs. Larkins, with corroborating cries from Minnie. " 'Ave a bit of a walk with the gals, and then come back to supper. You might all go and meet Annie while I straighten up, and lay things out."

" You're not to go touching the front room mind," said Miriam.

" *Who's* going to touch yer front room? " said Mrs. Larkins, apparently forgetful for a moment of Mr. Polly.

Both girls dressed with some care while Mrs. Larkins sketched the better side of their characters, and then the three young people went out to see something of Stamton. In the streets their risible mood gave way to a self-conscious propriety that was particularly evident in Miriam's bearing. They took Mr. Polly to the Stamton wreckery-ation ground—that at least was what they called it—with its handsome custodian's cottage, its asphalt paths, its Jubilee drinking fountain, its clumps of wallflower and daffodils, its charmingly artistic notice-boards with green borders and " art " lettering, and so to the new cemetery and a distant view of the Surrey hills, and round by the gasworks to the canal, to the factory that presently disgorged a surprised and radiant Annie.

" 'El-*lo*! " said Annie.

It is very pleasant to every properly constituted mind to be a centre of amiable interest for one's fellow-creatures; and when one is a young man conscious of becoming mourning and a certain wit, and the fellow-creatures are three young and ardent and sufficiently expressive young women who dispute for the honour of walking by one's side, one may be excused a secret exaltation. They did dispute.

" I'm going to 'ave 'im now," said Annie. " You two've been 'aving 'im all the safternoon. Besides, I've got something to say to 'im."

She had something to say to him. It came presently.

" I say," she said abruptly. " I *did* get them rings out of a prize packet."

" What rings? " asked Mr. Polly.

" What you saw at your poor father's funeral. You made out they meant something. They didn't—straight."

" Then some people have been very remiss about their chances," said Mr. Polly, understanding.

" They haven't had any chances," said Annie. " I don't believe in making oneself too free with people."

" Nor me," said Mr. Polly.

" I may be a bit larky and cheerful in my manner," Annie admitted. " But it don't *mean* anything. I ain't that sort."

" Right-o," said Mr. Polly.

4

It was past ten when Mr. Polly found himself riding back towards Easewood in a broad moonlight, and with a little Japanese lantern dangling from his handlebar, making a fiery circle of pinkish light on and round about his front wheel. He was mightily pleased with himself and the day. There had been four-ale to drink at supper mixed with ginger beer, very free and jolly in a jug. No shadow fell upon the agreeable excitement of his mind until he faced the anxious and reproachful face of Johnson, who had been sitting up for him, smoking and trying to read the odd volume of *Purchas his Pilgrimes*—about the monk who went into Sarmatia and saw those limitless Tartar carts that carried tents.

"Not had an accident, Elfrid?" said Johnson.

The weakness of Mr. Polly's character came out in his reply.

"Not much," he said. "Pedal got a bit loose in Stamton, O' Man. Couldn't ride it; so I looked up the cousins while I waited."

"Not the Larkins lot?"

"Yes."

Johnson yawned hugely, and asked for and was given friendly particulars.

"Well," he said, "better get to bed. I been reading that book of yours; rum stuff. Can't make it out quite. Quite out of date, I should say, if you asked me."

"That's all right, O' Man," said Mr. Polly.

"Not a bit of use for anything that I can see."

"Not a bit."

"See any shops in Stamton?"

"Nothing to speak of," said Mr. Polly. "Goo'-night, O' Man."

Before and after this brief conversation his mind ran on his cousins very warmly and prettily in the vein of high spring. Mr. Polly had been drinking at the poisoned fountains of English literature, fountains so unsuited to the needs of a decent clerk or shopman, fountains charged with the dangerous suggestion that it becomes a man of gaiety and spirit to make love gallantly and rather carelessly. It seemed to him that evening to be handsome and humorous and practicable to make love to all his cousins. It wasn't that he liked any of them particularly, but he liked something about them. He liked their youth and femininity, their resolute high spirits, and their interest in him.

They laughed at nothing and knew nothing, and Minnie had lost a tooth, and Annie screamed and shouted; but they were interesting, immensely interesting.

And Miriam wasn't so bad as the others. He had

kissed them all, and had been kissed in addition several times by Minnie—" oscoolatory exercises."

He buried his nose in his pillow and went to sleep—to dream of anything rather than getting on in the world, as a sensible young man in his position ought to have done.

5

And now Mr. Polly began to lead a double life. With the Johnsons he professed to be inclined, but not so conclusively inclined as to be inconvenient, to get a shop for himself—to be, to use the phrase he preferred, " looking for an opening." He would ride off in the afternoon upon that research, remarking that he was going to " cast a strategical eye " on Chertsey or Weybridge. But if not all roads, still a great majority of them led by however devious ways to Stamton, and to laughter and increasing familiarity. Relations developed with Annie and Minnie and Miriam. Their various characters were increasingly interesting. The laughter became perceptibly less abundant, something of the fizz had gone from the first opening, still these visits remained wonderfully friendly and upholding. Then back he would come to grave but evasive discussions with Johnson.

Johnson was really anxious to get Mr. Polly " into something." His was a reserved, honest character, and he would really have preferred to see his lodger doing things for himself than receive his money for house-keeping. He hated waste, anybody's waste, much more than he desired profit. But Mrs. Johnson was all for Mr. Polly's loitering. She seemed much the more human and likeable of the two to Mr. Polly.

He tried at times to work up enthusiasm for the various avenues to well-being his discussion with Johnson opened. But they remained disheartening

H.M.P. D

prospects. He imagined himself wonderfully smartened up, acquiring style and value in a London shop; but the picture was stiff and unconvincing. He tried to rouse himself to enthusiasm by the idea of his property increasing by leaps and bounds, by twenty pounds a year or so, let us say, each year, in a well-placed little shop, the corner shop Johnson favoured. There was a certain picturesque interest in imagining cut-throat economies, but his heart told him there would be little in practising them.

And then it happened to Mr. Polly that real Romance came out of dreamland into his life, intoxicated and gladdened him with sweetly beautiful suggestions—and left him. She came and left him as that dear lady leaves so many of us, alas! not sparing him one jot or one tittle of the hollowness of her retreating aspect.

It was all the more to Mr. Polly's taste that the thing should happen as things happen in books.

In a resolute attempt not to get to Stamton that day, he had turned due southward from Easewood towards a country where the abundance of bracken jungles, lady's smock, stitchwort, bluebells, and grassy stretches by the wayside under shady trees does much to compensate the lighter type of mind for the absence of promising " openings." He turned aside from the road, wheeled his machine along a faintly marked attractive trail through bracken until he came to a heap of logs against a high old stone wall with a damaged coping and wallflower plants already gone to seed. He sat down, balanced the straw hat on a convenient lump of wood, lit a cigarette, and abandoned himself to agreeable musings and the friendly observation of a cheerful little brown and gray bird his stillness presently encouraged to approach him.

" This is All Right," said Mr. Polly softly to the little brown and gray bird. " Business—later."

He reflected that he might go on in this way for

four or five years, and then be scarcely worse off than he had been in his father's lifetime.

" Vile Business," said Mr. Polly.

Then Romance appeared. Or to be exact, Romance became audible.

Romance began as a series of small but increasingly vigorous movements on the other side of the wall, then a voice murmuring, then as a falling of little fragments on the other side and as ten pink finger-tips, scarcely apprehended before Romance became startlingly and emphatically a leg, remained for a time a fine, slender, actively struggling limb, brown stockinged, and wearing a brown toe-worn shoe, and then. . . . A handsome, red-haired girl wearing a short dress of blue linen was sitting astride the wall, panting, considerably disarranged by her climbing, and as yet unaware of Mr. Polly. . . .

His fine instincts made him turn his head away and assume an attitude of negligent contemplation, with his ears and mind alive to every sound behind him.

" Goodness! " said a voice, with a sharp note of surprise.

Mr. Polly was on his feet in an instant. " Dear me! Can I be of any assistance? " he said, with deferential gallantry.

" I don't know," said the young lady, and regarded him calmly with clear blue eyes. " I didn't know there was any one here," she added.

" Sorry," said Mr. Polly, " if I am intrudacious. I didn't know you didn't want me to be here."

She reflected for a moment on the word.

" It isn't that," she said, surveying him. " I oughtn't to get over the wall," she explained. " It's out of bounds; at least in term time. But this being holidays——"

Her manner placed the matter before him.

" Holidays is different," said Mr. Polly.

" I don't want to actually *break* the rules," she said.

" Leave them behind you," said Mr. Polly, with a catch of the breath, " where they are safe." And marvelling at his own wit and daring, and indeed trembling within himself, he held out a hand for her.

She brought another brown leg from the unknown, and arranged her skirt with a dexterity altogether feminine.

" I think I'll stay on the wall," she decided. " So long as some of me's in bounds——"

She continued to regard him with an irresistible smile of satisfaction. Mr. Polly smiled in return.

" You bicycle? " she said.

Mr. Polly admitted the fact, and she said she did too.

" All my people are in India," she explained. " It's beastly rot—I mean it's frightfully dull being left here alone."

" All *my* people," said Mr. Polly, " are in Heaven! "

" I say! "

" Fact," said Mr. Polly. " Got nobody."

" And that's why——" She checked her artless comment on his mourning. " I say," she said in a sympathetic voice, " I *am* sorry. I really am. Was it a fire, or a ship—or something? "

Her sympathy was very delightful. He shook his head. " The ordinary tables of mortality," he said. " First one, and then another."

Behind this outward melancholy, delight was dancing wildly.

" Are *you* lonely? " asked the girl.

Mr. Polly nodded.

" I was just sitting there in melancholic rectro-spectatiousness," he said, indicating the logs ; and again a swift thoughtfulness swept across her face.

" There's no harm in our talking," she reflected.

" It's a kindness. Won't you get down? "

She reflected, and surveyed the turf below and the
scene around, and him.

" I'll stay on the wall," she said, " if only for bounds'
sake."

She certainly looked quite adorable on the wall. She
had a fine neck and pointed chin that was particularly
admirable from below, and pretty eyes and fine eye-
brows are never so pretty as when they look down upon
one. But no calculation of that sort, thank Heaven,
was going on beneath her ruddy shock of hair.

6

" Let's talk," she said, and for a time they were
both tongue-tied.

Mr. Polly's literary proclivities had taught him that
under such circumstances a strain of gallantry was
demanded. And something in his blood repeated that
lesson.

" You make me feel like one of those old knights," he
said, " who rode about the country looking for dragons
and beautiful maidens and chivalresque adventures."

" Oh! " she said. " Why? "

" Beautiful maiden," he said.

She flushed under her freckles with the quick bright
flush those pretty red-haired people have. " Non-
sense! " she said.

" You are. I'm not the first to tell you that. A
beautiful maiden imprisoned in an enchanted school."

" *You* wouldn't think it enchanted."

" And here am I—clad in steel. Well, not exactly,
but my fiery war-horse is, anyhow. Ready to absquatulate all the dragons, and rescue you."

She laughed, a jolly laugh, that showed delightfully
gleaming teeth. " I wish you could *see* the dragons,"
she said, with great enjoyment. Mr. Polly felt they
were a sun's distance from the world of every day.

" Fly with me! " he dared.

She stared for a moment, and then went off into peals of laughter. " You *are* funny! " she said. " Why, I haven't known you five minutes."

" One doesn't—in this medieval world. My mind is made up, anyhow."

He was proud and pleased with his joke, and quick to change his key neatly. " I wish one could," he said.

" I wonder if people ever did."

" If there were people like you."

" We don't even know each other's names," she remarked, with a descent to matters of fact.

" Your's is the prettiest name in the world."

" How do you know? "

" It must be—anyhow."

" It *is* rather pretty, you know. It's Christabel."

" What did I tell you? "

" And yours? "

" Poorer than I deserve. It's Alfred."

" *I* can't call you Alfred."

" Well, Polly."

" It's a girl's name! "

For a moment he went out of tune. " I wish it was," he said, and could have bitten out his tongue at the Larkins sound of it.

" I shan't forget it," she remarked consolingly.

" I say," she said, in the pause that followed, " why are you riding about the country on a bicycle? "

" I'm doing it because I like it."

She sought to estimate his social status on her limited basis of experience. He stood leaning with one hand against the wall, looking up at her and tingling with daring thoughts. He was a littleish man, you must remember, but neither mean-looking nor unhandsome in those days, sunburnt by his holiday and now warmly flushed. He had an inspiration to simple speech that no practised trifler with love could have bettered.

"There *is* love at first sight," he said, and said it sincerely.

She stared at him with eyes round and big with excitement.

"I think," she said slowly, and without any signs of fear or retreat, "I ought to get back over the wall."

"It needn't matter to you," he said; "I'm just a nobody. But I know you are the best and most beautiful thing I've ever spoken to." His breath caught against something. "No harm in telling you that," he said.

"I should have to go back if I thought you were serious," she said after a pause, and they both smiled together.

After that they talked in a fragmentary way for some time. The blue eyes surveyed Mr. Polly with kindly curiosity from under a broad, finely-modelled brow, much as an exceptionally intelligent cat might survey a new sort of dog. She meant to find out all about him. She asked questions that riddled the honest knight in armour below, and probed even nearer to the hateful secret of the shop and his normal servitude. And when he made a flourish and mispronounced a word, a thoughtful shade passed like the shadow of a cloud across her face.

"Booom!" came the sound of a gong.

"Lordy!" cried the girl, and flashed a pair of brown legs at him and was gone.

Then her pink finger-tips reappeared, and the top of her red hair. "Knight," she cried from the other side of the wall. "Knight there!"

"Lady!" he answered.

"Come again to-morrow."

"At your command. But——"

"Yes?"

"Just one finger."

"What do you mean?"

" To kiss."

The rustle of retreating footsteps and silence. . . .

But after he had waited next day for twenty minutes she reappeared, a little out of breath with the effort to surmount the wall, and head first this time. And it seemed to him she was lighter and more daring and altogether prettier than the dreams and enchanted memories that had filled the interval.

7

From first to last their acquaintance lasted ten days, but into that time Mr. Polly packed ten years of dreams.

" He don't seem," said Johnson, " to take a serious interest in anything. That shop at the corner's bound to be snapped up if he don't look out."

The girl and Mr. Polly did not meet on every one of those ten days; one was Sunday and she could not come, and on the eighth the school reassembled and she made vague excuses. All their meetings amounted to this, that she sat on the wall, more or less in bounds as she expressed it, and let Mr. Polly fall in love with her and try to express it below. She sat in a state of irresponsible exaltation, watching him, and at intervals prodding a vivisecting point of encouragement into him, with that strange passive cruelty which is natural and proper in her sex and age.

And Mr. Polly fell in love, as though the world had given way beneath him and he had dropped through into another, into a world of luminous clouds and of a desolate, hopeless wilderness of desiring and of wild valleys of unreasonable ecstasy, a world whose infinite miseries were finer and in some inexplicable way sweeter than the purest gold of the daily life, whose joys—they were indeed but the merest remote glimpses of joy—were brighter than a dying martyr vision of

heaven. Her smiling face looked down upon him out
of the sky, her careless pose was the living body of life.
It was senseless, it was utterly foolish, but all that was
best and richest in Mr. Polly's nature broke like a wave
and foamed up at the girl's feet, and died, and never
touched her. And she sat on the wall and marvelled
at him, and was amused, and once, suddenly moved
and wrung by his pleading, she bent down rather
shamefacedly and gave him a freckled, tennis-blistered
little paw to kiss. And she looked into his eyes and
suddenly felt a perplexity, a curious swimming of the
mind that made her recoil and stiffen, and wonder
afterwards and dream. . . .

And then with some instinct of self-protection she
went and told her three best friends, great students of
character all, of this remarkable phenomenon she had
discovered on the other side of the wall.

" Look here," said Mr. Polly, " I'm wild for the
love of you! I can't keep up this gesticulatious game
any more. I'm not a knight. Treat me as a human
man. You may sit up there smiling, but I'd die in
torments to have you mine for an hour. I'm nobody
and nothing. But look here! Will you wait for me
five years? You're just a girl yet, and it won't be hard."

" Shut up! " said Christabel, in an aside he did not
hear, and something he did not see touched her hand.

" I've always been just dillententytating about till
now, but I could work. I've just woke up. Wait till
I've got a chance with the money I've got."

" But you haven't got much money ! "

" I've got enough to take a chance with, some sort
of chance. I'd find a chance. I'll do that, anyhow.
I'll go away. I mean what I say. I'll stop trifling and
shirking. If I don't come back it won't matter. If
I do——"

Her expression had become uneasy. Suddenly she
bent down towards him.

" Don't! " she said in an undertone.

" Don't—what? "

" Don't go on like this! You're different. Go on being the knight who wants to kiss my hand as his—what did you call it? " The ghost of a smile curved her face. " Gurdrum! "

" But——! "

Then through a pause they both stared at each other, listening.

A muffled tumult on the other side of the wall asserted itself.

" Shut *up*, Rosie! " said a voice.

" I tell you I will see! I can't half hear. Give me a leg up! "

" You idiot! He'll see you. You're spoiling everything."

The bottom dropped out of Mr. Polly's world. He felt as people must feel who are going to faint.

" You've got someone—— " he said, aghast.

She found life inexpressible to Mr. Polly. She addressed some unseen hearers. " You filthy little Beasts! " she cried, with a sharp note of agony in her voice, and swung herself back over the wall and vanished. There was a squeal of pain and fear, and a swift, fierce altercation.

For a couple of seconds he stood agape.

Then a wild resolve to confirm his worst sense of what was on the other side of the wall made him seize a log, put it against the stones, clutch the parapet with insecure fingers, and lug himself to a momentary balance on the wall.

Romance and his goddess had vanished.

A red-haired girl with a pigtail was wringing the wrist of a schoolfellow, who shrieked with pain and cried, " Mercy! Mercy! O-o-o! Christabel! "

" You Idiot! " cried Christabel. " You giggling Idiot! "

Two other young ladies made off through the beech trees from this outburst of savagery.

Then the grip of Mr. Polly's fingers gave, and he hit his chin against the stones and slipped clumsily to the ground again, scraping his cheek against the wall, and hurting his shin against the log by which he had reached the top. Just for a moment he crouched against the wall.

He swore, staggered to the pile of logs, and sat down.

He remained very still for some time, with his lips pressed together.

"Fool!" he said at last. "You Blithering Fool!" and began to rub his shin as though he had just discovered his bruises.

Afterwards he found his face was wet with blood—which was none the less red stuff from the heart because it came from slight abrasions.

CHAPTER SIX

Miriam

I

It is an illogical consequence of one human being's ill-treatment that we should fly immediately to another, but that is the way with us. It seemed to Mr. Polly that only a human touch could assuage the smart of his humiliation. Moreover, it had, for some undefined reason, to be a feminine touch, and the number of women in his world was limited.

He thought of the Larkins family—the Larkins whom he had not been near now for ten long days. Healing people they seemed to him now—healing, simple people. They had good hearts, and he had neglected them for a mirage. If he rode over to them he would be able to talk bosh, and laugh, and forget the whirl of memories and thoughts that was spinning round and round so unendurably in his brain.

" Law! " said Mrs. Larkins, " come in! You're quite a stranger, Elfrid! "

" Been seeing to business," said the unveracious Polly.

" None of 'em ain't at 'ome, but Miriam's just out to do a bit of shopping. Won't let me shop, she won't, because I'm so keerless. She's a wonderful manager, that girl. Minnie's got some work at the carpet place. 'Ope it won't make 'er ill again. She's the loving delikit sort, is Minnie. . . . Come into the front parlour. It's a bit untidy, but you got to take us as you find us. Wot you been doing to your face? "

" Bit of a scraze with the bicycle," said Mr. Polly. " 'Ow? "

"Trying to pass a carriage on the wrong side, and he drew up and ran me against a wall."

Mrs. Larkins scrutinised it. "You ought to 'ave some one look after your scrazes," she said. "That's all red and rough. It ought to be cold-creamed. Bring your bicycle into the passage and come in."

She "straightened up a bit." That is to say, she increased the dislocation of a number of scattered articles, put a work-basket on the top of several books, swept two or three dogs'-eared numbers of *The Lady's Own Novelist* from the table into the broken armchair, and proceeded to sketch together the tea-things with various such interpolations as: "Law, if I ain't forgot the butter!" All the while she talked of Annie's good spirits and cleverness with her millinery, and of Minnie's affection, and Miriam's relative love of order and management. Mr. Polly stood by the window uneasily, and thought how good and sincere was the Larkins tone. It was well to be back again.

"You're a long time finding that shop of yours," said Mrs. Larkins.

"Don't do to be too precipitous," said Mr. Polly.

"No," said Mrs. Larkins, "once you got it you got it. Like choosing a 'usband. You better see you get it good. I kept Larkins 'esitating two years, I did, until I felt sure of him. A 'ansom man 'e was, as you can see by the looks of the girls, but 'ansom is as 'ansom does. You'd like a bit of jam for your tea, I expect? I 'ope they'll keep *their* men waiting when the time comes. I tell them if they think of marrying, it only shows they don't know when they're well off. Here's Miriam!"

Miriam entered with several parcels in a net, and a peevish expression. "Mother," she said, "you might 'ave prevented my going out with the net with the broken handle. I've been cutting my fingers with the string all the way 'ome." The she discovered Mr. Polly and her face brightened.

" 'Ello, Elfrid! " she said. " Where you been all this time? "

" Looking round," said Mr. Polly.

" Found a shop? "

" One or two likely ones. But it takes time."

" You've got the wrong cups, Mother."

She went into the kitchen, disposed of her purchases, and returned with the right cups. " What you done to your face, Elfrid? " she asked, and came and scrutinised his scratches. " All rough it is."

He repeated his story of the accident, and she was sympathetic in a pleasant, homely way.

" You *are* quiet to-day," she said, as they sat down to tea.

" Meditatious," said Mr. Polly.

Quite by accident he touched her hand on the table, and she answered his touch.

" Why not? " thought Mr. Polly, and looking up, caught Mrs. Larkins' eye and flushed guiltily. But Mrs. Larkins, with unusual restraint, said nothing. She made a grimace, enigmatical, but in its essence friendly.

Presently Minnie came in with some vague grievance against the manager of the carpet-making place about his method of estimating piece-work. Her account was redundant, defective, and highly technical, but redeemed by a certain earnestness. " I'm never within sixpence of what I reckon to be," she said. " It's a bit too 'ot." Then Mr. Polly, feeling that he was being conspicuously dull, launched into a description of the shop he was looking for and the shops he had seen. His mind warmed up as he talked.

" Found your tongue again," said Mrs. Larkins.

He had. He began to embroider the subject and work upon it. For the first time it assumed picturesque and desirable qualities in his mind. It stimulated him to see how readily and willingly they accepted hi

sketches. Bright ideas appeared in his mind from
nowhere. He was suddenly enthusiastic.

"When I get this shop of mine I shall have a cat.
Must make a home for a cat, you know."

"What, to catch the mice?" said Mrs. Larkins.

"No—sleep in the window. A venerable signor of
a cat. Tabby. Cat's no good if it isn't tabby. Cat
I'm going to have, and a canary! Didn't think of that
before, but a cat and a canary seem to go, you know.
Summer weather I shall sit at breakfast in the little
room behind the shop, sun streaming in the window
to rights, cat on a chair, canary singing, and—Mrs.
Polly. . . ."

"'Ello!" said Mrs. Larkins.

"Mrs. Polly frying an extra bit of bacon. Bacon
singing, cat singing, canary singing, kettle singing.
Mrs. Polly——"

"But who's Mrs. Polly going to be?" said Mrs.
Larkins.

"Figment of imagination, M'am," said Mr. Polly.
"Put in to fill up picture. No face to figure—as yet.
Still, that's how it will be. I can assure you. I think
I must have a bit of garden. Johnson's the man for a
garden, of course," he said, going off at a tangent,
"but I don't mean a fierce sort of garden. Earnest
industry. Anxious moments. Fervous digging. Shan't
go in for that sort of garden, M'am. No! Too much
backache for me. My garden will be just a patch of
'sturtiums and sweet-pea. Red-bricked yard, clothes-
line. Trellis put up in odd time. Humorous wind vane.
Creeper up the back of the house."

"Virginia creeper?" asked Miriam.

"Canary creeper," said Mr. Polly.

"You *will* 'ave it nice," said Miriam desirously.

"Rather," said Mr. Polly. "Ting-a-ling-a-ling.
Shop!"

He straightened himself up, and they all laughed.

" Smart little shop," he said. " Counter. Desk. All complete. Umbrella stand. Carpet on the floor. Cat asleep on the counter. Ties and hose on a rail over the counter. All right."

" I wonder you don't set about it right off," said Miriam.

" Mean to get it exactly right, M'am," said Mr. Polly.

" Have to have a Tom cat," said Mr. Polly, and paused for an expectant moment. " Wouldn't do to open shop one morning, you know, and find the window full of kittens. Can't sell kittens. . . ."

When tea was over he was left alone with Minnie for a few minutes, and an odd intimation of an incident occurred that left Mr. Polly rather scared and shaken. A silence fell between them—an uneasy silence. He sat with his elbows on the table looking at her. All the way from Easewood to Stamton his erratic imagination had been running upon neat ways of proposing marriage. I don't know why it should have done, but it had. It was a kind of secret exercise that had not had any definite aim at the time, but which now recurred to him with extraordinary force. He couldn't think of anything in the world that wasn't the gambit to a proposal. It was almost irresistibly fascinating to think how immensely a few words from him would excite and revolutionise Minnie. She was sitting at the table with a work-basket among the tea-things, mending a glove in order to avoid her share of clearing away.

" I like cats," said Minnie, after a thoughtful pause. " I'm always saying to Mother, I wish we 'ad a cat. But we couldn't 'ave a cat 'ere—not with no yard."

" Never had a cat myself," said Mr. Polly. " No! "

" I'm fond of them," said Minnie.

" I like the look of them," said Mr. Polly. " Can't exactly call myself fond."

" I expect I shall get one some day. When about you get your shop."

" I shall have my shop all right before long," said Mr. Polly. " Trust me. Canary bird and all."

She shook her head. " I shall get a cat first," she said. " You never mean anything you say."

" Might get 'em together," said Mr. Polly, with his sense of a neat thing outrunning his discretion.

" Why! 'ow do you mean? " said Minnie, suddenly alert.

" Shop and cat thrown in," said Mr. Polly in spite of himself, and his head swam, and he broke out into a cold sweat as he said it.

He found her eyes fixed on him with an eager expression. " Mean to say——? " she began, as if for verification. He sprang to his feet, and turned to the window. " Little dog! " he said, and moved doorward hastily. " Eating my bicycle tyre, I believe," he explained. And so escaped.

He saw his bicycle in the hall and cut it dead.

He heard Mrs. Larkins in the passage behind him as he opened the front door.

He turned to her. " Thought my bicycle was on fire," he said. " Outside. Funny fancy! All right reely. Little dog outside. . . . Miriam ready? "

" What for? "

" To go and meet Annie."

Mrs. Larkins stared at him. " You're stopping for a bit of supper! "

" If I may," said Mr. Polly.

" You're a rum un," said Mrs. Larkins, and called: " Miriam! "

Minnie appeared at the door of the room looking infinitely perplexed. " There ain't a little dog anywhere, Elfrid," she said.

Mr. Polly passed his hand over his brow. " I had a most curious sensation. Felt exactly as though something was up somewhere. That's why I said Little Dog. All right now."

He bent down and pinched his bicycle tyre.

" You was saying something about a cat, Elfrid," said Minnie.

" Give you one," he answered, without looking up. " The very day my shop is opened."

He straightened himself up and smiled reassuringly.

" Trust me," he said.

2

When, after imperceptible manœuvres by Mrs. Larkins, he found himself starting circuitously through the inevitable recreation ground with Miriam to meet Annie, he found himself quite unable to avoid the topic of the shop that had now taken such a grip upon him. A sense of danger only increased the attraction. Minnie's persistent disposition to accompany them had been crushed by a novel and violent and pungently expressed desire on the part of Mrs. Larkins to see her do something in the house sometimes. . . .

" You really think you'll open a shop? " said Miriam.

" I hate cribs," said Mr. Polly, adopting a moderate tone. " In a shop there's this drawback and that, but one *is* one's own master."

" That wasn't all talk ? "

" Not a bit of it."

" After all," he went on, " a little shop needn't be so bad."

" It's a 'ome," said Miriam.

" It's a home."

Pause.

" There's no need to keep accounts and that sort of thing if there's no assistant. I dare say I could run a shop all right if I wasn't interfered with."

" I should like to see you in your shop," said Miriam.
" I expect you'd keep everything tremendously neat."

The conversation flagged.

" Let's sit down on one of those seats over there past
that notice-board," said Miriam, " where we can see
those blue flowers."

They did as she suggested, and sat down in a corner
where a triangular bed of stock and delphinium brightened the asphalted traceries of the recreation ground.

" I wonder what they call those flowers," she said.
" I always like them. They're handsome."

" Delphicums and larkspurs," said Mr. Polly.
" They used to be in the park at Port Burdock."

" Floriferous corner," he added approvingly.

He put an arm over the back of the seat, and assumed
a more comfortable attitude. He glanced at Miriam,
who was sitting in a lax, thoughtful pose, with her eyes
on the flowers. She was wearing her old dress. She
had not had time to change, and the blue tones of her
old dress brought out a certain warmth in her skin, and
her pose exaggerated whatever was feminine in her
rather lean and insufficient body, and rounded her flat
chest delusively. A little line of light lay across her
profile. The afternoon was full of transfiguring sunshine, children were playing noisily in the adjacent
sand-pit, some Judas trees were abloom in the villa
gardens that bordered the recreation ground, and all
the place was bright with touches of young summer
colour. It all merged with the effect of Miriam in
Mr. Polly's mind.

Her thought found speech. " One did ought to be
happy in a shop," she said, with a note of unusual
softness in her voice.

It seemed to him that she was right. One did ought
to be happy in a shop. Folly not to banish dreams
that made one ache of townless woods and bracken
tangles and red-haired linen-clad figures sitting in

dappled sunshine upon gray and crumbling walls and looking queenly down on one with clear blue eyes. Cruel and foolish dreams they were, that ended in one's being laughed at and made a mock of. There was no mockery here.

" A shop's such a respectable thing to be," said Miriam thoughtfully.

" *I* could be happy in a shop," he said.

His sense of effect had made him pause.

" If I had the right company," he added.

She became very still.

Mr. Polly swerved a little from the conversational ice-run upon which he had embarked.

" I'm not such a blooming Geezer," he said, " as not to be able to sell goods a bit. One has to be nosy over one's buying, of course. But I shall do all right."

He stopped, and felt falling, falling through the aching silence that followed.

" If you get the right company," said Miriam.

" I shall get that all right."

" You don't mean you've got some one——? "

He found himself plunging.

" I've got some one in my eye this minute," he said.

" Elfrid! " she said, turning to him. " You don't mean—— "

Well, *did* he mean? " I do ! " he said.

" Not reely! " She clenched her hands to keep still. He took the conclusive step.

" Well, you and me, Miriam, in a little shop, with a cat and a canary—— " He tried too late to get back to a hypothetical note. " Just suppose it! "

" You mean," said Miriam, " you're in love with me, Elfrid? "

What possible answer can a man give to such a question but " Yes! "

Regardless of the public park, the children in the sandpit, and every one, she bent forward and seized his shoulder and kissed him on the lips. Something lit up in Mr. Polly at the touch. He put an arm about her and kissed her back, and felt an irrevocable act was sealed. He had a curious feeling that it would be very satisfying to marry and have a wife—only somehow he wished it wasn't Miriam. Her lips were very pleasant to him, and the feel of her in his arm.

They recoiled a little from each other, and sat for a moment flushed and awkwardly silent. His mind was altogether incapable of controlling its confusions.

"I didn't dream," said Miriam, "you cared—— Sometimes I thought it was Annie, sometimes Minnie——"

"Always I liked you better than them," said Mr. Polly.

"I love you, Elfrid," said Miriam, "since ever we met at your poor father's funeral. Leastways I *would* have done if I had thought—— You didn't seem to mean anything you said.

"I can't believe it!" she added.

"Nor I," said Mr. Polly.

"You mean to marry me and start that little shop?"

"Soon as ever I find it," said Mr. Polly.

"I had no more idea when I came out with you——"

"Nor me."

"It's like a dream."

They said no more for a little while.

"I got to pinch myself to think it's real," said Miriam. "What they'll do without me at 'ome I can't imagine. When I tell them——"

For the life of him Mr. Polly could not tell whether he was fullest of tender anticipations or regretful panic.

"Mother's no good at managing—not a bit. Annie don't care for housework, and Minnie's got no 'ead for it. What they'll do without me I can't imagine."

"They'll have to do without you," said Mr. Polly, sticking to his guns.

A clock in the town began striking.

" Lor! " said Miriam, " we shall miss Annie, sitting 'ere and love-making."

She rose and made as if to take Mr. Polly's arm. But Mr. Polly felt that their condition must be nakedly exposed to the ridicule of the world by such a linking, and evaded her movement.

Annie was already in sight before a flood of hesitation and terrors assailed Mr. Polly.

" Don't tell any one yet a bit," he said.

." Only Mother," said Miriam firmly.

3

Figures are the most shocking things in the world. The pettiest little squiggles of black, looked at in the right light; and yet consider the blow they can give you upon the heart. You return from a little careless holiday abroad, and turn over the page of a newspaper, and against the name of the distant, vague-conceived railway, in mortgages upon which you have embarked the bulk of your capital, you see, instead of the familiar, persistent 95-6 (varying at most to 93 *ex div.*), this slightly richer arrangement of marks, $76\frac{1}{2}$-$78\frac{1}{2}$.

It is like the opening of a pit just under your feet.

So, too, Mr. Polly's happy sense of limitless resources was obliterated suddenly by a vision of this tracery:—

`" 298 "`

instead of the

" 350 "

he had come to regard as the fixed symbol of his affluence.

It gave him a disagreeable feeling about the diaphragm, akin in a remote degree to the sensation he had when the perfidy of the red-haired schoolgirl became plain to him. It made his brow moist.

" Going down a Vorterex," he whispered.

By a characteristic feat of subtraction he decided that he must have spent sixty-two pounds.

" Funererial baked meats," he said, recalling possible items.

The happy dream in which he had been living, of long, warm days, of open roads, of limitless, unchecked hours, of infinite time to look about him, vanished like a thing enchanted. He was sudddenly back in the hard old economic world, that exacts work, that limits range, that discourages phrasing and dispels laughter. He saw Wood Street and its fearful suspenses yawning beneath his feet.

And also he had promised to marry Miriam, and on the whole rather wanted to.

He was distraught at supper. Afterwards, when Mrs. Johnson had gone to bed with a slight headache, he opened a conversation with Johnson.

" It's about time, O' Man, I saw about doing something," he said. " Riding about and looking at shops all very debonairious, O' Man, but it's time I took one for keeps."

" What did I tell you? " said Johnson.

" How do you think that corner shop of yours will figure out? " Mr. Polly asked.

" You're really meaning it? "

" If it's a practable proposition, O' Man. Assuming it's practable, what's your idea of the figures? "

Johnson went to the chiffonier, got out a letter, and tore off the back sheet. " Let's figure it out," he said, with solemn satisfaction. " Let's see the lowest you could do it on."

He squared himself to the task, and Mr. Polly sat beside him like a pupil, watching the evolution of the gray, distasteful figures that were to dispose of his little hoard.

" What running expenses have we got to provide

for?" said Johnson, wetting his pencil. "Let's have them first. Rent? . . ."

At the end of an hour of hideous speculations, Johnson decided, "It's close; but you'll have a chance."

"M'm," said Mr. Polly. "What more does a brave man want?"

"One thing you can do quite easily. I've asked about it."

"What's that, O' Man?" said Mr. Polly.

"Take the shop without the house above it."

"I suppose I might put my head in to mind it," said Mr. Polly, "and get a job with my body."

"Not exactly that. But I thought you'd save a lot if you stayed on here—being all alone, as you are."

"Never thought of that, O' Man," said Mr. Polly, and reflected silently upon the needlessness of Miriam.

"We were talking of eighty pounds for stock," said Johnson. "Of course seventy-five is five pounds less, isn't it? Not much else we can cut."

"No," said Mr. Polly.

"It's very interesting, all this," said Johnson, folding up the half sheet of paper and unfolding it. "I wish sometimes I had a business of my own instead of a fixed salary. You'll have to keep books, of course."

"One wants to know where one is."

"I should do it all by double entry," said Johnson. "A little troublesome at first, but far the best in the end."

"Lemme see that paper," said Mr. Polly, and took it with the feeling of a man who takes a nauseating medicine, and scrutinised his cousin's neat figures with listless eyes.

"Well," said Johnson, rising stretching, "Bed! Better sleep on it, O' Man."

"Right-o!" said Mr. Polly, without moving; but indeed he could as well have slept upon a bed of thorns.

He had a dreadful night. It was like the end of the annual holiday, only infinitely worse. It was like a newly arrived prisoner's backward glance at the trees and heather through the prison gates. He had to go back to harness, and he was as fitted to go in harness as the ordinary domestic cat. All night Fate, with the quiet complacency, and indeed at times the very face and gestures, of Johnson, guided him towards that undesired establishment at the corner near the station. "O Lord!" he cried, "I'd rather go back to cribs. I *should* keep my money anyhow." Fate never winced.

"Run away to sea," whispered Mr. Polly; but he knew he wasn't man enough. "Cut my blooming throat."

Some braver strain urged him to think of Miriam, and for a little while he lay still. . . .

"Well, O' Man?" said Johnson, when Mr. Polly came down to breakfast, and Mrs. Johnson looked up brightly. Mr. Polly had never felt breakfast so unattractive before.

"Just a day or so more, O' Man, to turn it over in my mind," he said.

"You'll get the place snapped up," said Johnson.

There were times in those last few days of coyness with his destiny when his engagement seemed the most negligible of circumstances; and times—and these happened for the most part at nights, after Mrs. Johnson had indulged everybody in a Welsh rarebit—when it assumed so sinister and portentous an appearance as to make him think of suicide. And there were times too when he very distinctly desired to be married, now that the idea had got into his head, at any cost. Also he tried to recall all the circumstances of his proposal time after time, and never quite succeeded in recalling what had brought the thing off. He went over to Stamton with a becoming frequency, and kissed all his cousins, and Miriam especially, a great deal, and found it very stirring and refreshing. They all appeared to know; and Minnie was tearful but resigned. Mrs. Larkins met him, and indeed enveloped him, with unwonted warmth, and there was a big pot of household jam for tea. And he could not make up his mind to sign his name to anything about the shop, though it crawled nearer and nearer to him, though the project had materialised now to the extent of a draft agreement, with the place for his signature indicated in pencil.

One morning, just after Mr. Johnson had gone to the station, Mr. Polly wheeled his bicycle out into the road, went up to his bedroom, packed his long white night-dress, a comb, and a tooth-brush in a manner that was as off-hand as he could make it, informed Mrs. Johnson, who was manifestly curious, that he was " off for a day or two to clear his head," and fled forthright into the road, and mounting, turned his wheel towards the tropics and the equator and the south coast of England, and indeed more particularly to where the little village of Fishbourne slumbers and sleeps.

When he returned, four days later, he astonished Johnson beyond measure by remarking, so soon as the shop project was reopened, " I've took a little con-traption at Fishbourne, O' Man, that I fancy suits me better."

He paused, and then added in a manner if possible even more off-hand, " Oh, and I'm going to have a bit of a nuptial over at Stamton—with one of the Larkins cousins."

" Nuptial? " said Johnson.

" Wedding bells, O' Man. Benedictine collapse."

On the whole Johnson showed great self-control. " It's your own affair, O' Man," he said, when things had been more clearly explained; " and I hope you won't feel sorry when it's too late."

But Mrs. Johnson was first of all angrily silent, and

then reproachful. " I don't see what we've done to be
made fools of like this," she said. " After all the trouble
we've 'ad to make you comfortable and see after you
—out late, and sitting up, and everything; and then
you go off as sly as sly, without a word, an' get a shop
behind our backs, as though you thought we meant to
steal your money. I 'aven't patience with such deceit-
fulness, and I didn't think it of you, Elfrid. And now
the letting season's 'arf gone by, and what I shall do
with that room of yours I've no idea. Frank is frank,
and fair play fair play; so *I* was told, any'ow, when I
was a girl. Just as long as it suits you to stay 'ere you
stay 'ere, and then it's off and no thank you whether
we like it or not. Johnson's too easy with you. 'E sits
there and doesn't say a word; and night after night
'e's been adding up and subtracting and multiplying
and dividing, and suggesting and thinkin' for you,
instead of seeing to his own affairs."

She paused for breath.

" Unfortunate amoor," said Mr. Polly apologetically
and indistinctly. " Didn't expect it myself."

4

Mr. Polly's marriage followed with a certain
inevitableness.

He tried to assure himself that he was acting upon
his own forceful initiative, but at the back of his mind
was the completest realisation of his powerlessness to
resist the gigantic social forces he had set in motion.
He had got to marry under the will of society, even as
in times past it had been appointed for other sunny
souls under the will of society that they should be led
out by serious and unavoidable fellow-creatures and
ceremoniously drowned or burnt or hung. He would
have preferred infinitely a more observant and less
conspicuous rôle, but the choice was no longer open to

him. He did his best to play his part, and he procured some particularly neat check trousers to do it in. The rest of his costume, except for some bright yellow gloves, a gray and blue mixture tie, and that the broad crape band was changed for a livelier piece of silk, were the things he had worn at the funeral of his father. So nearly akin are human joy and sorrow.

The Larkins sisters had done wonders with gray sateen. The idea of orange blossom and white veils had been abandoned reluctantly on account of the expense of the cabs. A novelette in which the heroine had stood at the altar in "a modest going-away dress" had materially assisted this decision. Miriam was frankly tearful, and so, indeed, was Annie, but with laughter as well to carry it off. Mr. Polly heard Annie say something vague about never getting a chance because of Miriam always sticking about at home like a cat at a mouse hole, that became, as people say, food for thought. Mrs. Larkins was from the first flushed, garrulous, and wet and smeared by copious weeping; an incredibly soaked and crumpled and used-up pocket-handkerchief never left the clutch of her plump red hand. "Goo' girls all of them," she kept on saying in a tremulous voice; "such Goo'-Goo'-Goo' girls!" She wetted Mr. Polly dreadfully when she kissed him. Her emotion affected the buttons down the back of her bodice, and almost the last filial duty Miriam did before entering on her new life was to close that gaping orifice for the eleventh time. Her bonnet was small and ill-balanced, black adorned with red roses, and first it got over her right eye until Annie told her of it, and then she pushed it over her left eye and looked ferocious for a space, and after that baptismal kissing of Mr. Polly the delicate millinery took fright and climbed right up to the back part of her head and hung on there by a pin, and flapped piteously at all the larger waves of emotion that filled the gathering. Mr. Polly became more and more aware of that bonnet as time went on, until he felt for it like a thing alive. Towards the end it had yawning fits.

The company did not include Mrs. Johnson, but Johnson came with a pervading surreptitiousness and backed against walls and watched Mr. Polly with doubt and speculation in his large gray eye, and whistled noiselessly and doubtfully on the edge of things. He was, so to speak, to be best man *sotto voce.* A sprinkling of girls in gray hats from Miriam's place of business appeared in church, great nudgers all of them, but only two came on afterwards to the house. Mrs. Punt brought her son with his ever-widening mind —it was his first wedding; and a Larkins uncle, a Mr. Voules, a licensed victualler, very kindly drove over in a high-hung dogcart from Sommershill with a plump, well-dressed wife, to give the bride away. One or two total strangers drifted into the church and sat down observantly in distant seats.

This sprinkling of people seemed only to enhance the cool brown emptiness of the church, the rows and rows of empty pews, disengaged Prayer Books, and abandoned hassocks. It had the effect of a preposterous misfit. Johnson consulted with a thin-legged short-skirted verger about the disposition of the party. The officiating clergy appeared distantly in the doorway of the vestry putting on his surplice, and relapsed into a contemplative cheek-scratching that was manifestly habitual. Before the bride arrived, Mr. Polly's sense of the church found an outlet in whispered criticisms of ecclesiastical architecture with Johnson. " Early Norman arches, eh? " he said, " or Perpendicular."

" Can't say," said Johnson.

" Telessated pavements all right."

" It's well laid anyhow."

" Can't say I admire the altar. Scrappy rather with those flowers."

He coughed behind his hand and cleared his throat. At the back of his mind he was speculating whether flight at this eleventh hour would be criminal or merely reprehensible bad taste. A murmur from the nudgers announced the arrival of the bridal party.

The little procession from a remote door became one of the enduring memories of Mr. Polly's life. The verger had bustled to meet it and arrange it according to tradition and morality. In spite of Mrs. Larkins' impassioned " Don't take her from me yet! " he made Miriam go first with Mr. Voules, the bridesmaids followed, and then himself, hopelessly unable to disentangle himself from the whispering, maternal anguish of Mrs. Larkins. Mrs. Voules, a compact, rounded woman with a square, expressionless face, imperturbable dignity, and a dress of considerable fashion, completed the procession.

Mr. Polly's eyes fell first upon the bride; the sight of her filled him with a curious stir of emotion. Alarm, desire, affection, respect—and a queer element of reluctant dislike, all played their part in that complex eddy. The gray dress made her a stranger to him, made her stiff and commonplace; she was not even the rather drooping form that had caught his facile sense of beauty when he had proposed to her in the recreation ground. There was something, too, that did not please him in the angle of her hat; it was, indeed, an ill-conceived hat with large, aimless rosettes of pink and gray. Then his mind passed to Mrs. Larkins and the bonnet that was to gain such a hold upon him; it seemed to be flag-signalling as she advanced, and to the two eager, unrefined sisters he was acquiring.

A freak of fancy set him wondering where and when in the future a beautiful girl with red hair might march along some splendid aisle—— Never mind! He became aware of Mr. Voules.

He became aware of Mr. Voules as a watchful, blue

eye of intense forcefulness. It was the eye of a man
who has got hold of a situation. He was a fat, short,
red-faced man, clad in a tight-fitting tail-coat of black
and white check, with a coquettish bow tie under the
lowest of a number of crisp little red chins. He held
the bride under his arm with an air of invincible
championship, and his free arm flourished a gray top-
hat of an equestrian type. Mr. Polly instantly learnt
from that eye that Mr. Voules knew all about his
longing for flight. Its azure-rimmed pupil glowed with
disciplined resolution. It said: " I've come to give
this girl away, and give her away I will. I'm here now,
and things have to go on all right. So don't think of
it any more "—and Mr. Polly didn't. A faint phantom
of a certain " lill dog " that had hovered just beneath
the threshold of consciousness vanished into black
impossibility. Until the conclusive moment of the
service was attained the eye of Mr. Voules watched
Mr. Polly relentlessly, and then instantly he relieved
guard, and blew his nose into a voluminous and richly-
patterned handkerchief, and sighed and looked round
for the approval and sympathy of Mrs. Voules, and
nodded to her brightly, like one who has always fore-
told a successful issue to things. Mr. Polly felt at last
like a marionette that has dropped off its wire. But
it was long before that release arrived.

He became aware of Miriam breathing close to him.

" Hallo! " he said, and feeling that was clumsy and
would meet the eye's disapproval: " Gray dress—suits
you no end."

Miriam's eyes shone under her hat brim.

" Not reely! " she whispered.

" You're all right," he said, with the feeling of the
eye's observation and criticism stiffening his lips. He
cleared his throat.

The verger's hand pushed at him from behind. Some
one was driving Miriam towards the altar rails and the

clergyman. "We're in for it," said Mr. Polly to her
sympathetically. "Where? Here? Right-o."

He was interested for a moment or so in something
indescribably habitual in the clergyman's pose. What
a lot of weddings he must have seen! Sick he must be
of them!

"Don't let your attention wander," said the eye.

"Got the ring?" whispered Johnson.

"Pawned it yesterday," answered Mr. Polly, with
an attempt at lightness, and then had a dreadful
moment under that pitiless scrutiny while he felt in
the wrong waistcoat pocket. . . .

The officiating clergy sighed deeply, began, and
married them wearily and without any hitch.

"D'bloved we gath'd gether sighto' Gard 'n face
this con'gation join gather Man Woom Ho Mat-mony
whichis on'bl state stooted by Gard in times mans
in'cency. . . ."

Mr. Polly's thoughts wandered wide and far and
once again something like a cold hand touched his
heart, and he saw a sweet face in sunshine under the
shadow of trees. Some one was nudging him. It was
Johnson's finger diverting his eyes to the crucial place
in the Prayer Book to which they had come.

"Wiltou lover, comfer, oner keeper sickness and
health. . . ."

"*Say, ' I will.*'"

Mr. Polly moistened his lips. "I will," he said
hoarsely.

Miriam, nearly inaudibly, answered some similar
demand.

Then the clergyman said: "Who gi's Mom mad't
this man?"

"Well, *I'm* doing that," said Mr. Voules in a
refreshingly full voice, and looking round the church.

"Pete arf me," said the clergyman to Mr. Polly.
"Take thee Mirum wed wife——"

" Take thee Mi'm wed wife," said Mr. Polly.

" Have hold this day ford."

" Have hold this day ford."

" Betworse, richypoo'."

" Bet worse, richypoo'. . . ."

Then came Miriam's turn.

" Lego hands," said the clergyman, " gothering? No! On book. So! Here! Pete arf me ' Wis ring Ivy wed.' "

" Wis ring Ivy wed——"

So it went on, blurried and hurried, like the momentary vision of a very beautiful thing seen through the smoke of a passing train. . . .

" Now my boy," said Mr. Voules at last, gripping Mr. Polly's elbow tightly, " you've got to sign the registry and there you are! Done! "

Before him stood Miriam, a little stiffly, the hat with a slight rake across her forehead, and a kind of questioning hesitation in her face. Mr. Voules urged her past him.

It was astounding. She was his wife!

And for some reason Miriam and Mrs. Larkins were sobbing, and Annie was looking grave. Hadn't they after all, wanted him to marry her? Because if that was the case——!

He became aware for the first time of the presence of Uncle Pentstemon in the background but approaching, wearing a tie of light mineral blue colour, and grinning and sucking enigmatically and judicially round his principal tooth.

5

It was in the vestry that the force of Mr. Voules' personality began to show at its true value. He seemed to open out, like the fisherman's Ginn from the pot, and spread over everything directly the restraints of the ceremony were at an end.

"Ceremony," he said to the clergyman, "excellent, excellent." He also shook hands with Mrs. Larkins, who clung to him for a space, and kissed Miriam on the cheek. "First kiss for me," he said, "anyhow."

He led Mr. Polly to the register by the arm, and then got chairs for Mrs. Larkins and his wife. He then turned on Miriam. "Now, young people," he said. "One! or *I* shall again.

"That's right," said Mr. Voules. "Same again, Miss."

Mr. Polly was overcome with modest confusion, and turning, found a refuge from this publicity in the arms of Mrs. Larkins. Then in a state of profuse moisture he was assaulted and kissed by Annie and Minnie, who were immediately kissed upon some indistinctly stated grounds by Mr. Voules, who then kissed the entirely impassive Mrs. Voules, and smacked his lips and remarked, "Home again safe and sound." Then with a strange harrowing cry, Mrs. Larkins seized upon and bedewed Miriam with kisses. Annie and Minnie kissed each other, and Johnson went abruptly to the door of the vestry and stared into the church, no doubt with ideas of sanctuary in his mind. "Like a bit of a kiss round sometimes," said Mr. Voules, and made a kind of hissing noise with his teeth, and suddenly smacked his hands together with great *éclat* several times. Meanwhile the clergyman scratched his cheek with one hand and fiddled the pen with the other, and the verger coughed protestingly.

"The dogcart's just outside," said Mr. Voules. "No walking home to-day for the bride, M'am."

"Not going to drive us?" cried Annie.

"The happy pair, Miss. *Your* turn soon."

"Get out!" said Annie. "I shan't marry—ever."

"You won't be able to help it. You'll have to do it,

just to disperse the crowd." Mr. Voules laid his hand on Mr. Polly's shoulder. "The bridegroom gives his arm to the bride. Hands across, and down the middle. Prump, Prump, Perump-pump-pump-pump-perump."

Mr. Polly found himself and the bride leading the way towards the western door.

Mrs. Larkins passed close to Uncle Pentstemon, sobbing, too earnestly to be aware of him. "Such a goo'-goo'-goo' girl," she sobbed.

"Didn't think I'd come, did you?" said Uncle Pentstemon; but she swept past him, too busy with the expression of her feelings to observe him.

"She didn't think I'd come, I lay," said Uncle Pentstemon, a little foiled, but effecting an auditory lodgment on Johnson.

"I don't know," said Johnson, uncomfortable. "I suppose you were asked. How are you getting on?"

"I was *arst*," said Uncle Pentstemon, and brooded for a moment.

"I goes about seeing wonders," he added, and then in a sort of enhanced undertone, "One of her girls gettin' married. That's what I means by wonders. Lord's goodness! Wow!"

"Nothing the matter?" asked Johnson.

"Got it in the back for a moment. Going to be a change of weather, I suppose," said Uncle Pentstemon. "I brought 'er a nice present, too, what I got in this passel. Vallyble old tea-caddy that uset' be my mother's. What I kep' my baccy in for years and years —till the hinge at the back got broke. It ain't been no use to me particular since, so thinks I, drat it! I may as well give it to 'er as not. . . ."

Mr. Polly found himself emerging from the western door.

Outside, a crowd of half a dozen adults and about fifty children had collected, and hailed the approach of the newly-wedded couple with a faint, indeterminate cheer. All the children were holding something in little bags, and his attention was caught by the expression of vindictive concentration upon the face of a small, big-eared boy in the foreground. He didn't for the moment realise what these things might import. Then he received a stinging handful of rice in the ear, and a great light shone.

"Not yet, you young fool," he heard Mr. Voules saying behind him, and then a second handful spoke against his hat.

"Not yet," said Mr. Voules, with increasing emphasis, and Mr. Polly became aware that he and Miriam were the focus of two crescents of small boys, each with the light of massacre in his eyes and a grubby fist clutching into a paper bag for rice, and that Mr. Voules was warding off probable discharges with a large red hand.

The dogcart was in charge of a loafer, and the horse and the whip were adorned with white favours, and the back seat was confused, but not untenable, with hampers. "Up we go," said Mr. Voules. "Old birds in front and young ones behind." An ominous group of ill-restrained rice-throwers followed them up as they mounted.

"Get your handkerchief for your face," said Mr. Polly to his bride, and took the place next the pavement with considerable heroism, held on, gripped his hat, shut his eyes, and prepared for the worst. "Off!" said Mr. Voules, and a concentrated fire came stinging Mr. Polly's face.

The horse shied, and when the bridegroom could look at the world again it was manifest the dogcart had just missed an electric tram by a hair's-breadth, and far away outside the church railings the verger and Johnson were battling with an active crowd of small boys for the life of the rest of the Larkins family. Mrs. Punt and her son had escaped across the road, the son trailing and stumbling at the end of a remorseless arm; but Uncle Pentstemon, encumbered by the tea-caddy, was the centre of a little circle of his own, and appeared to be dratting them all very heartily. Remoter, a policeman approached with an air of tranquil unconsciousness.

"Steady, you idiot, steady!" cried Mr. Voules; and then over his shoulder, "I brought that rice. I like old customs.—Whoa! steady-y."

The dogcart swerved violently, and then, evoking a shout of groundless alarm from a cyclist, took a corner, and the rest of the wedding party was hidden from Mr. Polly's eyes.

6

"We'll get the stuff into the house before the old gal comes along," said Mr. Voules, "if you'll hold the hoss."

"How about the key?" asked Mr. Polly.

"I got the key coming."

And while Mr. Polly held the sweating horse and dodged the foam that dripped from its bit, the house absorbed Miriam and Mr. Voules altogether. Mr. Voules carried in the various hampers he had brought with him, and finally closed the door behind him.

For some time Mr. Polly remained alone with his charge in the little blind alley outside the Larkins' house, while the neighbours scrutinised him from behind their blinds. He reflected that he was a married man, that he must look very like a fool, that the head of a horse is a silly shape and its eye a bulger; he wondered what the horse thought of him, and whether it really liked being held and patted on the neck, or whether it only submitted out of contempt. Did it know he was married? Then he wondered if the clergyman had thought him much of an ass, and whether the individual lurking behind the lace curtains of the front room next door was a man or a woman. A door opened over the way, an elderly gentleman in a kind of embroidered fez appeared smoking a pipe, with a quiet satisfied expression. He regarded Mr. Polly for some time with mild but sustained curiosity. Finally he called: " Hi! "

" Hallo! " said Mr. Polly.

" You needn't 'old that 'orse," said the old gentleman.

" Spirited beast," said Mr. Polly. " And "—with some faint analogy to ginger beer in his mind—" he's up to-day."

" 'E won't turn 'isself round," said the old gentleman, " any'ow. And there ain't no way through for 'im to go."

" *Verbum sap*," said Mr. Polly, and abandoned the horse and turned to the door. It opened to him just as Mrs. Larkins on the arm of Johnson, followed by Annie, Minnie, two friends, Mrs. Punt and her son, and at a slight distance Uncle Pentstemon, appeared round the corner.

" They're coming," he said to Miriam, and put an arm about her and gave her a kiss.

She was kissing him back, when they were startled violently by the shying of two empty hampers into the passage. Then Mr. Voules appeared holding a third.

" Here! you'll have plenty of time for that presently," he said; " get these hampers away before the old girl comes. I got a cold collation here to make her sit up. My eye! "

Miriam took the hampers, and Mr. Polly, under compulsion from Mr. Voules, went into the little front room. A profuse pie and a large ham had been added to the modest provision of Mrs. Larkins, and a number of select-looking bottles shouldered the bottle of sherry and the bottle of port she had got to grace the feast. They certainly went better with the iced wedding cake in the middle. Mrs. Voules, still impassive, stood by the window regarding these things with faint approval.

"Makes it look a bit thicker, eh?" said Mr. Voules, and blew out both his cheeks, and smacked his hands together violently several times. "Surprise the old girl no end."

He stood back and smiled and bowed with arms extended as the others came clustering at the door.

"Why, Un-cle Voules!" cried Annie, with a rising note.

It was his reward.

And then came a great wedging and squeezing and crowding into the little room. Nearly every one was hungry, and eyes brightened at the sight of the pie, and the ham, and the convivial array of bottles. "Sit down, every one," cried Mr. Voules. "Leaning against anything counts as sitting, and makes it easier to shake down the grub!"

The two friends from Miriam's place of business came into the room among the first, and then wedged themselves so hopelessly against Johnson in an attempt to get out again to take off their things upstairs, that they abandoned the attempt. Amid the struggle Mr. Polly saw Uncle Pentstemon relieve himself of his parcel by giving it to the bride. "Here!" he said, and handed it to her. "Weddin' present," he explained, and added with a confidential chuckle, "*I* never thought I'd 'ave to give one—ever."

"Who says steak-and-kidney pie? You 'ave a drop of old Tommy, Martha. That's what you want to steady you. . . .

"Sit down, every one, and don't all speak at once. Who says steak-and-kidney pie?" . . .

"Vocificeratious," whispered Mr. Polly. "Convivial vocificerations."

"Bit of 'am with it," shouted Mr. Voules, poising a slice of ham on his knife. "Any one 'ave a bit of 'am with it? Won't that little man of yours, Mrs. Punt—won't 'e 'ave a bit of 'am? "

" And now, ladies and gentlemen," said Mr. Voules, still standing and dominating the crammed roomful, " now you got your plates filled, and something I can warrant you good in your glasses, wot about drinking the 'ealth of the bride? "

" Eat a bit fust," said Uncle Pentstemon, speaking with his mouth full, amidst murmurs of applause. " Eat a bit fust."

So they did, and the plates clattered and the glasses clinked.

Mr. Polly stood shoulder to shoulder with Johnson for a moment. " In for it," said Mr. Polly cheeringly. " Cheer up, O' Man, and peck a bit. No reason why *you* shouldn't eat, you know."

The Punt boy stood on Mr. Polly's boots for a minute, struggling violently against the compunction of Mrs. Punt's grip.

" Pie," said the Punt boy, " Pie! "

" You sit 'ere and 'ave 'em, my lord! " said Mrs. Punt, prevailing. " Pie you can't 'ave and you won't."

" Lor' bless my heart, Mrs. Punt! " protested Mr. Voules, " let the boy 'ave a bit if he wants it—wedding and all! "

" You 'aven't 'ad 'im sick on your 'ands, Uncle Voules," said Mrs. Punt. " Else you wouldn't want to humour his fancies as you do. . . ."

" I can't help feeling it's a mistake, O' Man," said Johnson, in a confidential undertone. " I can't help feeling you've been rash. Let's hope for the best."

" Always glad of good wishes, O' Man," said Mr. Polly. " You'd better have a drink of something. Anyhow, sit down to it."

Johnson subsided gloomily, and Mr. Polly secured some ham and carried it off, and sat himself down on the sewing machine on the floor in the corner to devour it. He was hungry, and a little cut off from the rest of the company by Mrs. Voules' hat and back, and he occupied himself for a time with ham and his own thoughts. He became aware of a series of jangling concussions on the table. He craned his neck, and discovered that Mr. Voules was standing up and leaning forward over the table in the manner distinctive of after-dinner speeches, tapping upon the table with a black bottle. "Ladies and gentlemen," said Mr. Voules, raising his glass solemnly in the empty desert of sound he had made, and paused for a second or so. "Ladies and gentlemen—the Bride." He searched his mind for some suitable wreath of speech, and brightened at last with discovery. "Here's luck to her!" he said at last.

"Here's luck!" said Johnson hopelessly but resolutely, and raised his glass. Everybody murmured, "Here's luck."

"Luck!" said Mr. Polly, unseen in his corner, lifting a forkful of ham.

"That's all right," said Mr. Voules, with a sigh of relief at having brought off a difficult operation. "And now, who's for a bit more pie?"

For a time conversation was fragmentary again. But presently Mr. Voules rose from his chair again, and produced a silence by renewed hammering; he had subsided with a contented smile after his first oratorical effort. "Ladies and gents," he said, "fill up for a second toast: the happy Bridegroom!" He stood for half a minute searching his mind for the apt phrase that came at last in a rush. "Here's (hic) luck to *him*," said Mr. Voules.

"Luck to him!" said every one; and Mr. Polly, standing up behind Mrs. Voules, bowed amiably, amidst enthusiasm.

"He may say what he likes," said Mrs. Larkins, "he's *got* luck. That girl's a treasure of treasures, and always has been ever since she tried to nurse her own little sister being but three at the time and fell the full flight of stairs from top to bottom, no hurt that any outward eye 'as ever seen but always ready and helping, always tidying and busy. A treasure I must say, and a treasure I will say, giving her no more than her due. . . ."

She was silenced altogether by a rapping sound that would not be denied. Mr. Voules had been struck by a fresh idea, and was standing up and hammering with the bottle again.

" The third Toast, ladies and gentlemen," he said; " fill up, please. The Mother of the Bride. I—er . . . Uoo . . . Ere! . . . Ladies and gem, 'Ere's Luck to 'er! . . ."

7

The dingy little room was stuffy and crowded to its utmost limit, and Mr. Polly's skies were dark with the sense of irreparable acts. Everybody seemed noisy and greedy, and doing foolish things. Miriam, still in that unbecoming hat—for presently they had to start off to the station together—sat just beyond Mrs. Punt and her son, doing her share in the hospitalities, and ever and again glancing at him with a deliberately encouraging smile. Once she leant over the back of the chair to him and whispered cheeringly, " Soon be together now." Next to her sat Johnson, profoundly silent, and then Annie, talking vigorously to a friend. Uncle Pentstemon was eating voraciously opposite, but with a kindling eye for Annie. Mrs. Larkins sat next Mr. Voules. She was unable to eat a mouthful, she declared, it would choke her; but ever and again Mr. Voules wooed her to swallow a little drop of liquid refreshment.

There seemed a lot of rice upon everybody, in their hats and hair and the folds of their garments.

Presently Mr. Voules was hammering the table for the fourth time in the interests of the Best Man. . . .

All feasts come to an end at last, and the break-up of things was precipitated by alarming symptoms on the part of Master Punt. He was taken out hastily after a whispered consultation; and since he had got into the corner between the fireplace and the cupboard, that meant every one moving to make way for him. Johnson took the opportunity to say, " Well, so long," to any one who might be listening, and disappeared. Mr. Polly found himself smoking a cigarette and walking up and down outside in the company of Uncle Pentstemon, while Mr. Voules replaced bottles in the hampers, and prepared for departure, and the women-kind of the party crowded upstairs with the bride. Mr. Polly felt taciturn, but the events of the day had stirred the mind of Uncle Pentstemon to speech. And so he spoke, discursively and disconnectedly, a little heedless of his listener, as wise old men will.

" They do say," said Uncle Pentstemon, " one funeral makes many. This time it's a wedding. But it's all very much of a muchness. . . .

" 'Am *do* get in my teeth nowadays," said Uncle Pentstemon, " I can't understand it. 'Tisn't like there was nubblicks or strings or such in 'am. It's a plain food, surely.

" You *got* to get married," said Uncle Pentstemon, resuming his discourse. " That's the way of it. Some has. Some hain't. I done it long before I was your age. It hain't for me to blame you. You can't 'elp being the marrying sort any more than me. It's nat'ral —like poaching or drinking, or wind on the stummik. You can't 'elp it, and there you are! As for the good of it, there ain't no particular good in it as I can see. It's a toss up. The hotter come, the sooner cold; but

they all gets tired of it sooner or later. . . . I hain't
no grounds to complain. Two I've 'ad and buried,
and might 'ave 'ad a third, and never no worrit with
kids—never. . . .

"You done well not to 'ave the big gal. I will say
that for ye. She's a gad-about grinny, she is, if ever
was. A gad about grinny. Mucked up my mushroom
bed to rights, she did, and I 'aven't forgot it. Got the
feet of a centipede, she 'as—all over everything and
neither with your leave nor by your leave. Like a
stray 'en in a pea patch. Cluck! cluck! Trying to
laugh it off. *I* laughed 'er off, I did. Dratted lumpin'
baggage! . . ."

For a while he mused malevolently upon Annie,
and routed out a reluctant crumb from some coy
sitting-out place in his tooth.

"Wimmin's a toss up," said Uncle Pentstemon.
"Prize packets they are, and you can't tell what's in
'em till you took 'em 'ome and undone 'em. Never
was a bachelor married yet that didn't buy a pig in
a poke. Never! Marriage seems to change the very
natures in 'em through and through. You can't tell
what they won't turn into—nohow.

"I seen the nicest girls go wrong," said Uncle
Pentstemon, and added with unusual thoughtfulness,
"Not that I mean *you* got one of that sort."

He sent another crumb on to its long home with a
sucking, encouraging noise.

"The wust sort's the grizzler," Uncle Pentstemon
resumed. "If ever I'd 'ad a grizzler, I'd up and 'it
'er on the 'ead with sumpthin' pretty quick. I don't
think I *could* abide a grizzler," said Uncle Pentstemon.

"I'd liefer 'ave a lump-about like that other gal. I
would indeed. I lay I'd make 'er stop laughing after
a bit for all 'er airs. And mind where her clumsy
great feet went . . .

"A man's got to tackle 'em, whatever they be," said

Uncle Pentstemon, summing up the shrewd observation of an old-world lifetime. "Good or bad," said Uncle Pentstemon, raising his voice fearlessly, "a man's got to tackle 'em."

8

At last it was time for the two young people to catch the train for Waterloo *en route* for Fishbourne. They had to hurry, and as a concluding glory of matrimony they travelled second class, and were seen off by all the rest of the party except the Punts, Master Punt being now beyond all question unwell.

"Off!" The train moved out of the station.

Mr. Polly remained waving his hat and Mrs. Polly her handkerchief until they were hidden under the bridge. The dominating figure to the last was Mr. Voules. He had followed them along the platform, waving the equestrian gray hat and kissing his hand to the bride.

They subsided into their seats.

"Got a compartment to ourselves, anyhow," said Mrs. Polly, after a pause.

Silence for a moment.

"The rice 'e must 'ave bought. Pounds and pounds!"

Mr. Polly felt round his collar at the thought.

"Ain't you going to kiss me, Elfrid, now we're alone together?"

He roused himself to sit forward, hands on knees, cocked his hat over one eye, and assumed an expression of avidity becoming to the occasion.

"Never!" he said. "Ever!" and feigned to be selecting a place to kiss with great discrimination.

"Come here," he said, and drew her to him.

"Be careful of my 'at," said Mrs. Polly, yielding awkwardly.

CHAPTER SEVEN

The Little Shop at Fishbourne

I

FOR fifteen years Mr. Polly was a respectable shop-keeper in Fishbourne.

Years they were in which every day was tedious, and when they were gone it was as if they had gone in a flash. But now Mr. Polly had good looks no more. He was, as I have described him in the beginning of this story, thirty-seven, and fattish in a not very healthy way, dull and yellowish about the complexion, and with discontented wrinkles round his eyes. He sat on the stile above Fishbourne and cried to the Heavens above him: "Oh, Roöötten Beëëastly Silly Hole!" And he wore a rather shabby black morning coat and vest, and his tie was richly splendid, being from stock, and his golf cap aslant over one eye.

Fifteen years ago, and it might have seemed to you that the queer little flower of Mr. Polly's imagination might be altogether withered and dead, and with no living seed left in any part of him. But, indeed, it still lived as an insatiable hunger for bright and delightful experiences, for the gracious aspect of things, for beauty. He still read books when he had a chance—books that told of glorious places abroad and glorious times, that wrung a rich humour from life, and contained the delight of words freshly and expressively grouped. But, alas! there are not many such books, and for the newspapers and the cheap fiction that abounded more and more in the world, Mr. Polly had little taste. There was no epithet in them. And there was no one to talk to, as he loved to talk. And he had to mind his shop.

142

It was a reluctant little shop from the beginning.

He had taken it to escape the doom of Johnson's choice, and because Fishbourne had a hold upon his imagination. He had disregarded the ill-built, cramped rooms behind it in which he would have to lurk and live, and the relentless limitations of its dimensions, the inconvenience of an underground kitchen that must necessarily be the living room in winter—the narrow yard behind giving upon the yard of the Royal Fishbourne Hotel—the tiresome sitting and waiting for custom, the restricted prospects of trade. He had visualised himself and Miriam first as at breakfast on a clear, bright, winter morning, amidst a tremendous smell of bacon, and then as having muffins for tea. He had also thought of sitting on the beach on Sunday afternoons, and of going for a walk in the country behind the town and picking marguerites and poppies. But, in fact, Miriam and he were usually extremely cross at breakfast, and it did not run to muffins at tea. And she didn't think it looked well, she said, to go trapesing about the country on Sundays.

It was unfortunate that Miriam never took to the house from the first. She did not like it when she saw it, and liked it less as she explored it. " There's too many stairs," she said, " and the coal being indoors will make a lot of work."

" Didn't think of that," said Mr. Polly, following her round.

" It'll be a hard house to keep clean," said Miriam.

" White paint's all very well in its way," said Miriam, " but it shows the dirt something fearful. Better 'ave 'ad it nicely grained."

" There's a kind of place here," said Mr. Polly, " where we might have some flowers in pots."

" Not me," said Miriam. " I've 'ad trouble enough with Minnie and 'er musk. . . ."

They stayed for a week in a cheap boarding-house

before they moved in. They had bought some furniture in Stamton, mostly second-hand, but with new cheap cutlery and china and linen, and they supplemented this from the Fishbourne shops. Miriam, relieved from the hilarious associations of home, developed a meagre and serious quality of her own, and went about with knitted brows pursuing some ideal of " 'aving everything right." Mr. Polly gave himself to the arrangement of the shop with a certain zest, and whistled a great deal, until Miriam appeared and said that it went through her head. So soon as he had taken the shop he had filled the window with aggressive posters, announcing in no measured terms that he was going to open; and, now he was getting his stuff put out, he was resolved to show Fishbourne what window-dressing could do. He meant to give them boater straws, imitation Panamas, bathing dresses with novelties in stripes, light flannel shirts, summer ties, and ready-made flannel trousers for men, youths, and boys. Incidentally he watched the small fishmonger over the way, and had a glimpse of the china dealer next door, and wondered if a friendly nod would be out of place. And on the first Sunday in this new life he and Miriam arrayed themselves with great care, he in his wedding-funeral hat and coat and she in her going-away dress, and went processionally to church—a more respectable looking couple you could hardly imagine—and looked about them.

Things began to settle down next week into their places. A few customers came, chiefly for bathing-suits and hat-guards, and on Saturday night the cheapest straw hats and ties, and Mr. Polly found himself more and more drawn towards the shop door and the social charm of the street. He found the china-dealer unpacking a crate at the edge of the pavement, and remarked that it was a fine day. The china-dealer gave a reluctant assent, and plunged into the crate in a manner that presented no encouragement to a loquacious neighbour.

" Zealacious commerciality," whispered Mr. Polly to that unfriendly back view. . . .

2

Miriam combined earnestness of spirit with great practical incapacity. The house was never clean nor tidy, but always being frightfully disarranged for cleaning or tidying up, and she cooked because food had to be cooked, and with a sound moralist's entire disregard of the quality or the consequences. The food came from her hands done rather than improved, and looking as uncomfortable as savages clothed under duress by a missionary with a stock of out-sizes. Such food is too apt to behave resentfully, rebel, and work Obi. She ceased to listen to her husband's talk from the day she married him, and ceased to unwrinkle the kink in her brow at his presence, giving herself up to mental states that had a quality of preoccupation. And she developed an idea, for which, perhaps, there was legitimate excuse, that he was lazy. He seemed to stand about a great deal to read—an indolent habit— and presently to seek company for talking. He began to attend the bar parlour of the God's Providence Inn with some frequency, and would have done so regularly in the evening if cards, which bored him to death, had not arrested conversation. But the perpetual foolish variation of the permutations and combinations of two-and-fifty cards taken five at a time, and the meagre surprises and excitements that ensue, had no charm for Mr. Polly's mind, which was at once too vivid in its impressions and too easily fatigued.

It was soon manifest the shop paid only in the most exacting sense, and Miriam did not conceal her opinion that he ought to bestir himself and " do things," though what he was to do was hard to say. You see, when you have once sunken your capital in a shop you do not very easily get it out again. If customers will not come to you cheerfully and freely, the law sets limits upon the compulsion you may exercise. You cannot pursue people about the streets of a watering-place, compelling them either by threats or importunity to buy flannel trousers. Additional sources of income for a tradesman are not always easy to find. Wintershed, at the bicycle and gramophone shop to the right, played the organ in the church, and Clamp of the toy-shop was a pew-opener and so forth; Gambell, the greengrocer, waited at table and his wife cooked, and Carter, the watch-maker, left things to his wife while he went about the world winding clocks; but Mr. Polly had none of these arts, and wouldn't in spite of Miriam's quietly persistent protests, get any other. And on summer evenings he would ride his bicycle about the country, and if he discovered a sale where there were books, he would as often as not waste half the next day in going to acquire a job lot of them haphazard, and bring them home tied about with string, and hide them from Miriam under the counter in the shop. That is a heartbreaking thing for any wife with a serious in-vestigatory turn of mind to discover. She was always thinking of burning these finds, but her natural turn of economy prevailed with her.

The books he read during those fifteen years! He read everything he got except theology, and, as he read, his little unsuccessful circumstances vanished and the wonder of life returned to him; the routine of reluctant getting up, opening shop, pretending to dust it with zest, breakfasting with a shop egg underdone or over-done, or a herring raw or charred, and coffee made Miriam's way, and full of little particles, the return to the shop, the morning paper, the standing, standing at the door saying " How do! " to passers-by, or getting a bit of gossip, or watching unusual visitors, all these things vanished as the auditorium of a theatre vanishes when the stage is lit. He acquired hundreds of books at last—old, dusty books, books with torn covers and broken covers, fat books whose backs were naked string and glue—an inimical litter to Miriam.

There was, for example, the voyages of La Perouse, with many careful, explicit woodcuts and the frankest revelations of the ways of the eighteenth-century sailor-man, homely, adventurous, drunken, incontinent, and delightful, until he floated, smooth and slow, with all sails set and mirrored in the glassy water, until his head was full of the thought of shining, kindly, brown-skinned women, who smiled at him and wreathed his head with unfamiliar flowers. He had, too, a piece of a book about the lost palaces of Yucatan, those vast terraces buried in primordial forest, of whose makers there is now no human memory. With La Perouse he linked *The Island Nights' Entertainments*, and it never palled upon him that in the dusky stabbing of the "Island of Voices" something poured over the stabber's hands "like warm tea." Queer, incommunicable joy it is, the joy of the vivid phrase that turns the statement of the horridest fact to beauty.

And another book which had no beginning for him was the second volume of the travels of the Abbés Huc and Gabet. He followed those two sweet souls from their lessons in the Thibetan under Sandura the Bearded (who called them donkeys, to their infinite benefit, and stole their store of butter through a hundred misadventures to the very heart of Lhasa), and it was a thirst in him that was never quenched to find the other volume and whence they came, and who in fact they were. He read Fenimore Cooper and *Tom Cringle's Log* side by side with Joseph Conrad, and dreamt of the many-hued humanity of the East and West Indies until his heart ached to see those sun-

soaked lands before he died. Conrad's prose had a
pleasure for him that he was never able to define, a
peculiar, deep-coloured effect. He found, too, one day,
among a pile of soiled sixpenny books at Port Burdock,
to which place he sometimes rode on his ageing bicycle,
Bart Kennedy's *A Sailor Tramp*, all written in vivid
jerks, and had for ever after a kindlier and more
understanding eye for every burly rough who slouched
through Fishbourne High Street. Sterne he read with
a wavering appreciation and some perplexity, but
except for the *Pickwick Papers*, for some reason that I
do not understand, he never took at all kindly to
Dickens. Yet he liked Lever, and Thackeray's *Catherine*,
and all Dumas until he got to the *Vicomte de Bragelonne*.
I am puzzled by his insensibility to Dickens, and I
record it, as a good historian should, with an admission
of my perplexity. It is much more understandable
that he had no love for Scott. And I suppose it was
because of his ignorance of the proper pronunciation
of words that he infinitely preferred any prose to any
metrical writing.

A book he browsed over with a recurrent pleasure
was Waterton's *Wanderings in South America*. He would
even amuse himself by inventing descriptions of other
birds in the Watertonian manner, new birds that he
invented, birds with peculiarities that made him chuckle
when they occurred to him. He tried to make Rusper,
the ironmonger, share this joy with him. He read
Bates, too, about the Amazon; but when he discovered
that you could not see one bank from the other, he
lost, through some mysterious action of the soul, that
again I cannot understand, at least a tithe of the
pleasure he had taken in that river. But he read all
sorts of things; a book of old Keltic stories collected
by Joyce charmed him, and Mitford's *Tales of old
Japan*, and a number of paper-covered volumes, *Tales
from Blackwood*, he had acquired at Easewood, remained

a stand-by. He developed a quite considerable acquaintance with the plays of William Shakespeare, and in his dreams he wore cinque cento or Elizabethan clothes, and walked about a stormy, ruffling, taverning, teeming world. Great land of sublimated things, thou World of Books, happy asylum, refreshment, and refuge from the world of every day! . . .

The essential thing of those fifteen long years of shopkeeping is Mr. Polly, well athwart the counter of his rather ill-lit shop, lost in a book, or rousing himself with a sigh to attend to business.

And meanwhile he got little exercise; indigestion grew with him until it ruled all his moods; he fattened and deteriorated physically, great moods of distress invaded and darkened his skies, little things irritated him more and more, and casual laughter ceased in him. His hair began to come off until he had a large bald space at the back of his head. Suddenly, one day it came to him—forgetful of those books and all he had lived and seen through them—that he had been in his shop for exactly fifteen years, that he would soon be forty, and that his life during that time had not been worth living, that it had been in apathetic and feebly hostile and critical company, ugly in detail and mean in scope, and that it had brought him at last to an outlook utterly hopeless and gray.

3

I have already had occasion to mention, indeed I have quoted, a certain high-browed gentleman living at Highbury, wearing a golden *pince-nez*, and writing for the most part in that very beautiful room, the library of the Climax Club. There he wrestled with what he calls " social problems " in a bloodless but at times, I think one must admit, an extremely illuminating manner. He had a fixed idea that something called a collective "intelligence" is wanted in the world, which means in practice that you and I and every one have to think about things frightfully hard and pool the results, and oblige ourselves to be shamelessly and persistently clear and truthful, and support and respect (I suppose) a perfect horde of professors and writers and artists and ill-groomed, difficult people, instead of using our brains in a moderate and sensible manner to play golf and bridge (pretending a sense of humour prevents our doing anything else with them), and generally taking life in a nice, easy, gentlemanly way, confound him! Well, this dome-headed monster of intellect alleges that Mr. Polly was unhappy entirely through that.

"A rapidly complicating society," he writes, "which, as a whole, declines to contemplate its future or face the intricate problems of its organisation, is in exactly the position of a man who takes no thought of dietary or regimen, who abstains from baths and exercise and gives his appetites free play. It accumulates useless and aimless lives, as a man accumulates fat and morbid products in his blood; it declines in its collective efficiency and vigour, and secretes discomfort and misery. Every phase of its evolution is accompanied by a maximum of avoidable distress and inconvenience and human waste. . . .

"Nothing can better demonstrate the collective dullness of our community, the crying need for a strenuous, intellectual renewal, than the consideration of that vast mass of useless, uncomfortable, under-educated, under-trained, and altogether pitiable people we contemplate when we use that inaccurate and misleading term, the Lower Middle Class. A great proportion of the lower middle class should properly be assigned to the unemployed and the unemployable. They are not only that, because the possession of some small hoard of money, savings during a period of wage-earning, an insurance policy or such like capital, prevents a direct appeal to the rates. But they are doing little or nothing for the community in return for what they consume; they have no understanding of any relation of service to the community, they have never been trained nor their imaginations touched to any social purpose. A great proportion of small shopkeepers, for example, are people who have, through their inefficiency that comes from inadequate training and sheer aimlessness, or through improvements in machinery or the drift of trade, been thrown out of employment, and who set up in needless shops as a method of ekeing out the savings upon which they count. They contrive to make sixty or seventy per cent. of their expenditure, the rest is drawn from the shrinking capital. Essentially their lives are failures, not the sharp and tragic failure of the labourer who gets out of work and starves, but the slow, chronic process of consecutive small losses which may end, if the individual is exceptionally fortunate, in an impoverished death-bed before actual bankruptcy or destitution supervenes. Their chances of ascendant means are less in their shops than in any lottery that was ever planned. The secular development of transit and communications has made the organisation of distributing businesses upon large and economical lines inevitable; except in the chaotic confusions of newly opened countries, the day when a man might earn an independent living by unskilled, or practically un-skilled, retailing has gone for ever. Yet every year sees the melancholy procession towards petty bankruptcy and imprisonment for debt go on, and there is no statesmanship in us to avert it. Every issue of every trade journal has its four or five columns of abridged bankruptcy proceedings, nearly every item in which means the final collapse of another struggling family upon the resources of the community, and continually a fresh supply of superfluous artisans and shop-assistants, coming out of employment with savings or " help " from relations, of widows with a husband's insurance money, of the ill-trained sons of parsimonious fathers, replaces the fallen in the ill-equipped, jerry-built shops that everywhere abound. . . ."

I quote these fragments from a gifted if unpleasant contemporary for what they are worth. I feel this has to come in here as the broad aspect of this History. I come back to Mr. Polly, sitting upon his gate and swearing in the east wind, and so returning I have a sense of floating across unbridged abysses between the general and the particular. There, on the one hand, is the man of understanding seeing clearly—I suppose he sees clearly—the big process that dooms millions of lives to thwarting and discomfort and unhappy circum-stances, and giving us no help, no hint, by which we may get that better " collective will and intelligence " which would dam that stream of human failure; and on the other hand, Mr. Polly, sitting on his gate, un-trained, unwarned, confused, distressed, angry, seeing nothing except that he is, as it were, netted in grayness and discomfort—with life dancing all about him; Mr. Polly with a capacity for joy and beauty at least as keen and subtle as yours and mine.

4

I have hinted that our Mother England had equipped Mr. Polly for the management of his internal concerns no whit better than she had for the direction of his external affairs. With a careless generosity she affords her children a variety of foods unparalleled in the world's history, including many condiments and preserved preparations novel to the human economy. And Miriam did the cooking. Mr. Polly's system, like a confused and ill-governed democracy, had been brought to a state of perpetual clamour and disorder, demanding now evil and unsuitable internal satisfactions such as pickles and vinegar and the crackling on pork, and now vindictive external expressions, such as war and bloodshed through the world. So that Mr. Polly had been led into hatred and a series of disagreeable quarrels with his landlord, his wholesalers, and most of his neighbours.

Rumbold, the china-dealer next door, seemed hostile from the first for no apparent reason, and always unpacked his crates with a full back to his new neighbour, and from the first Mr. Polly resented and hated that uncivil breadth of expressionless humanity, wanted to prod it, kick it, satirise. But you cannot satirise a back, if you have no friend to nudge while you do it.

At last Mr. Polly could stand it no longer. He approached and prodded Rumbold.

" 'Ello! " said Rumbold, suddenly erect and turned about.

" Can't we have some other point of view? " said Mr. Polly. " I'm tired of the end elevation."

" Eh? " said Mr. Rumbold, frankly puzzled.

" Of all the vertebracious animals man alone raises his face to the sky, O' Man. Well, why avert it? "

Rumbold shook his head with a helpless expression.

" Don't like so much Arreary Pensy."

Rumbold, distressed, in utter obscurity.

" In fact, I'm sick of your turning your back on me, see? "

A great light shone on Rumbold. " *That's* what you're talking about! " he said.

" That's it," said Mr. Polly.

Rumbold scratched his ear with the three strawy jampots he held in his hand. " Way the wind blows, I expect," he said. " But what's the fuss? "

" No fuss! " said Mr. Polly. " Passing remark. I don't like it, O' Man, that's all."

" Can't help it, if the wind blows my stror," said Mr. Rumbold, still far from clear about it.

" It isn't ordinary civility," said Mr. Polly.

" Got to unpack 'ow it suits me. Can't unpack with stror blowing into one's eyes."

" Needn't unpack like a pig rooting for truffles, need you? "

" Truffles? "

" Needn't unpack like a pig."

Mr. Rumbold apprehended something.

" Pig! " he said, impressed. " You calling me a pig? "

" It's the side I seem to get of you."

" 'Ere," said Mr. Rumbold, suddenly fierce, and shouting and making his points with gesticulated jampots, " you go indoors. I don't want no row with you, and I don't want you to row with me. I don't know what you're after, but I'm a peaceful man— teetotaller, too, and a good thing if *you* was. See? You go indoors! "

" You mean to say—— I'm asking you civilly to stop unpacking—with your back to me."

" Pig ain't civil and you ain't sober. You go indoors and lemme go on unpacking. You—you're excited."

" D'you mean——! " Mr. Polly was foiled.

He perceived an immense solidity about Rumbold.

" Get back to your shop and lemme get on with my business," said Mr. Rumbold. " Stop calling me pigs. See? Sweep your pavemint."

" I came here to make a civil request."

" You came 'ere to make a row. I don't want no truck with you. See? I don't like the looks of you. See? And I can't stand 'ere all day arguing. See? "

Pause of mutual inspection.

It occurred to Mr. Polly that probably he was to some extent in the wrong.

Mr. Rumbold, blowing heavily, walked past him,

deposited the jampots in his shop with an immense affectation that there was no Mr. Polly in the world, returned, turned a scornful back on Mr. Polly, and dived to the interior of the crate. Mr. Polly stood baffled. Should he kick this solid mass before him? Should he administer a resounding kick?

No!

He plunged his hands deeply into his trousers pockets, began to whistle, and returned to his own doorstep with an air of profound unconcern. There, for a time, to the tune of " Men of Harlech," he contemplated the receding possibility of kicking Mr. Rumbold hard. It would be splendid—and for the moment satisfying. But he decided not to do it. For indefinable reasons he could not do it. He went indoors and straightened up his dress ties very slowly and thoughtfully. Presently he went to the window and regarded Mr. Rumbold obliquely. Mr. Rumbold was still unpacking. . . .

Mr. Polly had no human intercourse thereafter with Rumbold for fifteen years. He kept up a Hate.

There was a time when it seemed as if Rumbold might go, but he had a meeting of his creditors and then went on unpacking as before, obtusely as ever.

5

Hinks, the saddler, two shops farther down the street, was a different case. Hinks was the aggressor —practically.

Hinks was a sporting man in his way, with that taste for checks in costume and tight trousers which is, under Providence, so mysteriously and invariably associated with equestrian proclivities. At first Mr. Polly took to him as a character, became frequent in the God's Providence Inn under his guidance, stood and was stood drinks, and concealed a great ignorance of horses until Hinks became urgent for him to play billiards or bet.

Then Mr. Polly took to evading him, and Hinks ceased to conceal his opinion that Mr. Polly was in reality a softish sort of flat.

He did not, however, discontinue conversation with Mr. Polly. He would come along to him whenever he appeared at his door and converse about sport and women and fisticuffs and the pride of life with an air of extreme initiation, until Mr. Polly felt himself the faintest under-developed simulacrum of man that had ever hovered on the verge of non-existence.

So he invented phrases for Hink's clothes and took Rusper, the ironmonger, into his confidence upon the weakness of Hinks. He called him the " chequered Careerist," and spoke of his patterned legs as " shivery shakys." Good things of this sort are apt to get round to people.

He was standing at his door one day, feeling bored, when Hinks appeared down the street, stood still, and regarded him with a strange, malignant expression for a space.

Mr. Polly waved a hand in a rather belated salutation.

Mr. Hinks spat on the pavement and appeared to reflect. Then he came towards Mr. Polly portentously and paused, and spoke between his teeth in an earnest, confidential tone.

" You been flapping your mouth about me, I'm told," he said.

Mr. Polly felt suddenly spiritless. " Not that I know of," he answered.

" Not that you know of, be blowed! You been flapping your mouth."

" Don't see it," said Mr. Polly.

" Don't see it, be blowed! You go flapping your silly mouth about me, and I'll give you a poke in the eye. See? "

Mr. Hinks regarded the effect of this coldly but firmly, and spat again.

" Understand me? " he inquired.

" Don't recollect," began Mr. Polly.

" Don't recollect, be blowed! You flap your mouth a damn sight too much. This place gets more of your mouth than it wants. . . . Seen this? "

And Mr. Hinks, having displayed a freckled fist of extraordinary size and pugginess in an ostentatiously familiar manner to Mr. Polly's close inspection by sight or smell, turned it about this way and that, shaking it gently for a moment or so, replaced it carefully in his pocket as if for future use, receded slowly and watchfully for a pace, and then turned away as if to other matters, and ceased to be, even in outward seeming, a friend. . . .

6

Mr. Polly's intercourse with all his fellow-tradesmen was tarnished sooner or later by some such adverse incident, until not a friend remained to him, and loneliness made even the shop door terrible. Shops bankrupted all about him, and fresh people came, and new acquaintances sprang up, but sooner or later a discord was inevitable—the tension under which these badly-fed, poorly-housed, bored, and bothered neighbours lived made in inevitable. The mere fact that Mr. Polly had to see them every day, that there was no getting away from them, was in itself sufficient to make them almost unendurable to his frettingly active mind.

Among other shopkeepers in the High Street there was Chuffles, the grocer, a small, hairy, silent intent polygamist, who was given rough music by the youth of the neighbourhood because of the scandal about his wife's sister, and who was nevertheless totally uninteresting, and Tonks, the second grocer, an old man with an older, very enfeebled wife, both submerged by piety. Tonks went bankrupt, and was succeeded by a branch of the National Provision Company, with a young manager exactly like a fox, except that he barked. The toy and sweetstuff shop was kept by an old woman of repellent manners, and so was the little fish shop at the end of the street. The Berlin-wool shop having gone bankrupt, became a newspaper shop, then fell to a haberdasher in consumption, and finally to a stationer; the three shops at the end of the street wallowed in and out of insolvency in the hands of a bicycle repairer and dealer, a gramophone dealer, a tobacconist, a sixpenny-halfpenny bazaar keeper, a shoemaker, a greengrocer, and the exploiter of a cinematograph peep-show—but none of them supplied friendship to Mr. Polly.

These adventurers in commerce were all more or less distraught souls, driving without intelligible comment before the gale of fate. The two milkmen of Fishbourne were brothers, who had quarrelled about their father's will, and started in opposition to each other. One was stone deaf and no use to Mr. Polly, and the other was a sporting man with a natural dread of epithet, who sided with Hinks. So it was all about him ; on every hand, it seemed, were uncongenial people, uninteresting people, or people who conceived the deepest distrust and hostility towards him—a magic circle of suspicious, preoccupied, and dehumanised humanity. So the poison in his system poisoned the world without.

But Boomer, the wine merchant, and Tashingford, the chemist, be it noted, were fraught with pride, and held themselves to be a cut above Mr. Polly. They never quarrelled with him, preferring to bear themselves from the outset as though they had already done so.

As his internal malady grew upon Mr. Polly, and he

became more and more a battle-ground of fermenting foods and warring juices, he came to hate the very sight, as people say, of every one of these neighbours. There they were, every day and all the days just the same, echoing his own stagnation. They pained him all round the top and back of his head; they made his legs and arms weary and spiritless. The air was tasteless by reason of them. He lost his human kindliness.

In the afternoons he would hover in the shop, bored to death with his business and his home and Miriam, and yet afraid to go out because of his inflamed and magnified dislike and dread of these neighbours. He could not bring himself to go out and run the gauntlet of the observant windows and the cold and estranged eyes.

One of his last friendships was with Rusper, the ironmonger. Rusper took over Worthington's shop about three years after Mr. Polly opened. He was a tall, lean, nervous, convulsive man, with an upturned, backthrown, oval head, who read newspapers and the *Review of Reviews* assiduously, had belonged to a Literary Society somewhere once, and had some defect of the palate that at first gave his lightest word a charm and interest for Mr. Polly. It caused a peculiar clinking sound, as though he had something between a giggle and a gas-meter at work in his neck.

His literary admirations were not precisely Mr. Polly's literary admirations; he thought books were written to enshrine Great Thoughts, and that art was pedagogy in fancy dress; he had no sense of phrase or epithet or richness of texture, but still he knew there were books. He did know there were books, and he was full of large, windy ideas of the sort he called " Modern (kik) Thought," and seemed needlessly and helplessly concerned about " (kik) the Welfare of the Race."

Mr. Polly would dream about that (kik) at night.

It seemed to that undesirable mind of his that Rusper's head was the most egg-shaped head he had ever seen; the similarity weighed upon him, and when he found an argument growing warm with Rusper he would say, " Boil it some more, O' Man; boil it harder! " or " Six minutes at least," allusions Rusper could never make head or tail of, and got at last to disregard as a part of Mr. Polly's general eccentricity. For a long time that little tendency threw no shadow over their intercourse, but it contained within it the seeds of an ultimate disruption.

Often during the days of this friendship Mr. Polly would leave his shop and walk over to Mr. Rusper's establishment and stand in his doorway and inquire, " Well, O' Man, how's the Mind of the Age working? " and get quite an hour of it; and sometimes Mr. Rusper would come into the outfitter's shop with " Heard the (kik) latest? " and spend the rest of the morning.

Then Mr. Rusper married, and he married, very inconsiderately, a woman who was totally uninteresting to Mr. Polly. A coolness grew between them from the first intimation of her advent. Mr. Polly couldn't help thinking when he saw her that she drew her hair back from her forehead a great deal too tightly, and that her elbows were angular. His desire not to mention these things in the apt terms that welled up so richly in his mind made him awkward in her presence, and that gave her an impression that he was hiding some guilty secret from her. She decided he must have a bad influence upon her husband, and she made it a point to appear whenever she heard him talking to Rusper.

One day they became a little heated about the German peril.

" I lay (kik) they'll invade us," said Rusper.

" Not a bit of it. William's not the Xerxiacious sort."

" You'll see, O'Man."

" Just what I shan't do."

" Before (kik) five years are out."

" Not it."

" Yes."

" No."

" Yes."

" Oh, boil it hard! " said Mr. Polly.

Then he looked up and saw Mrs. Rusper standing behind the counter, half hidden by a trophy of spades and garden shears and a knife-cleaning machine, and by her expression he knew instantly that she understood.

The conversation palled, and presently Mr. Polly withdrew.

After that estrangement increased steadily.

Mr. Rusper ceased altogether to come over to the outfitter's, and Mr. Polly called upon the ironmonger only with the completest air of casualty. And everything they said to each other led now to flat contradiction and raised voices. Rusper had been warned in vague and alarming terms that Mr. Polly insulted and made game of him, he couldn't discover exactly where; and so it appeared to him now that every word of Mr. Polly's might be an insult meriting his resentment, meriting it none the less because it was masked and cloaked.

Soon Mr. Polly's calls upon Mr. Rusper ceased also; and then Mr. Rusper, pursuing incomprehensible lines of thought, became afflicted with a specialised short-sightedness that applied only to Mr. Polly. He would look in other directions when Mr. Polly appeared, and his large, oval face assumed an expression of conscious serenity and deliberate happy unawareness that would have maddened a far less irritable person than Mr. Polly. It evoked a strong desire to mock and ape, and produced in his throat a cough of singular scornfulness, more particularly when Mr. Rusper also assisted with an assumed unconsciousness that was all his own.

Then one day Mr. Polly had a bicycle accident.

His bicycle was now very old, and it is one of the concomitants of a bicycle's senility that its free-wheel should one day obstinately cease to be free. It corresponds to that epoch in human decay when an old gentleman loses an incisor tooth. It happened just as Mr. Polly was approaching Mr. Rusper's shop, and the untoward chance of a motor-car trying to pass a wagon on the wrong side gave Mr. Polly no choice but to get on to the pavement and dismount. He was always accustomed to take his time and step off his left pedal at its lowest point, but the jamming of the free-wheel gear made that lowest moment a transitory one, and the pedal was lifting his foot for another revolution before he realised what had happened. Before he could dismount according to his habit the pedal had to make a revolution, and before it could make a revolution Mr. Polly found himself among the various sonorous things with which Mr. Rusper adorned the front of his shop—zinc dust bins, household pails, lawn mowers, rakes, spades, and all manner of clattering things. Before he got among them he had one of those agonising moments of helpless wrath and suspense that seem to last ages, in which one seems to perceive everything and think of nothing but words that are better forgotten. He sent a column of pails thundering across the doorway, and dismounted with one foot in a sanitary dustbin, amidst an enormous uproar of falling ironmongery.

" Put all over the place! " he cried, and found Mr. Rusper emerging from his shop with the large tranquillities of his countenance puckered to anger, like the frowns in the brow of a reefing sail. He gesticulated speechlessly for a moment.

" (kik) Jer doing? " he said at last.

" Tin mantraps! " said Mr. Polly.

" Jer (kik) doing? "

" Dressing all over the pavement as though the blessed town belonged to you! Ugh! "

And Mr. Polly, in attempting a dignified movement, realised his entanglement with the dustbin for the first time. With a low, embittering expression, he kicked his foot about in it for a moment very noisily, and finally sent it thundering to the kerb. On its way it struck a pail or so. Then Mr. Polly picked up his bicycle and proposed to resume his homeward way. But the hand of Mr. Rusper arrested him.

" Put it (kik) all (kik) back (kik)."

" Put it (kik) back yourself."

" You got (kik) put it back."

" Get out of the (kik) way."

Mr. Rusper laid one hand on the bicycle handle, and the other gripped Mr. Polly's collar urgently. Whereupon Mr. Polly said " Leggo! " and again, " D'you *hear*? Leggo! " and then drove his elbow with considerable force into the region of Mr. Rusper's midriff. Whereupon Mr. Rusper, with a loud, impassioned cry resembling " Woo kik " more than any other combination of letters, released the bicycle handle, seized Mr. Polly by the cap and hair, and bore his head and shoulders downwards. Thereat Mr. Polly, emitting such words as every one knows and nobody prints, butted his utmost into the concavity of Mr. Rusper, entwined a leg about him, and, after terrific moments of swaying instability, fell headlong beneath him amidst the bicycle and pails. There on the pavement these inexpert children of a pacific age, untrained in arms and uninured to violence, abandoned themselves to amateurish and absurd efforts to hurt and injure one another—of which the most palpable consequences were dusty backs, ruffled hair, and torn and twisted collars. Mr. Polly by accident got his finger into Mr. Rusper's mouth, and strove earnestly for some time to prolong that aperture in the direction of Mr. Rusper's ear before it occurred to Mr. Rusper to bite him (and even then he didn't bite very hard), while Mr. Rusper concentrated his mind almost entirely on an effort to rub Mr. Polly's face on the pavement. (And their positions bristled with chances of the deadliest sort!) They didn't, from first to last, draw blood.

Then it seemed to each of them that the other had become endowed with many hands and several voices and great accessions of strength. They submitted to fate and ceased to struggle. They found themselves torn apart and held up by outwardly scandalised and inwardly delighted neighbours, and invited to explain what it was all about.

"Got to (kik) puttem all back," panted Mr. Rusper, in the expert grasp of Hinks. "Merely asked him to (kik) puttem all back."

Mr. Polly was under restraint of little Clamp of the toyshop, who was holding his hands in a complex and uncomfortable manner that he afterwards explained to Wintershed was a combination of something romantic called " Jiu-jitsu " and something else still more romantic called the " Police Grip."

"Pails," explained Mr. Polly, in breathless fragments. "All over the road. Pails. Bungs up the street with his pails. Look at them! "

"Deliber (kik) lib (kik) liberately rode into my goods (kik). Constantly (kik) annoying me (kik)! " said Mr. Rusper.

They were both tremendously earnest and reasonable in their manner. They wished every one to regard them as responsible and intellectual men acting for the love of right and the enduring good of the world. They felt they must treat this business as a profound and publicly significant affair. They wanted to explain and orate and show the entire necessity of everything they had done. Mr. Polly was convinced he had never been so absolutely correct in all his life as when he planted his foot in the sanitary dustbin, and Mr. Rusper considered his clutch at Mr. Polly's hair as the one faultless impulse in an otherwise undistinguished career. But it was clear in their minds they might easily become ridiculous if they were not careful, if for a second they stepped over the edge of the high spirit and pitiless dignity they had hitherto maintained. At any cost they perceived they must not become ridiculous.

Mr. Chuffles, the scandalous grocer, joined the throng about the principal combatants, mutely, as became an outcast, and with a sad, distressed, helpful expression picked up Mr. Polly's bicycle. Gambell's summer errand boy, moved by example, restored the dustbin and pails to their self-respect.

" '*E* ought—'*E* ought (kik) pick them up," protested Mr. Rusper.

" What's it all about? " said Mr. Hinks for the third time, shaking Mr. Rusper gently. " 'As 'e been calling you names? "

" Simply ran into his pails—as any one might," said Mr. Polly, " and out he comes and scrags me."

" (kik) Assault! " said Mr. Rusper.

" He assaulted *me*," said Mr. Polly.

" Jumped (kik) into my dus'bin," said Mr. Rusper. " That assault? Or isn't it? "

" You better drop it," said Mr. Hinks.

" Great pity they can't be'ave better, both of 'em," said Mr. Chuffles, glad for once to find himself morally unassailable.

" Any one see it begin? " said Mr. Wintershed.

" *I* was in the shop," said Mrs. Rusper suddenly, from the doorstep, piercing the little group of men and boys with the sharp horror of a woman's voice. " If a witness is wanted, I suppose I've got a tongue. I suppose I got a voice in seeing my own husband injured. My husband went out and spoke to Mr. Polly, who was jumping off and on his bicycle all among our pails and things, and immediately 'E butted him in the stomach—immediately—most savagely—butted him. Just after his dinner, too, and him far from strong. I could have screamed. But Rusper caught hold of him right way, I will say that for Rusper——"

" I'm going," said Mr. Polly suddenly, releasing himself from the Anglo-Japanese grip and holding out his hands for his bicycle.

" Teach you (kik) to leave things alone," said Mr. Rusper, with an air of one who has given a lesson.

The testimony of Mrs. Rusper continued relentlessly in the background.

" You'll hear of me through a summons," said Mr. Polly, preparing to wheel his bicycle.

" (kik) Me too," said Mr. Rusper.

Some one handed Mr. Polly a collar. " This yours? "

Mr. Polly investigated his neck. " I suppose it is. Any one seen a tie? "

A small boy produced a grimy strip of spotted blue silk.

" Human life isn't safe with you," said Mr. Polly as a parting shot.

" (kik) Yours isn't," said Mr. Rusper.

And they got small satisfaction out of the Bench, which refused altogether to perceive the relentless correctitude of the behaviour of either party, and reproved the eagerness of Mrs. Rusper—speaking to her gently, firmly but exasperatingly as " My Good Woman," and telling her to " Answer the Question! Answer the Question! "

" Seems a pity," said the chairman, when binding them over to keep the peace, " you can't behave like Respectable Tradesmen. Seems a Great Pity. Bad Example to the young and all that. Don't do any Good to the town, don't do any Good to yourselves, don't do any manner of Good, to have all the Tradesmen in the Place scrapping about the Pavement of an

Afternoon. Think we're letting you off very easily this time, and hope it will be a Warning to you. Don't expect men of your position to come up before us. Very Regrettable Affair. Eh?"

He addressed the latter inquiry to his two colleagues.

" Exactly, exactly," said the colleague to the right.

" Err (kik)," said Mr. Rusper.

7

But the disgust that overshadowed Mr. Polly's being as he sat upon the stile had other and profounder justification than his quarrel with Rusper and the indignity of appearing before the county bench. He was, for the first time in his business career, short with his rent for the approaching quarter day; and, so far as he could trust his own handling of figures, he was sixty or seventy pounds on the wrong side of solvency. And that was the outcome of fifteen years of passive endurance of dullness throughout the best years of his life. What would Miriam say when she learnt this, and was invited to face the prospect of exile—Heaven knows what sort of exile—from their present home? She would grumble and scold and become limply unhelpful, he knew, and none the less so because he could not help things. She would say he ought to have worked harder, and a hundred such exasperating, pointless things. Such thoughts as these require no aid from undigested pork and cold potatoes and pickles to darken the soul, and with these aids his soul was black indeed.

" May as well have a bit of a walk," said Mr. Polly at last, after nearly intolerable meditations, and sat round and put a leg over the stile.

He remained still for some time before he brought over the other leg.

" Kill myself," he murmured at last.

It was an idea that came back to his mind nowadays with a continually increasing attractiveness, more particularly after meals. Life, he felt, had no further happiness for him. He hated Miriam, and there was no getting away from her, whatever might betide. And for the rest, there was toil and struggle, toil and struggle with a failing heart and dwindling courage, to sustain that dreary duologue. " Life's insured," said Mr. Polly; " place is insured. I don't see it does any harm to her or any one."

He stuck his hands in his pockets. " Needn't hurt much," he said. He began to elaborate a plan.

He found it was quite interesting elaborating his plan. His countenance became less miserable and his pace quickened.

There is nothing so good in all the world for melancholia as walking, and the exercise of the imagination in planning something presently to be done, and soon the wrathful wretchedness had vanished from Mr. Polly's face. He would have to do the thing secretly and elaborately, because otherwise there might be difficulties about the life insurance. He began to scheme how he could circumvent that difficulty. . . .

He took a long walk, for, after all, what is the good of hurrying back to shop when you are not only insolvent but very soon to die? His dinner and the east wind lost their sinister hold upon his soul, and when at last he came back along the Fishbourne High Street his face was unusually bright and the craving hunger of the dyspeptic was returning. So he went into the grocer's and bought a ruddily decorated tin of a brightly pink fish-like substance known as " Deep Sea Salmon." This he resolved to consume, regardless of cost, with vinegar and salt and pepper as a relish to his supper.

He did, and since he and Miriam rarely talked, and Miriam thought honour and his recent behaviour demanded a hostile silence, he ate fast and copiously and soon gloomily. He ate alone, for she refrained, to mark her sense of his extravagance. Then he prowled into the High Street for a time, thought it an infernal place, tried his pipe and found it foul and bitter, and retired wearily to bed.

He slept for an hour or so, and then woke up to the contemplation of Miriam's hunched back and the riddle of life, and this bright and attractive idea of ending for ever and ever and ever all the things that were locking him in, this bright idea that shone like a baleful star above all the reek and darkness of his misery. . . .

CHAPTER EIGHT

Making an End to Things

I

MR. POLLY designed his suicide with considerable care and a quite remarkable altruism.

His passionate hatred for Miriam vanished directly the idea of getting away from her for ever became clear in his mind. He found himself full of solicitude then for her welfare. He did not want to buy his release at her expense. He had not the remotest intention of leaving her unprotected, with a painfully dead husband and a bankrupt shop on her hands. It seemed to him that he could contrive to secure for her the full benefit of both his life insurance and his fire insurance if he managed things in a tactful manner. He felt happier than he had done for years scheming out this undertaking, albeit it was, perhaps, a larger and sombrer kind of happiness than had fallen to his lot before. It amazed him to think he had endured his monotony of misery and failure for so long.

But there were some queer doubts and questions in the dim, half-lit background of his mind that he had very resolutely to ignore.

" Sick of it," he had to repeat to himself aloud to keep his determination clear and firm. His life was a failure; there was nothing more to hope for but unhappiness. Why shouldn't he?

His project was to begin the fire with the stairs that led from the ground floor to the underground kitchen and scullery. This he would soak with paraffin, and assist with firewood and paper and a brisk fire in the coal cellar underneath. He would smash a hole or so in the stairs to ventilate the blaze, and have a good pile of boxes and paper, and a convenient chair or so, in the shop above. He would have the paraffin can upset, and the shop lamp, as if awaiting refilling, at convenient distances in the scullery ready to catch. Then he would smash the house lamp on the staircase—a fall with that in his hand was to be the ostensible cause of the blaze—and he would cut his throat at the top of the kitchen stairs, which would then become his funeral pyre. He would do all this on Sunday evening while Miriam was at church, and it would appear that he had fallen down stairs with the lamp and been burnt to death. There was really no flaw whatever that he could see in the scheme. He was quite sure he knew how to cut his throat, deep at the side and not to saw at the windpipe, and he was reasonably sure it wouldn't hurt him very much. And then everything would be at an end.

There was no particular hurry to get the thing done, of course, and meanwhile he occupied his mind with possible variations of the scheme. . . .

It needed a particularly dry and dusty east wind, a Sunday dinner of exceptional virulence, a conclusive letter from Konk, Maybrick, Ghool, and Gabbitas, his principal and most urgent creditors, and a conversation with Miriam, arising out of arrears of rent and leading on to mutual character sketching, before Mr. Polly could be brought to the necessary pitch of despair to carry out his plans. He went for an embittering walk, and came back to find Miriam in a bad temper over the tea things, with the brewings of three-quarters of an hour in the pot and hot buttered muffins gone leathery. He sat eating in silence with his resolution made.

"Coming to church?" said Miriam after she had cleared away.

"Rather. I got a lot to be grateful for," said Mr. Polly.

"You got what you deserve," said Miriam.

" Suppose I have," said Mr. Polly, and went and stared out of the back window at a despondent horse in the hotel yard.

He was still standing there when Miriam came down stairs dressed for church. Something in his immobility struck home to her. " You'd better come to church than mope," she said.

" I shan't mope," he answered.

She remained still. Her presence irritated him. He felt that in another moment he would say something absurd to her, make some last appeal for that understanding she had never been able to give. " Oh! *go* to church," he said.

In another moment the outer door slammed upon her. " Good riddance! " said Mr. Polly.

He turned about. " I've had my whack," he said.

He reflected. " I don't see she'll have any cause to holler," he said. " Beastly Home! Beastly Life! "

For a space he remained thoughtful. " Here goes! " he said at last.

2

For twenty minutes Mr. Polly busied himself about the house, making his preparations very neatly and methodically.

He opened the attic windows in order to make sure of a good draught through the house, and drew down the blinds at the back and shut the kitchen door to conceal his arrangements from casual observation. At the end he would open the door on the yard and so make a clean, clear draught right through the house. He hacked at, and wedged off, the tread of a stair. He cleared out the coals from under the staircase, and built a neat fire of firewood and paper there; he splashed about paraffin and arranged the lamps and can even as he had designed, and made a fine, inflammable pile of things in the little parlour behind the shop. " Looks pretty arsenical," he said, as he surveyed it all. " Wouldn't do to have a caller now. Now for the stairs! "

" Plenty of time," he assured himself, and took the lamp which was to explain the whole affair, and went to the head of the staircase between the scullery and the parlour. He sat down in the twilight, with the unlit lamp beside him, and surveyed things. He must light the fire in the coal cellar under the stairs, open the back door, then come up them very quickly and light the paraffin puddles on each step, then sit down here again and cut his throat. He drew his razor from his pocket and felt the edge. It wouldn't hurt much, and in ten minutes he would be indistinguishable ashes in the blaze.

And this was the end of life for him!

The end! And it seemed to him now that life had never begun for him, never! It was as if his soul had been cramped and his eyes bandaged from the hour of his birth. Why had he lived such a life? Why had he submitted to things, blundered into things? Why had he never insisted on the things he thought beautiful and the things he desired, never sought them, fought for them, taken any risk for them, died rather than abandon them? They were the things that mattered. Safety did not matter. A living did not matter unless there were things to live for. . . .

He had been a fool, a coward and a fool; he had been fooled, too, for no one had ever warned him to take a firm hold upon life, no one had ever told him of the littleness of fear or pain or death. But what was the good of going through it now again? It was over and done with.

The clock in the back parlour pinged the half-hour.

" Time! " said Mr. Polly, and stood up.

For an instant he battled with an impulse to put it

all back, hastily, guiltily, and abandon this desperate plan of suicide for ever.

But Miriam would smell the paraffin!

"No way out this time, O' Man," said Mr. Polly, and went slowly down stairs, matchbox in hand.

He paused for five seconds, perhaps, to listen to noises in the yard of the Royal Fishbourne Hotel before he struck his match. It trembled a little in his hand. The paper blackened, and an edge of blue flame ran outward and spread.

The fire burnt up readily, and in an instant the wood was crackling cheerfully.

Some one might hear. He must hurry.

He lit a pool of paraffin on the scullery floor, and instantly a nest of wavering blue flame became agog for prey. He went up the stairs three steps at a time, with one eager blue flicker in pursuit of him. He seized the lamp at the top. "Now!" he said, and flung it smashing. The chimney broke, but the glass receiver stood the shock and rolled to the bottom, a potential bomb. Old Rumbold would hear that and wonder what it was. . . He'd know soon enough!

Then Mr. Polly stood hesitating, razor in hand, and then sat down. He was trembling violently, but quite unafraid.

He drew the blade lightly under one ear. "Lord!" but it stung like a nettle!

Then he perceived a little blue thread of flame running up his leg. It arrested his attention, and for a moment he sat, razor in hand, staring at it. It must be paraffin! On his trousers that had caught fire on the stairs. Of course his legs were wet with paraffin! He smacked the flicker with his hand to put it out, and felt his leg burn as he did so. But his trousers still charred and glowed. It seemed to him necessary that he must put this out before he cut his throat. He put down the razor beside him to smack with both hands very eagerly. And as he did so a thin, tall, red flame came up through the hole in the stairs he had made and stood still, quite still, as it seemed, and looked at him. It was a strange-looking flame, a flattish, salmon colour, redly streaked. It was so queer and quiet-mannered that the sight of it held Mr. Polly agape.

" Whuff! " went the can of paraffin below, and boiled over with stinking white fire. At the outbreak, the salmon-coloured flames shivered and ducked and then doubled and vanished, and instantly all the staircase was noisily ablaze.

Mr. Polly sprang up and backwards, as though the uprushing tongues of fire were a pack of eager wolves.

" Good Lord! " he cried, like a man who wakes up from a dream.

He swore sharply, and slapped again at a recrudescent flame upon his leg.

" What the deuce shall I do? I'm soaked with the confounded stuff! "

He had nerved himself for throat-cutting but this was fire!

He wanted to delay things, to put the fire out for a moment while he did his business. The idea of arresting all this hurry with water occurred to him.

There was no water in the little parlour and none in the shop. He hesitated for a moment whether he should not run upstairs to the bedroom and get a ewer of water to throw on the flames. At this rate Rumbold's would be ablaze in five minutes. Things were going all too fast for Mr. Polly. He ran towards the staircase door, and its hot breath pulled him up sharply. Then he dashed out through the shop. The catch of the front door was sometimes obstinate; it was now, and instantly he became frantic. He rattled and stormed and felt the parlour already ablaze behind him. In another moment he was in the High Street with the door wide open.

The staircase behind him was crackling now like horsewhips and pistol-shots.

He had a vague sense that he wasn't doing as he had proposed, but the chief thing was his sense of that uncontrolled fire within. What was he going to do? There was the fire-brigade station next door but one.

The Fishbourne High Street had never seemed so empty.

Far off, at the corner by the God's Providence Inn, a group of three stiff hobbledehoys in their black, neat clothes conversed intermittently with Taplow, the policeman.

" Hi! " bawled Mr. Polly to them. " Fire! Fire! " and, struck by a horrible thought, the thought of Rumbold's deaf mother-in-law upstairs, began to bang and kick and rattle with the utmost fury at Rumbold's shop door.

" Hi! " he repeated, " Fire! "

3

That was the beginning of the great Fishbourne fire, which burnt its way sideways into Mr. Rusper's piles of crates and straw, and backwards to the petrol and stabling of the Royal Fishbourne Hotel, and spread from that basis until it seemed half Fishbourne would be ablaze. The east wind, which had been gathering in strength all that day, fanned the flames; everything was dry and ready, and the little shed beyond Rumbold's, in which the local fire brigade kept its manual, was alight before the Fishbourne fire-hose could be saved from disaster. In marvellously little time a great column of black smoke, shot with red streamers, rose out of the middle of the High Street, and all Fishbourne was alive with excitement.

Much of the more respectable elements of Fishbourne society was in church or chapel; many, however, had been tempted by the blue sky and the hard freshness of spring to take walks inland, and there had been the usual disappearance of loungers and conversationalists from the beach and the back streets when, at the hour of six, the shooting of bolts and the turning of keys had ended the British Ramadan, that weekly interlude of drought our law imposes. The youth of the place were scattered on the beach or playing in the backyards, under threat if their clothes were dirtied; and the adolescent were disposed in pairs among the more secluded corners to be found upon the outskirts of the place. Several godless youths, seasick, but fishing steadily, were tossing upon the sea in old Tarbold the infidel's boat, and the Clamps were entertaining cousins from Port Burdock. Such few visitors as Fishbourne could boast in the spring were at church or on the beach. To all these that column of smoke did in a manner address itself. " Look here! " it said, " this, within limits, is your affair; what are you going to do?"

The three hobbledehoys, had it been a week-day and they in working clothes, might have felt free to act, but the stiffness of black was upon them, and they simply moved to the corner by Rusper's to take a better view of Mr. Polly beating at his door. The policeman was a young, inexpert constable with far too lively a sense of the public-house. He put his head inside the Private Bar, to the horror of every one there. But there was no breach of the law, thank Heaven! " Polly's and Rumbold's on fire! " he said, and vanished again. A window in the top-storey over Boomer's shop opened, and Boomer, captain of the fire brigade, appeared, staring out with a blank expression. Still staring, he began to fumble with his collar and tie; manifestly he had to put on his uniform. Hinks' dog, which had been lying on the pavement outside Wintershed's, woke up, and having regarded Mr. Polly suspiciously for some time, growled nervously and went round the corner into Granville Alley. Mr. Polly continued to beat and kick at Rumbold's door.

Then the public-houses began to vomit forth the less desirable elements of Fishbourne society; boys and men were moved to run and shout, and more windows went up as the stir increased. Tashingford, the chemist, appeared at his door, in shirt sleeves and an apron, with his photographic plate-holders in his hand. And then, like a vision of purpose, came Mr. Gambell, the greengrocer, running out of Gayford's Alley and buttoning on his jacket as he ran. His great brass fireman's helmet was on his head, hiding it all but the sharp nose, the firm mouth, the intrepid chin. He ran straight to the fire station and tried the door, and turned about and met the eye of Boomer still at his upper window. " The key! " cried Mr. Gambell, " the key! "

Mr. Boomer made some inaudible explanation about his trousers and half a minute.

" Seen old Rumbold? " cried Mr. Polly, approaching Mr. Gambell.

" Gone over Downford for a walk," said Mr. Gambell. " He told me! But look 'ere! We 'aven't got the key! "

" Lord! " said Mr. Polly, and regarded the china shop with open eyes. He knew the old woman must be there alone. He went back to the shop front, and stood surveying it in infinite perplexity. The other activities in the street did not interest him. A deaf old lady somewhere upstairs there! Precious moments passing! Suddenly he was struck by an idea, and vanished from public vision into the open door of the Royal Fishbourne Tap.

And now the street was getting crowded, and people were laying their hands to this and that.

Mr. Rusper had been at home reading a number of tracts upon Tariff Reform, during the quiet of the wife's absence in church, and trying to work out the application of the whole question to ironmongery. He heard a clattering in the street, and for a time disregarded it, until a cry of " Fire! " drew him to the window. He pencil-marked the tract of Chiozza Money's that he was reading side by side with one by Mr. Holt Schooling, made a hasty note, " Bal of Trade say 12,000,000," and went to look out. Instantly he opened the window and ceased to believe the Fiscal Question the most urgent of human affairs.

" Good (kik) Gud! " said Mr. Rusper.

For now the rapidly spreading blaze had forced the partition into Mr. Rumbold's premises, swept across his cellar, clambered his garden wall by means of his well-tarred mushroom shed, and assailed the engine-house. It stayed not to consume, but ran as a thing that seeks a quarry. Polly's shop and upper parts were already a furnace, and black smoke was coming out of Rumbold's cellar gratings. The fire in the engine-house showed only as a sudden rush of smoke from the back, like something suddenly blown up. The fire brigade, still much under strength, were now hard at work in front of the latter building. They had got the door open all too late; they had rescued the fire-escape and some buckets, and were now lugging out their manual, with the hose already a dripping mass of molten, flaring, stinking rubber. Boomer was dancing about and swearing and shouting; this direct attack upon his apparatus outraged his sense of chivalry. His subordinates hovered in a disheartened state about the rescued fire-escape, and tried to piece Boomer's comments into some tangible instructions.

" Hi! " said Rusper from the window. " (kik) What's up? "

Gambell answered him out of his helmet. " Hose! " he cried. " Hose gone! "

" I (kik) got hose," cried Rusper.

He had. He had a stock of several thousand feet of garden hose of various qualities and calibres, and now, he felt, was the time to use it. In another moment his shop door was open, and he was hurling pails, garden syringes, and rolls of garden hose out upon the pavement. " (kik) Undo it! " he cried to the gathering crowd in the roadway.

They did. Presently a hundred ready hands were unrolling and spreading and tangling up and twisting and hopelessly involving Mr. Rusper's stock of hose, sustained by an unquenchable assurance that presently it would in some manner contain and convey water; and Mr. Rusper on his knees (kiking violently), became incredibly busy with wire and brass junctions and all sorts of mysteries.

" Fix it to the (kik) bathroom tap! " said Mr. Rusper.

Next door to the fire station was Mantell and Throbsons', the little Fishbourne branch of that celebrated firm, and Mr. Boomer, seeking in a teeming mind for a plan of action, had determined to save this building. " Some one telephone to the Port Burdock and Hampstead-on-Sea fire brigades," he cried to the crowd, and then to his fellows: " Cut away the woodwork of the fire station! " and so led the way into the blaze with a whirling hatchet that effected wonders of ventilation in no time.

But it was not, after all, such a bad idea of his. Mantell and Throbsons' was separated from the fire station in front by a covered glass passage, and at the back the roof of a big outhouse sloped down to the fire station leads. The sturdy longshoremen, who made up the bulk of the fire brigade, assailed the glass roof of the passage with extraordinary gusto, and made a smashing of glass that drowned for a time the rising uproar of the flames.

A number of willing volunteers started off to the new

telephone office in obedience to Mr. Boomer's request, only to be told, with cold official politeness by the young lady at the exchange, that all that had been done on her own initiative ten minutes ago. She parleyed with these heated enthusiasts for a space, and then returned to the window.

And, indeed, the spectacle was well worth looking at. The dusk was falling, and the flames were showing brilliantly at half a dozen points. The Royal Fishbourne Hotel Tap, which adjoined Mr. Polly to the west, was being kept wet by the enthusiastic efforts of a string of volunteers with buckets of water, and above at a bathroom window, the little German waiter was busy with the garden hose. But Mr. Polly's establishment looked more like a house afire than most houses on fire contrive to look from start to finish. Every window showed eager, flickering flames, and flames like serpents' tongues were licking out of three large holes in the roof, which was already beginning to fall in. Behind, larger and abundantly spark-shot gusts of fire rose from the fodder that was now getting alight in the Royal Fishbourne Hotel stables. Next door to Mr. Polly, Mr. Rumbold's house was disgorging black smoke from the gratings that protected its underground windows, and smoke and occasional shivers of flame were also coming out of its first-floor windows. The fire station was better alight at the back than in front, and its woodwork burnt pretty briskly with peculiar greenish flickerings, and a pungent flavour. In the street an inaggressively disorderly crowd clambered over the rescued fire-escape, and resisted the attempts of the three local constables to get it away from the danger of Mr. Polly's tottering façade; a cluster of busy forms danced and shouted and advised on the noisy and smashing attempt to cut off Mantell and Throbsons' from the fire station that was still in effectual progress. Further, a number of people appeared to be destroying interminable red and gray snakes under the heated direction of Mr. Rusper—it was as if the High Street had a plague of worms; and beyond again, the more timid and less active crowded in front of an accumulation of arrested traffic. Most of the men were in Sabbatical black, and this, and the white and starched quality of the women and children in their best clothes, gave a note of ceremony to the whole affair.

For a moment the attention of the telephone clerk was held by the activities of Mr. Tashingford, the chemist, who, regardless of every one else, was rushing across the road hurling fire grenades into the fire station and running back for more, and then her eyes lifted to the slanting outhouse roof that went up to a ridge behind the parapet of Mantell and Throbsons'. An expression of incredulity came into the telephone operator's eye, and gave place to hard activity. She flung up the window and screamed out, " Two people on the roof up there! Two people on the roof! "

4

Her eyes had not deceived her. Two figures which had emerged from the upper staircase window of Mr. Rumbold's and had got, after a perilous paddle in his cistern, on to the fire station, were now slowly but resolutely clambering up the outhouse roof towards the back of the main premises of Messrs. Mantell and Throbsons'. They clambered slowly, and one urged and helped the other, slipping and pausing ever and again amidst a constant trickle of fragments of broken tile.

One was Mr. Polly, with his hair wildly disordered, his face covered with black smudges and streaked with perspiration, and his trouser legs scorched and blackened; the other was an elderly lady, quietly but becomingly dressed in black with small white frills at her neck and wrists, and a Sunday cap of écru lace enlivened with a black velvet bow. Her hair was brushed back from her wrinkled brow and plastered down tightly, meeting in a small knob behind; her wrinkled mouth bore that expression of supreme resolution common with the toothless aged. She was shaky, not with fear, but with the vibrations natural to her years, and she spoke with a slow, quavering firmness.

"I don't mind scrambling," she said with piping inflexibility, "but I can't jump, and I won't jump."

"Scramble, old lady, then, scramble!" said Mr. Polly, pulling her arm. "It's one up and two down on these blessed tiles."

"It's not what I'm used to," she said.

"Stick to it," said Mr. Polly. "Live and learn," and got to the ridge and grasped her arm to pull her after him.

"I can't jump, mind ye," she repeated, pressing her lips together. "And old ladies like me mustn't be hurried."

"Well, let's get as high as possible, anyhow," said Mr. Polly, urging her gently upwards. "Shinning up a waterspout in your line? Near as you'll get to Heaven."

"I *can't* jump," she said. "I can do anything but jump."

"Hold on," said Mr. Polly, "while I give you a boost. That's—wonderful."

"So long as it isn't jumping. . . ."

The old lady grasped the parapet above, and there was a moment of intense struggle.

"Urup!" said Mr. Polly. "Hold on! Gollys! where's she gone to? . . ,"

Then an ill-mended, wavering, yet very reassuring spring-side boot appeared for an instant.

"Thought perhaps there wasn't any roof there!" he explained, scrambling up over the parapet beside her.

"I've never been out on a roof before," said the old lady. "I'm all disconnected. It's very bumpy. Especially that last bit. Can't we sit here for a bit and rest? I'm not the girl I used to be."

"You sit here ten minutes," shouted Mr. Polly, "and you'll pop like a roast chestnut. Don't understand me? *Roast Chestnut!* ROAST CHESTNUT! POP! There ought to be a limit to deafness. Come on round to the front and see if we can find an attic window. Look at this smoke!"

"Nasty!" said the old lady, her eyes following his gesture, puckering her face into an expression of great distaste.

"Come on!"

"Can't hear a word you say."

He pulled her arm. "Come on!"

She paused for a moment to relieve herself of a series of entirely unexpected chuckles. "Sich goings on!" she said. "I never did! Where's he going now?" and came along behind the parapet to the front of the drapery establishment.

Below, the street was now fully alive to their presence, and encouraged the appearance of their heads by shouts and cheers. A sort of free fight was going on round the fire-escape, order represented by Mr. Boomer and the very young policeman, and disorder by some partially intoxicated volunteers with views of their own about the manipulation of the apparatus. Two or three lengths of Mr. Rusper's garden hose appeared to have twined themselves round the ladder. Mr. Polly watched the struggle with a certain impatience, and glanced ever and again over his shoulder at the increasing volume of smoke and steam that was pouring up from the burning fire station. He decided to break an attic window and get in, and so try and get down through the shop. He found himself in a little bedroom, and returned to fetch his charge. For some time he could not make her understand his purpose.

"Got to come at once!" he shouted.

"I hain't 'ad sich a time for years!" said the old lady.

"We'll have to get down through the house!"

"Can't do no jumping," said the old lady. "No!" She yielded reluctantly to his grasp.

She stared over the parapet. "Runnin' and scurrying about like black beetles in a kitchen," she said.

"We've got to hurry."

"Mr. Rumbold. 'E's a very Quiet man. 'E likes everything Quiet. He'll be surprised to see me 'ere! Why! there 'E is!" She fumbled in her garments mysteriously, and at last produced a wrinkled pocket-handkerchief and began to wave it.

"Oh, come *ON*!" cried Mr. Polly, and seized her.

He got her into the attic, but the staircase, he found, was full of suffocating smoke, and he dared not venture below the next floor. He took her into a long dormitory, shut the door on those pungent and pervasive fumes, and opened the window, to discover the fire-escape was now against the house, and all Fishbourne boiling with excitement as an immensely helmeted and active and resolute little figure ascended. In another moment the rescuer stared over the window-sill, heroic but just a trifle self-conscious and grotesque.

"Lawks-a-mussy!" said the old lady. "Wonders and Wonders! Why! it's Mr. Gambell! 'Iding 'is 'ead in that thing! I *never* did!"

"Can we get her out?" said Mr. Gambell. "There's not much time."

"He might get stuck in it."

"*You'll* get stuck in it," said Mr. Polly; "come along!"

" Not for jumpin' I don't," said the old lady, under-standing his gestures rather than his words. " Not a bit of it. I bain't no good at jumping, and I *wun't*."

They urged her gently but firmly towards the window.

" You lemme do it my own way," said the old lady at the sill. . . .

" I could do it better if 'e'd take 'it off."

" Oh, *carm* on! "

" It's wuss than Carter's stile," she said, " before they mended it—with a cow looking at you."

Mr. Gambell hovered protectingly below. Mr. Polly steered her aged limbs from above. An anxious crowd below babbled advice and did its best to upset the fire-escape. Within, streamers of black smoke were pouring up through the cracks in the floor. For some seconds the world waited while the old lady gave herself up to reckless mirth again. " Sich times! " she said. " Poor Rumbold! "

Slowly they descended, and Mr. Polly remained at the post of danger, steadying the long ladder until the old lady was in safety below and sheltered by Mr. Rumbold (who was in tears) and the young policeman from the urgent congratulations of the crowd. The crowd was full of an impotent passion to participate. Those nearest wanted to shake her hand, those remoter cheered.

" The fust fire I was ever in, and likely to be my last. It's a scurryin', 'urryin' business, but I'm real glad I haven't missed it," said the old lady, as she was borne rather than led towards the refuge of the Temperance Hotel.

Also she was heard to remark: " 'E was saying something about 'ot chestnuts. *I* haven't 'ad no 'ot chestnuts."

Then the crowd became aware of Mr. Polly awk-wardly negotiating the top rungs of the fire-escape.

" 'Ere 'e comes! " cried a voice; and Mr. Polly descended into the world again out of the conflagration he had lit to be his funeral-pyre, moist, excited, and tremendously alive, amidst a tempest of applause. As he got lower and lower, the crowd howled like a pack of dogs at him. Impatient men, unable to wait for him, seized and shook his descending boots, and so brought him to earth with a run. He was rescued with difficulty from an enthusiast who wished to slake at his own expense and to his own accompaniment a thirst altogether heroic. He was hauled into the Temperance Hotel and flung like a sack, breathless and helpless, into the tear-wet embrace of Miriam.

5

With the dusk and the arrival of some county constabulary, and first one and presently two other fire-engines from Port Burdock and Hampstead-on-Sea, the local talent of Fishbourne found itself forced back into a secondary, less responsible, and more observant rôle. I will not pursue the story of the fire to its ashes, nor will I do more than glance at the unfortunate Mr. Rusper, a modern Laocoon, vainly trying to retrieve his scattered hose amidst the tramplings and rushings of the Port Burdock experts.

In a small sitting-room of the Fishbourne Temperance Hotel a little group of Fishbourne tradesmen sat and conversed in fragments, and anon went to the window and looked out upon the smoking desolation of their houses across the way, and anon sat down again. They and their families were the guests of old Lady Bargrave, who had displayed the utmost sympathy and interest in their misfortunes. She had taken several people into her own house at Everdean, had engaged the Temperance Hotel as a temporary refuge, and personally superintended the housing of Mantell and

Throbsons' homeless assistants. The Temperance Hotel became and remained extremely noisy and congested **with** people sitting about anywhere, conversing in fragments, and totally unable to get themselves to bed. The manager was an old soldier, and, following the best traditions of the service, saw that every one had hot cocoa. Hot cocoa seemed to be about everywhere, and it was no doubt very heartening and sustaining to every one. When the manager detected any one disposed to be drooping or pensive he exhorted that person at once to drink further hot cocoa and maintain a stout heart.

The hero of the occasion, the centre of interest, was Mr. Polly. For he had not only caused the fire by upsetting a lighted lamp, scorching his trousers and narrowly escaping death, as indeed he had now explained in detail about twenty times, but he had further thought at once of that amiable but helpless old lady next door, had shown the utmost decision in making his way to her over the yard wall of the Royal Fishbourne Hotel, and had rescued her with persistence and vigour, in spite of the levity natural to her years. Every one thought well of him and was anxious to show it, more especially by shaking his hand painfully and repeatedly. Mr. Rumbold, breaking a silence of nearly fifteen years, thanked him profusely, said that he had never understood him properly, and declared he ought to have a medal. There seemed to be a widely diffused idea that Mr. Polly ought to have a medal. Hinks thought so. He declared, moreover, and with the utmost emphasis, that Mr. Polly had a crowded and richly decorated interior—or words to that effect. There was something apologetic in this persistence; it was as if he regretted past intimations that Mr. Polly was internally defective and hollow. He also said that Mr. Polly was a " white man " albeit, as he developed it, with a liver of the deepest chromatic satisfactions.

Mr. Polly wandered centrally through it all, with his face washed and his hair carefully brushed and parted, looking modest and more than a little absent-minded, and wearing a pair of black dress trousers belonging to the manager of the Temperance Hotel—a larger man than himself in every way.

He drifted upstairs to his fellow-tradesmen, and stood for a time staring into the littered street, with its pools of water and extinguished gas lamps. His companions in misfortune resumed a fragmentary disconnected conversation. They touched now on one aspect of the disaster and now on another, and there were intervals of silence. More or less empty cocoa cups were distributed over the table, mantelshelf, and piano, and in the middle of the table was a tin of biscuits, into which Mr. Rumbold, sitting round-shouldered, dipped ever and again in an absent-minded way, and munched like a distant shooting of coals. It added to the solemnity of the affair that nearly all of them were in their black Sunday clothes; little Clamp was particularly impressive and dignified in a wide open frock-coat, a Gladstone-shaped paper collar, and a large white-and-blue tie. They felt that they were in the presence of a great disaster, the sort of disaster that gets into the papers, and is even illustrated by blurred photographs of the crumbling ruins. In the presence of that sort of disaster all honourable men are lugubrious and sententious.

And yet it is impossible to deny a certain element of elation. Not one of those excellent men but was already realising that a great door had opened, as it were, in the opaque fabric of destiny, that they were to get their money again that had seemed sunken for ever beyond any hope in the deeps of retail trade. Life was already in their imagination rising like a Phœnix from the flames.

" I suppose there'll be a public subscription," said Mr. Clamp.

" Not for those who're insured," said Mr. Winter-shed.

" I was thinking of them assistants from Mantell and Throbsons'. They must have lost nearly everything."

" They'll be looked after all right," said Mr. Rumbold. " Never fear."

Pause.

" *I'm* insured," said Mr. Clamp with unconcealed satisfaction. " Royal Salamander."

" Same here," said Mr. Wintershed.

" Mine's the Glasgow Sun," Mr. Hinks remarked. " Very good company."

" You insured, Mr. Polly? "

" He deserves to be," said Rumbold.

" Ra—ther," said Hinks. " Blowed if he don't. Hard lines it *would* be—if there wasn't something for him."

" Commercial and General," answered Mr. Polly over his shoulder, still staring out of the window. " Oh! I'm all right."

The topic dropped for a time, though manifestly it continued to exercise their minds.

" It's cleared me out of a lot of old stock," said Mr. Wintershed; " that's one good thing."

The remark was felt to be in rather questionable taste, and still more so was his next comment.

" Rusper's a bit sick it didn't reach '*im*.' "

Every one looked uncomfortable, and no one was willing to point the reason why Rusper should be a bit sick.

" Rusper's been playing a game of his own," said Hinks. " Wonder what he thought he was up to! Sittin' in the middle of the road with a pair of tweezers he was, and about a yard of wire—mending somethin'.

Wonder he warn't run over by the Port Burdock engine."

Presently a little chat sprang up upon the causes of fires, and Mr. Polly was moved to tell for the one-and-twentieth time how it had happened. His story had now become as circumstantial and exact as the evidence of a police witness. " Upset the lamp," he said. " I'd just lighted it. I was going upstairs, and my foot slipped against where one of the treads were a bit rotten, and down I went. Thing was aflare in a moment! . . ."

He yawned at the end of the discussion, and moved doorward.

" So long," said Mr. Polly.

" Good night," said Mr. Rumbold. " You played a brave man's part! If you don't get a medal——"

He left an eloquent pause.

" 'Ear, 'ear! " said Mr. Wintershed and Mr. Clamp.

" Goo'-night, O' Man," said Mr. Hinks.

" Goo'-night, All," said Mr. Polly. . . .

He went slowly upstairs. The vague perplexity common to popular heroes pervaded his mind. He entered the bedroom and turned up the electric light. It was quite a pleasant room, one of the best in the Temperance Hotel, with a nice clean flowered wall-paper, and a very large looking-glass. Miriam appeared to be asleep, and her shoulders were humped up under the clothes in a shapeless, forbidding lump that Mr. Polly had found utterly loathsome for fifteen years. He went softly over to the dressing-table and surveyed himself thoughtfully. Presently he hitched up the trousers. " Miles too big for me," he remarked. " Funny not to have a pair of breeches of one's own. . . . Like being born again. Naked came I into the world."

Miriam stirred and rolled over, and stared at him.

" Hallo! " she said.

" Hallo? "

" Come to bed? "

" It's three."

Pause while Mr. Polly disrobed slowly.

" I been thinking," said Miriam. " It isn't going to be so bad after all. We shall get your insurance. We can easy begin all over again."

" H'm," said Mr. Polly.

She turned her face away from him and reflected.

" Get a better house," said Miriam, regarding the wallpaper pattern. " I've always 'ated them stairs."

Mr. Polly removed a boot.

" Choose a better position where there's more doing," murmured Miriam. . . .

" Not half so bad," she whispered. . . .

" You *wanted* stirring up," she said, half asleep. . . .

It dawned upon Mr. Polly for the first time that he had forgotten something.

He ought to have cut his throat!

The fact struck him as remarkable, but as now no longer of any particular urgency. It seemed a thing far off in the past, and he wondered why he had not thought of it before. Odd thing life is! If he had done it he would never have seen this clean and agreeable apartment with the electric light. . . . His thoughts wandered into a question of detail. Where could he have put down the razor? Somewhere in the little room behind the shop, he supposed, but he could not think where more precisely. Anyhow, it didn't matter now.

He undressed himself calmly, got into bed, and fell asleep almost immediately.

CHAPTER NINE

The Potwell Inn

I

BUT when a man has once broken through the paper walls of everyday circumstance, those unsubstantial walls that hold so many of us securely prisoned from the cradle to the grave, he has made a discovery. If the world does not please you, *you can change it.* Determine to alter it at any price, and you can change it altogether. You may change it into something sinister and angry, to something appalling, but it may be you will change it to something brighter, something more agreeable, and at the worst something much more interesting. There is only one sort of man who is absolutely to blame for his own misery, and that is the man who finds life dull and dreary. There are no circumstances in the world that determined action cannot alter, unless, perhaps, they are the walls of a prison cell, and even those will dissolve and change, I am told, into the infirmary compartment, at any rate, for the man who can fast with resolution. I give these things as facts and information, and with no moral intimations. And Mr. Polly, lying awake at nights, with a renewed indigestion, with Miriam sleeping sonorously beside him, and a general air of inevitableness about his situation, saw through it, understood there was no inevitable any more, and escaped his former despair.

He could, for example, " clear out."

It became a wonderful and alluring phrase to him— " Clear out! "

Why had he never thought of clearing out before?

He was amazed and a little shocked at the un-imaginative and superfluous criminality in him that had turned old, cramped, and stagnant Fishbourne into a blaze and new beginnings. (I wish from the bottom of my heart I could add that he was properly sorry.) But something constricting and restrained seemed to have been destroyed by that flare. *Fishbourne wasn't the world.* That was the new, the essential fact of which he had lived so lamentably in ignorance. Fishbourne, as he had known it and hated it, so that he wanted to kill himself to get out of it, *wasn't the world.*

The insurance money he was to receive made every-thing humane and kindly and practicable. He would " clear out " with justice and humanity. He would take exactly twenty-one pounds, and all the rest he would leave to Miriam. That seemed to him absolutely fair. Without him, she could do all sorts of things— all the sorts of things she was constantly urging him to do. . . .

And he would go off along the white road that led to Garchester, and on to Crogate and so to Tunbridge Wells, where there was a Toad Rock he had heard of but never seen. (It seemed to him this must needs be a marvel.) And so to other towns and cities. He would walk and loiter by the way, and sleep in inns at night, and get an odd job here and there, and talk to strange people.

Perhaps he would get quite a lot of work, and prosper; and if he did not do so he would lie down in front of a train, or wait for a warm night and then fall into some smooth, broad river. Not so bad as sitting down to a dentist—not nearly so bad. And he would never open a shop any more.

So the possibilities of the future presented themselves to Mr. Polly, as he lay awake at nights.

It was springtime, and in the woods, so soon as one

got out of reach of the sea wind, there would be
anemones and primroses.

2

A month later a leisurely and dusty tramp, plump
equatorially and slightly bald, with his hands in his
pockets and his lips puckered to a contemplative
whistle, strolled along the river bank between Upping-
don and Potwell. It was a profusely budding spring
day, and greens such as God had never permitted in
the world before in human memory (though, indeed,
they come every year and we forget) were mirrored
vividly in a mirror of equally unprecedented brown.
For a time the wanderer stopped and stood still, and
even the thin whistle died away from his lips as he
watched a water-vole run to and fro upon a little headland across the stream. The vole plopped into the
water, and swam and dived, and only when the last
ring of its disturbance had vanished did Mr.
Polly resume his thoughtful course to nowhere in
particular.

For the first time in many years he had been leading
a healthy human life, living constantly in the open air,
walking every day for eight or nine hours, eating sparingly, accepting every conversational opportunity, not
even disdaining the discussion of possible work. And
beyond mending a hole in his coat, that he had made
while negotiating barbed wire, with a borrowed needle
and thread in a lodging-house, he had done no real
work at all. Neither had he worried about business nor
about times and seasons. And for the first time in his
life he had seen the Aurora Borealis.

So far, the holiday had cost him very little. He had
arranged it on a plan that was entirely his own. He
had started with four five-pound notes and a pound

divided into silver, and he had gone by train from Fishbourne to Ashington. At Ashington he had gone to the post office, obtained a registered letter envelope and sent his four five-pound notes with a short, brotherly note addressed to himself at Gilhampton post office. He sent this letter to Gilhampton for no other reason in the world than that he liked the name of Gilhampton and the rural suggestion of its containing county, which was Sussex; and having so despatched it, he set himself to discover, mark down, and walk to Gilhampton, and so recover his resources. And having got to Gilhampton at last, he changed a five-pound note, bought four pound postal orders, and repeated his manœuvre with nineteen pounds.

After a lapse of fifteen years he rediscovered this interesting world, about which so many people go incredibly blind and bored. He went along country roads while all the birds were piping and chirruping and cheeping and singing, and looked at fresh new things, and felt as happy and irresponsible as a boy with an unexpected half-holiday. And if ever the thought of Miriam returned to him, he controlled his mind. He came to country inns and sat for unmeasured hours talking of this and that to those sage carters who rest for ever in the taps of the country inns, while the big, sleek, brass-jingling horses wait patiently outside with their wagons. He got a job with some van people who were wandering about the country with swings and a steam roundabout, and remained with them three days, until one of their dogs took a violent dislike to him, and made his duties unpleasant. He talked to tramps and wayside labourers. He snoozed under hedges by day, and in outhouses and hayricks at night, and once, but only once, he slept in a casual ward. He felt as the etiolated grass and daisies must do when you move the garden roller away to a new place.

He gathered a quantity of strange and interesting memories.

He crossed some misty meadows by moonlight and the mist lay low on the grass, so low that it scarcely reached above his waist, and houses and clumps of trees stood out like islands in a milky sea, so sharply defined was the upper surface of the mist-bank. He came nearer and nearer to a strange thing that floated like a boat upon this magic lake, and behold, something moved at the stern, and a rope was whisked at the prow, and it had changed into a pensive cow, drowsy-eyed, regarding him. . . .

He saw a remarkable sunset in a new valley near Maidstone, a very red and clear sunset, a wide redness under a pale, cloudless heaven, and with the hills all round the edge of the sky a deep purple blue and clear and flat, looking exactly as he had seen mountains painted in pictures. He seemed transported to some strange country, and would have felt no surprise if the old labourer he came upon leaning silently over a gate had addressed him in an unfamiliar tongue. . . .

Then one night, just towards dawn, his sleep upon a pile of brushwood was broken by the distant rattle of a racing motor-car breaking all the speed regulations, and as he could not sleep again, he got up and walked into Maidstone as the day came. He had never been abroad in a town at four o'clock in his life before, and the stillness of everything in the bright sunrise impressed him profoundly. At one corner was a startling policeman, standing up in a doorway quite motionless like a waxen image. Mr. Polly wished him " good-morning " unanswered, and went down to the bridge over the Medway, and sat on the parapet, very still and thoughtful, watching the town awaken, and wondering what he should do if it didn't, if the world of men never woke again. . . .

One day he found himself going along a road, with

a wide space of sprouting bracken and occasional trees on either side, and suddenly this road became strangely and perplexingly familiar. "Lord!" he said, and turned about and stood. "It can't be."

He was incredulous, then left the road and walked along a scarcely perceptible track to the left, and came in half a minute to an old lichenous stone wall. It seemed exactly the bit of wall he had known so well. It might have been but yesterday he was in that place; there remained even a little pile of wood. It became absurdly the same wood. The bracken, perhaps, was not so high, and most of its fronds were still coiled up, that was all. Here he had stood, it seemed, and there she had sat and looked down upon him. Where was she now, and what had become of her? He counted the years back, and marvelled that beauty should have called to him with so imperious a voice—and signified nothing.

He hoisted himself with some little difficulty to the top of the wall, and saw far off under the beech trees two schoolgirls—small, insignificant, pig-tailed creatures with heads of blond and black, with their arms twined about each other's necks, no doubt telling each other the silliest secrets.

But that girl with the red hair—was she a countess? was she a queen? Children, perhaps? Had sorrow dared to touch her?

Had she forgotten altogether? . . .

A tramp sat by the roadside, thinking, and it seemed to the man in the passing motor-car he must needs be plotting for another pot of beer. But, as a matter of fact, what the tramp was saying to himself over and over again, was a variant upon a well-known Hebrew word.

"Itchabod," the tramp was saying in the voice of one who reasons on the side of the inevitable. "It's

Fair Itchabod, O' Man. There's no going back to things like that."

3

It was about two o'clock in the afternoon, one hot day in May, when Mr. Polly, unhurrying and serene, came upon that broad bend of the river to which the little lawn and garden of the Potwell Inn run down. He stopped at the sight of the place and surveyed its deep tiled roof, nestling under big trees—you never get a decently big, decently shaped tree by the sea-side—its sign towards the roadway, its sun-blistered green bench and tables, its shapely white windows and its row of upshooting hollyhock plants in the garden. A hedge separated the premises from a buttercup-yellow meadow, and beyond stood three poplars in a group against the sky, three exceptionally tall, graceful, and harmonious poplars. It is hard to say what there was about them that made them so beautiful to Mr. Polly, but they seemed to him to touch a pleasant scene with a distinction almost divine. He stood admiring them quietly for a long time.

At last the need for coarser æsthetic satisfactions arose in him.

" Provender," he whispered, drawing near to the inn. " Cold sirloin, for choice. And nutbrown brew and wheaten bread."

The nearer he came to the place the more he liked it. The windows on the ground floor were long and low, and they had pleasing red blinds. The green tables outside were agreeably ringed with memories of former drinks, and an extensive grape vine spread level branches across the whole front of the place. Against the wall was a broken oar, two boat-hooks, and the stained and faded red cushions of a pleasure boat. One went up three steps to the glass-panelled door and peeped into a broad, low room with a bar and a beer engine, behind which were many bright and helpful-looking bottles against mirrors, and great and little pewter measures, and bottles fastened in brass wire upside down, with their corks replaced by taps, and a white china cask labelled " Shrub," and cigar boxes, and boxes of cigarettes, and a couple of Toby jugs and a beautifully coloured hunting scene framed and glazed, showing the most elegant people taking Piper's Cherry Brandy, and cards such as the law requires about the dilution of spirits and the illegality of bringing children into bars, and satirical verses about swearing and asking for credit, and three very bright, red-checked wax apples and a round shaped clock.

But these were the mere background to the really pleasant thing in the spectacle which was quite the plumpest woman Mr. Polly had ever seen, seated in an arm-chair in the midst of all those bottles and glasses and glittering things, peacefully, and tranquilly, and without the slightest loss of dignity, asleep. Many people would have called her a fat woman, but Mr. Polly's innate sense of epithet told him from the outset that plump was the word. She had shapely brows and a straight, well-shaped nose, kind lines and content-ment about her mouth, and beneath it the jolly chins clustered like chubby little cherubim about the feet of an Assumption-ing Madonna. Her plumpness was firm and pink and wholesome, and her hands, dimpled at every joint, were clasped in front of her; she seemed, as it were, to embrace herself with infinite confidence and kindliness, as one who knew herself good in substance, good in essence, and would show her gratitude to God by that ready acceptance of all that He had given her. Her head was a little on one side, not much, but just enough to speak of trustfulness, and rob her of the stiff effect of self-reliance. And she slept.

"*My* sort," said Mr. Polly, and opened the door very softly, divided between the desire to enter and come nearer, and an instinctive indisposition to break slumbers so manifestly sweet and satisfying.

She awoke with a start, and it amazed Mr. Polly to see swift terror flash into her eyes. Instantly it had gone again.

"Law!" she said, her face softening with relief. "I thought you was Jim."

"I'm never Jim," said Mr. Polly.

"You've got his sort of hat."

"Ah!" said Mr. Polly, and leant over the bar.

"It just came into my head you was Jim," said the plump lady, dismissed the topic and stood up. "I believe I was having forty winks," she said, "if all the truth was told. What can I do for you?"

"Cold meat?" said Mr. Polly.

"There *is* cold meat," the plump woman admitted.

"And room for it."

The plump woman came and leant over the bar and regarded him judicially but kindly. "There's some cold boiled beef," she said, and added, "A bit of crisp lettuce?"

"New mustard," said Mr. Polly.

"And a tankard!"

"A tankard."

They understood each other perfectly.

"Looking for work?" asked the plump woman.

"In a way," said Mr. Polly.

They smiled like old friends.

Whatever the truth may be about love, there is certainly such a thing as friendship at first sight. They liked each other's voices, they liked each other's way of smiling and speaking.

" It's such beautiful weather this spring," said Mr.
Polly, explaining everything.

" What sort of work do you want? " she asked.

" I've never properly thought that out," said Mr.
Polly. " I've been looking around—for ideas."

" Will you have your beef in the tap or outside?
That's the tap."

Mr. Polly had a glimpse of an oaken settle. " In the
tap will be handier for you," he said.

" Hear that? " said the plump lady.

" Hear what? "

" Listen."

Presently the silence was broken by a distant howl—
" Oooooover! "   " Eh? " she said.

He nodded.

" That's the ferry.   And there isn't a ferryman."

" Could I? "

" Can you punt? "

" Never tried."

" Well—pull the pole out before you reach the end
of the punt, that's all.   Try."

Mr. Polly went out again into the sunshine.

At times one can tell so much so briefly.   Here are
the facts then—bare.   He found a punt and a pole,
got across to the steps on the opposite side, picked up
an elderly gentleman in an alpaca jacket and a pith
helmet, cruised with him vaguely for twenty minutes,
conveyed him tortuously into the midst of a thicket
of forget-me-not spangled sedges, splashed some water-
weed over him, hit him twice with the punt pole, and
finally landed him, alarmed but abusive, in the
treacherous soil at the edge of a hay meadow about
forty yards down-stream, where he immediately got
into difficulties with a noisy, aggressive little white dog,
which was guarding a jacket.

Mr. Polly returned in a complicated manner, but
with perfect dignity, to his moorings.

He found the plump woman rather flushed and tearful, and seated at one of the green tables outside.

" I been laughing at you," she said.

" What for? " asked Mr. Polly.

" I ain't 'ad such a laugh since Jim come 'ome. When you 'it 'is 'ead, it 'urt my side."

" It didn't hurt his head—not particularly."

" Did you charge him anything? "

" Gratis," said Mr. Polly. " I never thought of it."

The plump woman pressed her hands to her sides and laughed silently for a space. " You ought to 'ave charged 'im Sumthing," she said. " You better come and have your cold meat before you do any more puntin'. You and me'll get on together."

Presently she came and stood watching him eat. " You eat better than you punt," she said; and then, " I dessay you could learn to punt."

" Wax to receive and marble to retain," said Mr. Polly. " This beef is a Bit of All Right, M'am. I could have done differently if I hadn't been punting on an empty stomach. There's a lear feeling as the pole goes in——"

" I've never held with fasting," said the plump woman.

" You want a ferryman? "

" I want an odd man about the place."

" I'm odd all right. What's the wages? "

" Not much, but you gets tips and pickings. I've a sort of feeling it would suit you."

" I've a sort of feeling it would. What's the duties? Fetch and carry? Ferry? Garden? Wash bottles? *Ceteris paribus?* "

" That's about it," said the fat woman.

" Give me a trial."

" I've more than half a mind. Or I wouldn't have said anything about it. I suppose you're all right.

You've got a sort of half-respectable look about you. I suppose you 'aven't *done* anything? "

" Bit of Arson," said Mr. Polly, as if he jested.

" So long as you haven't the habit," said the plump woman.

" My first time, M'am," said Mr. Polly, munching his way through an excellent big leaf of lettuce. " And my last."

" It's all right if you haven't been to prison," said the plump woman. " It isn't what a man's happened to do makes 'im bad. We all happen to do things at times. It's bringing it home to him and spoiling his self-respect does the mischief. You don't *look* a wrong 'un. 'Ave you been to prison? "

" Never."

" Nor a Reformatory? Nor any Institution? "

" Not me. Do I *look* reformed? "

" Can you paint and carpenter a bit? "

" Ripe for it."

" Have a bit of cheese? "

" If I might."

And the way she brought the cheese showed Mr. Polly that the business was settled in her mind.

He spent the afternoon exploring the premises of the Potwell Inn and learning the duties that might be expected of him, such as Stockholm tarring fences, digging potatoes, swabbing out boats, helping people land, embarking, landing, and time-keeping for the hirers of two rowing boats and one Canadian canoe, bailing out the said vessels and concealing their leaks and defects from prospective hirers, persuading inexperienced hirers to start down-stream rather than up, repairing rowlocks and taking inventories of returning boats with a view to supplementary charges, cleaning boots, sweeping chimneys, house painting, cleaning windows, sweeping out and sanding the Tap and Bar, cleaning pewter, washing glasses, turpentining wood-

work, white washing generally, plumbing and engin-
eering, repairing locks and clocks, waiting and tapster's
work generally, beating carpets and mats, cleaning
bottles and saving corks, taking into the cellar, moving,
tapping, and connecting beer casks with their engines,
blocking and destroying wasps' nests, doing forestry
with several trees, drowning superfluous kittens, dog-
fancying as required, assisting in the rearing of
ducklings and the care of various poultry, bee-keeping,
stabling, baiting and grooming horses and asses,
cleaning and " garing " motor-cars and bicycles,
inflating tyres and repairing punctures, recovering the
bodies of drowned persons from the river as required,
and assisting people in trouble in the water, first-aid
and sympathy, improvising and superintending a
bathing station for visitors, attending inquests and
funerals in the interests of the establishment, scrubbing
floors and all the ordinary duties of a scullion, the
Ferry, chasing hens and goats from the adjacent
cottages out of the garden, making up paths and superintending drainage, gardening generally, delivering
bottled beer and soda-water siphons in the neighbourhood, running miscellaneous errands, removing drunken
and offensive persons from the premises by tact or
muscle, as occasion required, keeping in with the local
policeman, defending the premises in general and the
orchard in particular from nocturnal depredators. . . .

" Can but try it," said Mr. Polly towards tea-time.
" When there's nothing else on hand I suppose I
might do a bit of fishing."

4

Mr. Polly was particularly charmed by the ducklings.
They were piping about among the vegetables in the
company of their foster mother, and as he and the
plump woman came down the garden path the little

creatures mobbed them, and ran over their boots and in between Mr. Polly's legs, and did their best to be trodden upon and killed after the manner of ducklings all the world over. Mr. Polly had never been near young ducklings before, and their extreme blondness and the delicate completeness of their feet and beaks filled him with admiration. It is open to question whether there is anything more friendly in the world than a very young duckling. It was with the utmost difficulty that he tore himself away to practise punting, with the plump woman coaching from the banks. Punting, he found, was difficult, but not impossible, and towards four o'clock he succeeded in conveying a second passenger across the sundering flood from the inn to the unknown.

As he returned, slowly indeed, but now one might almost say surely, to the peg to which the punt was moored, he became aware of a singularly delightful human being awaiting him on the bank. She stood with her legs very wide apart, her hands behind her back, and her head a little on one side, watching his gestures with an expression of disdainful interest. She had black hair and brown legs and a buff short frock and very intelligent eyes. And when he had reached a sufficient proximity she remarked, " Hallo! "

" Hallo," said Mr. Polly, and saved himself in the nick of time from disaster.

" Silly," said the young lady, and Mr. Polly lunged nearer.

" What are you called? "

" Polly."

" Liar! "

" Why? "

" I'm Polly."

" Then I'm Alfred. But I meant to be Polly."

" I was first."

" All right. I'm going to be the ferryman."

" I see. You'll have to punt better."

" You should have seen me early in the afternoon."

" I can imagine it . . . I've seen the others."

" What others? " Mr. Polly had landed now and was fastening up the punt.

" What Uncle Jim has scooted."

" Scooted? "

" He comes and scoots them. He'll scoot you, too, I expect."

A mysterious shadow seemed to fall athwart the sunshine and pleasantness of the Potwell Inn.

" I'm not a scooter," said Mr. Polly.

" Uncle Jim is."

She whistled a little flatly for a moment, and threw small stones at a clump of meadowsweet that sprang from the bank. Then she remarked—

" When Uncle Jim comes back he'll cut your insides out. . . . P'r'aps, very likely, he'll let me see."

There was a pause.

" *Who's* Uncle Jim? " Mr. Polly asked in a faded voice.

" Don't know who Uncle Jim is! He'll show you. He's a scorcher, is Uncle Jim. He only came back just a little time ago, and he's scooted three men. He don't like strangers about, don't Uncle Jim. He *can* swear. He's going to teach me, soon as I can whistle properly."

" Teach you to swear! " cried Mr. Polly, horrified.

" *And* spit," said the little girl proudly. " He says I'm the gamest little beast he ever came across— ever."

For the first time in his life it seemed to Mr. Polly that he had come across something sheerly dreadful. He stared at the pretty thing of flesh and spirit in front of him, lightly balanced on its stout little legs and looking at him with eyes that had still to learn the expression of either disgust or fear.

"I say," said Mr. Polly. "How old are you?"

"Nine," said the little girl.

She turned away and reflected. Truth compelled her to add one other statement.

"He's not what I should call handsome, not Uncle Jim," she said. "But he's a Scorcher and no Mistake. . . . Gramma don't like him."

5

Mr. Polly found the plump woman in the big bricked kitchen lighting a fire for tea. He went to the root of the matter at once.

"I say," he asked, "who's Uncle Jim?"

The plump woman blanched and stood still for a moment. A stick fell out of the bundle in her hand unheeded. "That little granddaughter of mine been saying things?" she asked faintly.

"Bits of things," said Mr. Polly.

"Well, I suppose I must tell you sooner or later. He's—It's Jim. He's the Drorback to this place, that's what he is. The Drorback. I hoped you mightn't hear so soon. . . . Very likely he's gone."

"*She* don't seem to think so."

"'E 'asn't been near the place these two weeks and more," said the plump woman.

"But who is he?"

"I suppose I got to tell you," said the plump woman.

"She says he scoots people," Mr. Polly remarked after a pause.

"He's my own sister's son." The plump woman watched the crackling fire for a space. "I suppose I got to tell you," she repeated.

She softened towards tears. "I try not to think of it, and night and day he's haunting me. I try not to think of it. I've been for easy going all my life. But

I'm that worried and afraid, with death and ruin threatened and evil all about me! I don't know what to do! My own sister's son, and me a widow woman and 'elpless against his doin's!"

She put down the sticks she held upon the fender, and felt for her handkerchief. She began to sob and talk quickly.

" I wouldn't mind nothing else half so much if he'd leave that child alone. But he goes talking to her—if I leave her a moment he's talking to her, teaching her Words, and giving her ideas!"

"That's a Bit Thick," said Mr. Polly.

"Thick!" cried the plump woman; "it's 'orrible! And what am I to do? He's been here three times now, six days, and a week, and a part of a week, and I pray to God night and day he may never come again. Praying! Back he's come, sure as fate. He takes my money and he takes my things. He won't let no man stay here to protect me or do the boats or work the ferry. The ferry's getting a scandal. They stand and shout and scream and use language. . . . If I complain they'll say I'm helpless to manage here, they'll take away my licence, out I shall go—and it's all the living I can get—and he knows it, and he plays on it, and he don't care. And here I am. I'd send the child away, but I got nowhere to send the child. I buys him off when it comes to that, and back he comes, worse than ever, prowling round and doing evil. And not a soul to help me. Not a soul! I just hoped there might be a day or so. Before he comes back again. I was just hoping—— I'm the sort that hopes."

Mr. Polly was reflecting on the flaws and drawbacks that seem to be inseparable from all the more agreeable things of life.

"Biggish sort of man, I expect?" asked Mr. Polly, trying to get the situation in all its bearings.

But the plump woman did not heed him. She was

going on with her fire-making, and retailing in disconnected fragments the fearfulness of Uncle Jim.

"There was always something a bit wrong with him," she said; "but nothing you mightn't have hoped for, not till they took him, and carried him off and reformed him. . . .

"He was cruel to the hens and chickens, it's true, and stuck a knife into another boy; but then I've seen him that nice to a cat, nobody could have been kinder. I'm sure he didn't do no 'arm to that cat whatever any one tries to make out of it. I'd never listen to that. . . . It was that Reformatory ruined him. They put him along of a lot of London boys full of ideas of wickedness, and because he didn't mind pain—and he don't, I *will* admit, try as I would—they made him think himself a hero. Them boys laughed at the teachers they set over them, laughed and mocked at them—and I don't suppose they *was* the best teachers in the world; I don't suppose, and I don't suppose any one sensible does suppose that every one who goes to be a teacher or a chaplain or a warder in a Reformatory Home goes and changes right away into an Angel of Grace from Heaven—and, oh Lord! Where was I?"

"What did they send him to the Reformatory for?"

"Playing truant and stealing. He stole right enough —stole the money from an old woman, and what was I to do when it came to the trial, but say what I knew. And him like a viper alooking at me—more like a viper than a human boy. He leans on the bar and looks at me. 'All right, Aunt Flo,' he says; just that, and nothing more. Time after time I've dreamt of it, and now he's come. 'They've Reformed me,' he says, ' and made me a devil, and a devil I mean to be to you. So out with it,' he says."

"What did you give him last time?" asked Mr. Polly.

" Three golden pounds," said the plump woman. " ' That won't last very long,' he says. ' But there ain't no hurry. I'll be back in a week about.' If I wasn't one of the hoping sort——"

She left the sentence unfinished.

Mr. Polly reflected. " What sort of a size is he? " he asked. " I'm not one of your Herculaceous sort, if you mean that. Nothing very wonderful bicepitally."

" You'll scoot," said the plump woman, with conviction rather than bitterness. " You'd better scoot now, and I'll try and find some money for him to go away again when he comes. It ain't reasonable to expect you to do anything but scoot. But I suppose it's the way of a woman in trouble to try and get help from a man, and hope and hope."

" How long's he been about? " asked Mr. Polly, ignoring his own outlook.

" Three months it is come the seventh since he come in by that very back door—and I hadn't set eyes on him for seven long years. He stood in the door watchin' me, and suddenly he let off a yelp—like a dog, and there he was grinning at the fright he'd given me. ' Good old Aunty Flo,' he says, ' ain't you dee-lighted to see me? ' he says, ' now I'm Reformed.' "

The plump lady went to the sink and filled the kettle.

" I never did like him," she said, standing at the sink. " And seeing him there, with his teeth all black and broken—— P'r'aps I didn't give him much of a welcome at first. Not what would have been kind to him. ' Lord! ' I said, ' It's Jim.' "

" ' It's Jim,' he said. ' Like a bad shillin'—like a damned bad shilling. Jim and trouble. You all of you wanted me Reformed, and now you got me Reformed. I'm a Reformatory Reformed Character, warranted all right, and turned out as such. Ain't you going to ask me in, Aunty dear? ' "

" ' Come in,' I said. ' I won't have it said I wasn't ready to be kind to you! ' "

" He comes in and shuts the door. Down he sits in that chair. ' I come to torment you,' he says, ' you old Sumpthing! ' and begins at me. . . . No 'uman being could ever have been called such things before. It made me cry out. ' And now,' he says, ' just to show I ain't afraid of 'urting you,' he says, and ups and twists my wrists."

Mr. Polly gasped.

" I could stand even his vi'lence," said the plump woman, " if it wasn't for the child."

Mr. Polly went to the kitchen window and surveyed his namesake, who was away up the garden path, with her hands behind her back, and wisps of black hair in disorder about her little face, thinking, thinking profoundly, about ducklings.

" You two oughtn't to be left," he said.

The plump woman stared at his back with hard hope in her eyes.

" I don't see that It's *my* affair," said Mr. Polly.

The plump woman resumed her business with the kettle.

" I'd like to have a look at him before I go," said Mr. Polly, thinking aloud, and added, " somehow. Not my business, of course."

" Lord! " he cried, with a start, at a noise in the bar, " who's that? "

" Only a customer," said the plump woman.

6

Mr. Polly made no rash promises, and thought a great deal.

" It seems a good sort of Crib," he said, and added, " for a chap who's looking for Trouble."

But he stayed on, and did various things out of the

list I have already given, and worked the ferry, and
it was four days before he saw anything of Uncle Jim.
And so resistant is the human mind to things not yet
experienced, that he could easily have believed in that
time that there was no such person in the world as
Uncle Jim. The plump woman, after her one outbreak
of confidences, ignored the subject, and little Polly
seemed to have exhausted her impressions in her first
communication, and engaged her mind now, with a
simple directness, in the study and subjugation of the
new human being Heaven had sent into her world.
The first unfavourable impression of his punting was
soon effaced; he could nickname ducklings very amus-
ingly, create boats out of wooden splinters, and stalk
and fly from imaginary tigers in the orchard, with a
convincing earnestness that was surely beyond the
power of any other human being. She conceded at last
that he should be called Mr. Polly, in honour of her,
Miss Polly, even as he desired.

Uncle Jim turned up in the twilight.

Uncle Jim appeared with none of the disruptive
violence Mr. Polly had dreaded. He came quite softly.
Mr. Polly was going down the lane behind the church,
that led to the Potwell Inn, after posting a letter to the
lime-juice people at the post office. He was walking
slowly, after his habit, and thinking discursively. With
a sudden tightening of the muscles he became aware
of a figure walking noiselessly beside him.

His first impression was of a face singularly broad
above, and with a wide, empty grin as its chief feature
below, of a slouching body and dragging feet.

"'Arf a mo'," said the figure, as if in response to
his start, and speaking in a hoarse whisper. "'Arf a
mo', mister. You the noo bloke at the Potwell Inn?"

Mr. Polly felt evasive. "S'pose I am," he replied
hoarsely, and quickened his pace.

"'Arf a mo'," said Uncle Jim, taking his arm.

"We ain't doing a (sanguinary) Marathon. It ain't a (decorated) cinder track. I want a word with you, mister. See?"

Mr. Polly wriggled his arm free and stopped. "What is it?" he asked, and faced the terror.

"I jest want a (decorated) word wive you. See? —just a friendly word or two. Just to clear up any blooming errors. That's all I want. No need to be so (richly decorated) proud, if you *are* the noo bloke at Potwell Inn. Not a bit of it. See?"

Uncle Jim was certainly not a handsome person. He was short, shorter than Mr. Polly, with long arms and lean, big hands; a thin and wiry neck stuck out of his grey flannel shirt, and supported a big head that had something of the snake in the convergent lines of its broad, knobby brow, meanly proportioned face, and pointed chin. His almost toothless mouth seemed a cavern in the twilight. Some accident had left him with one small and active, and one large and expressionless reddish eye, and wisps of straight hair strayed from under the blue cricket cap he had pulled down obliquely over the latter. He spat between his teeth, and wiped his mouth untidily with the soft side of his fist.

"You got to blurry well shift," he said. "See?"

"Shift!" said Mr. Polly. "How?"

"'Cos the Potwell Inn's *my* beat. See?"

Mr. Polly had never felt less witty. "How's it your beat?" he asked.

Uncle Jim thrust his face forward and shook his open hand, bent like a claw, under Mr. Polly's nose. "Not your blooming business," he said. "You got to shift."

"S'pose I don't," said Mr. Polly.

"You got to shift."

The tone of Uncle Jim's voice became urgent and confidential.

"You don't know who you're up against," he said.

" It's a kindness I'm doing to warn you. See? I'm just one of those blokes who don't stick at things, see? I don't stick at nuffin."

Mr. Polly's manner became detached and confidential —as though the matter and the speaker interested him greatly, but didn't concern him over much. " What do you think you'll do? " he asked.

" If you don't clear out? "

" Yes."

" *Gaw!* " said Uncle Jim. " You'd better! '*Ere!* "

He gripped Mr. Polly's wrist with a grip of steel, and in an instant Mr. Polly understood the relative quality of their muscles. He breathed, an uninspiring breath, into Mr. Polly's face.

" What *won't* I do," he said, " once I start in on you? "

He paused, and the night about them seemed to be listening. " I'll make a mess of you," he said, in his hoarse whisper. " I'll do you—injuries. I'll 'urt you. I'll kick you ugly, see? I'll 'urt you in 'orrible ways— 'orrible ugly ways. . . ."

He scrutinised Mr. Polly's face.

" You'll cry," he said, " to see yourself. See? Cry, you will."

" You got no right," began Mr. Polly.

" Right! " His note was fierce. " Ain't the old woman me aunt? "

He spoke still closelier. " I'll make a gory mess of you. I'll cut bits orf you——"

He receded a little. " I got no quarrel with *you*," he said.

" It's too late to go to-night," said Mr. Polly.

" I'll be round to-morrer—'bout eleven. See? And if I finds you——"

He produced a blood-curdling oath.

" H'm," said Mr. Polly, trying to keep things light. " We'll consider your suggestions."

" You better," said Uncle Jim, and suddenly, noiselessly, was going.

His whispering voice sank until Mr. Polly could hear only dim fragments of sentences. " 'Orrible things to you—'Orrible things. . . . Kick yer Ugly. . . . Cut yer —liver out. . . . spread it all about, I will. . . . See? I don't care a dead rat one way or the uvver."

And with a curious twisting gesture of the arm, Uncle Jim receded until his face was a still, dim thing that watched, and the black shadows of the hedge seemed to have swallowed up his body altogether.

7

Next morning about half-past ten Mr. Polly found himself seated under a clump of fir-trees by the roadside, and about three miles and a half from the Potwell Inn. He was by no means sure whether he was taking a walk to clear his mind, or leaving that threat-marred Paradise for good and all. His reason pointed a lean, unhesitating finger along the latter course.

For, after all, the thing was not *his* quarrel.

That agreeable, plump woman—agreeable, motherly, comfortable as she might be—wasn't his affair; that child with the mop of black hair, who combined so magically the charm of mouse and butterfly and flitting bird, who was daintier than a flower and softer than a peach, was no concern of his. Good Heavens! What were they to him? Nothing! . . .

Uncle Jim, of course, *had* a claim, a sort of claim.

If it came to duty and chucking up this attractive, indolent, observant, humorous, tramping life, there were those who had a right to him, a legitimate right, a prior claim on his protection and chivalry.

Why not listen to the call of duty and go back to Miriam now? . . .

He had had a very agreeable holiday. . . .

And while Mr. Polly sat thinking these things as well as he could, he knew that if only he dared to look up, the Heavens had opened, and the clear judgment on his case was written across the sky.

He knew—he knew now as much as a man can know of life. He knew he had to fight or perish.

Life had never been so clear to him before. It had always been a confused, entertaining spectacle. He had responded to this impulse and that, seeking agreeable and entertaining things, evading difficult and painful things. Such is the way of those who grow up to a life that has neither danger nor honour in its texture. He had been muddled and wrapped about and entangled, like a creature born in the jungle who has never seen sea or sky. Now he had come out of it suddenly into a great exposed place. It was as if God and Heaven waited over him, and all the earth was expectation.

"Not my business," said Mr. Polly, speaking aloud. "Where the devil do I come in?"

And again, with something between a whine and a snarl in his voice, "Not my blasted business!"

His mind seemed to have divided itself into several compartments, each with its own particular discussion busily in progress, and quite regardless of the others. One was busy with the detailed interpretation of the phrase, "Kick you ugly." There's a sort of French wrestling in which you use and guard against feet. Watch the man's eye, and as his foot comes up, grip, and over he goes—at your mercy, if you use the advantage rightly. But how do you use the advantage rightly?

When he thought of Uncle Jim the inside feeling of his body faded away rapidly to a blank discomfort.

"Old cadger! She hadn't no business to drag me into her quarrels. Ought to go to the police and ask for help! Dragging me into a quarrel that don't concern me."

"Wish I'd never set eyes on the rotten inn!"

The reality of the case arched over him like the vault of the sky, as plain as the sweet blue heaven above and the wide spread of hill and valley about him. Man comes into life to seek and find his sufficient beauty, to serve it, to win and increase it, to fight for it, to face anything and dare anything for it, counting death as nothing so long as the dying eyes still turn to it. And fear and dullness and indolence and appetite, which, indeed, are no more than fear's three crippled brothers, who make ambushes and creep by night, are against him, to delay him, to hold him off, to hamper and beguile and kill him in that quest. He had but to lift his eyes to see all that, as much a part of his world as the driving clouds and the bending grass; but he kept himself downcast, a grumbling, inglorious, dirty, fattish little tramp, full of dreams and quivering excuses.

"Why the hell was I ever born?" he said, with the truth almost winning him.

What do you do when a dirty man, who smells, gets you down and under, in the dirt and dust, with a knee below your diaphragm, and a large hairy hand squeezing your windpipe tighter and tighter in a quarrel that isn't, properly speaking, yours?

"If I had a chance against him——" protested Mr. Polly.

"It's no Good, you see," said Mr. Polly.

He stood up as though his decision was made, and was for an instant struck still by doubt.

There lay the road before him, going this way to the east, and that to the west.

Westward, one hour away now, was the Potwell Inn. Already things might be happening there. . . .

Eastward was the wise man's course, a road dipping

etween hedges to a hop garden and a wood, and
resently, no doubt, reaching an inn, a picturesque
iurch, perhaps, a village, and fresh company. The
ise man's course. Mr. Polly saw himself going along
, and tried to see himself going along it with all the
elf-applause a wise man feels. But somehow it wouldn't
ome like that. The wise man fell short of happiness
r all his wisdom. The wise man had a paunch, and
und shoulders, and red ears and excuses. It was a
leasant road, and why the wise man should not go
long it merry and singing, full of summer happiness,
as a miracle to Mr. Polly's mind. But, confound it!
ie fact remained: the figure went slinking—slinking
as the only word for it—and would not go otherwise
ian slinking. He turned his eyes westward as if for
n explanation, and if the figure was no longer ignoble,
ie prospect was appalling.

" One kick in the stummick would settle a chap like
ie," said Mr. Polly.

" Oh, God! " cried Mr. Polly, and lifted his eyes
) heaven, and said for the last time in that struggle,
It isn't my affair! "

And so saying, he turned his face towards the
otwell Inn.

He went back, neither halting nor hastening in his
ace after this last decision, but with a mind feverishly
usy.

" If I get killed I get killed, and if he gets killed I
et hung. Don't seem just somehow."

" Don't suppose I shall *frighten* him off."

8

The private war between Mr. Polly and Uncle Jim
or the possession of the Potwell Inn fell naturally into
hree chief campaigns. There was, first of all, the great
ampaign which ended in the triumphant eviction of

Uncle Jim from the inn premises; there came next, after a brief interval, the futile invasions of the premises by Uncle Jim that culminated in the Battle of the Dead Eel; and, after some months of involuntary truce, there was the last supreme conflict of the Night Surprise. Each of these campaigns merits a section to itself.

Mr. Polly re-entered the inn discreetly.

He found the plump woman seated in her bar, her eyes astare, her face white and wet with tears. " O God! " she was saying over and over again—" O God! "

The air was full of spirituous reek, and on the sanded boards in front of the bar were the fragments of a broken bottle, and an overturned glass.

She turned her despair at the sound of his entry, and despair gave place to astonishment.

" You come back? " she said.

" Ra-ther," said Mr. Polly.

" He's—he's mad drunk and looking for her."

" Where is she? "

" Locked upstairs."

" Haven't you sent for the police? "

" No one to send."

" I'll see to it," said Mr. Polly. " Out this way? "

She nodded.

He went to the crinkly paned window and peered out. Uncle Jim was coming down the garden path towards the house, his hands in his pockets, and singing hoarsely. Mr. Polly remembered afterwards, with pride and amazement, that he felt neither faint nor rigid. He glanced round him, seized a bottle of beer by the neck as an improvised club, and went out by the garden door. Uncle Jim stopped, amazed. His brain did not instantly rise to the new posture of things. " You! " he cried, and stopped for a moment. " You —*scoot*! "

" *Your* job," said Mr. Polly, and advanced some paces.

Uncle Jim stood swaying with wrathful astonishment, and then darted forward with clutching hands. Mr. Polly felt that if his antagonist closed, he was lost, and smote with all his force at the ugly head before him. Smash went the bottle and Uncle Jim staggered, half stunned by the blow, and blinded with beer.

The lapses and leaps of the human mind are for ever mysterious. Mr. Polly had never expected that bottle to break. In an instant he felt disarmed and helpless. Before him was Uncle Jim, infuriated and evidently still coming on, and for defence was nothing but the neck of a bottle.

For a time our Mr. Polly has figured heroic. Now comes the fall again; he sounded abject terror; he dropped that ineffectual scrap of glass and turned and fled round the corner of the house.

" Bolls! " came the thick voice of the enemy behind him, as one who accepts a challenge, and bleeding but indomitable, Uncle Jim entered the house.

" Bolls! " he said, surveying the bar. " Fightin' with bolls. I'll show 'im fightin' with bolls! "

Uncle Jim had learnt all about fighting with bottles in the Reformatory Home. Regardless of his terror-stricken aunt, he ranged among the bottled beer and succeeded, after one or two failures, in preparing two bottles to his satisfaction by knocking off the bottom, and gripping them dagger-wise, by the necks. So prepared, he went forth again to destroy Mr. Polly.

Mr. Polly, freed from the sense of urgent pursuit, had halted beyond the raspberry canes, and rallied his courage. The sense of Uncle Jim victorious in the house restored his manhood. He went round by the outhouses to the riverside, seeking a weapon, and found an old paddle boathook. With this he smote Uncle

Jim as he emerged by the door of the tap, Uncle Jim, blaspheming dreadfully, and with dire stabbing intimations in either hand, came through the splintering paddle like a circus rider through a paper hoop, and once more Mr. Polly dropped his weapon and fled.

A careless observer, watching him spring round and round the inn in front of the lumbering and reproachful pursuit of Uncle Jim, might have formed an altogether erroneous estimate of the issue of the campaign. Certain compensating qualities of the very greatest military value were appearing in Mr. Polly, even as he ran; if Uncle Jim had strength and brute courage, and the rich toughening experience a Reformatory Home affords, Mr. Polly was nevertheless sober, more mobile, and with a mind now stimulated to an almost incredible nimbleness. So that he not only gained on Uncle Jim but thought what use he might make of this advantage. The word " strategious " flamed red across the tumult of his mind. As he came round the house for the third time, he darted suddenly into the yard, swung the door to behind himself, and bolted it, seized the pig's zinc pail and stood by the entrance to the kitchen, and had it neatly and resonantly over Uncle Jim's head, as he came belatedly in round the outhouse on the other side. One of the splintered bottles jabbed Mr. Polly's ear—at the time it seemed of no importance—and then Uncle Jim was down and writhing dangerously and noisily upon the yard tiles with his head still in the pig pail, and his bottle gone to splinters, and Mr. Polly was fastening the kitchen door against him.

" Can't go on like this for ever," said Mr. Polly, whooping for breath, and selecting a weapon from among the brooms that stood behind the kitchen door. Uncle Jim was losing his head. He was up and kicking the door, and bellowing unamiable proposals and invitations, so that a strategist emerging silently by the tap door could locate him without difficulty, steal upon him unawares, and——!

But before that felling blow could be delivered, Uncle Jim's ear had caught a footfall, and he turned. Mr. Polly quailed, and lowered his broom—a fatal hesitation.

"*Now* I got you!" cried Uncle Jim, dancing forward in a disconcerting zigzag.

He rushed to close, and Mr. Polly stopped him neatly, as it were a miracle, with the head of the broom across his chest. Uncle Jim seized the broom with both hands. "Lea go," he said, and tugged. Mr. Polly shook his head, tugged, and showed pale, compressed lips. Both tugged. Then Uncle Jim tried to get round the end of the broom; Mr. Polly circled away. They began to circle about one another, both tugging hard, both intensely watchful of the slightest initiative on the part of the other. Mr. Polly wished brooms were longer—twelve or thirteen feet, for example; Uncle Jim was clearly for shortness in brooms. He wasted breath in saying what was to happen shortly—sanguinary, oriental, soul-blenching things—when the broom no longer separated them. Mr. Polly thought he had never seen an uglier person. Suddenly Uncle Jim flashed into violent activity, but alcohol slows movement, and Mr. Polly was equal to him. Then Uncle Jim tried jerks, and, for a terrible instant, he seemed to have the broom out of Mr. Polly's hands. But Mr. Polly recovered it with the clutch of a drowning man. Then Uncle Jim drove suddenly at Mr. Polly's midriff; but again Mr. Polly was ready, and swept him round in a circle. Then suddenly a wild hope filled Mr. Polly. He saw the river was very near, the post to which the punt was tied not three yards away. With a wild yell he sent the broom home under his antagonist's ribs. "Woosh!" he cried, as the resistance gave.

" Oh! *Gaw!* " said Uncle Jim, going backward
helplessly, and Mr. Polly thrust hard, and abandoned
the broom to the enemy's despairing clutch.

Splash! Uncle Jim was in the water, and Mr. Polly
had leapt like a cat aboard the ferry punt, and grasped
the pole.

Up came Uncle Jim spluttering and dripping.
" You (unprofitable matter, and printing it might lead
to a Censorship of Novels)—You know I got a weak
chess! "

The pole took him in the throat and drove him
backward and downwards.

" Lea go! " cried Uncle Jim, staggering, and with
real terror in his once awful eyes.

Splash! Down he fell backwards into a frothing
mass of water, with Mr. Polly jabbing at him. Under
water he turned round, and came up again, as if in
flight towards the middle of the river. Directly his
head reappeared, Mr. Polly had him between his
shoulders and under again, bubbling thickly. A hand
clutched and disappeared.

It was stupendous! Mr. Polly had discovered the
heel of Achilles. Uncle Jim had no stomach for cold
water. The broom floated away, pitching gently on
the swell. Mr. Polly, infuriated by victory, thrust
Uncle Jim under again, and drove the punt round on
its chain in such a manner, that when Uncle Jim
came up for the fourth time—and now he was nearly
out of his depth, too buoyed up to walk, and apparently
nearly helpless—Mr. Polly, fortunately for them both,
could not reach him.

Uncle Jim made the clumsy gestures of those who
struggle insecurely in the water. " Keep out," said
Mr. Polly. Uncle Jim, with a great effort, got a
footing, emerged until his armpits were out of water,
until his waistcoat buttons showed, one by one, till

scarcely two remained, and made for the camp-sheeting.

"Keep out!" cried Mr. Polly, and leapt off the punt and followed the movements of his victim along the shore.

"I tell you I got a weak chess," said Uncle Jim moistly. "I 'ate worter. This ain't fair fightin'.''

"Keep out," said Mr. Polly.

"This ain't fair fightin'," said Uncle Jim, almost weeping, and all his terrors had gone.

"Keep out!" said Mr. Polly, with an accurately poised pole.

"I tell you I got to land, you Fool," said Uncle Jim, with a sort of despairing wrathfulness, and began moving down-stream.

"You keep out," said Mr. Polly in parallel movement. "Don't you ever land on this place again! . . ."

Slowly, argumentatively, and reluctantly, Uncle Jim waded down-stream. He tried threats, he tried persuasion, he even tried a belated note of pathos; Mr. Polly remained inexorable, if in secret a little perplexed as to the outcome of the situation. "This cold's getting to my marrer!" said Uncle Jim.

"You want cooling. You keep out in it," said Mr. Polly.

They came round the bend into sight of Nicholson's ait, where the backwater runs down to the Potwell Mill. And there, after much parley and several feints, Uncle Jim made a desperate effort and struggled into clutch of the overhanging osiers on the island, and so got out of the water, with the mill-stream between them. He emerged dripping and muddy and vindictive. "By *Gaw*!" he said. "I'll skin you for this!"

"You keep off, or I'll do worse to you," said Mr. Polly.

The spirit was out of Uncle Jim for the time, and he turned away to struggle through the osiers towards the mill, leaving a shining trail of water among the green-gray stems.

Mr. Polly returned slowly and thoughtfully to the inn, and suddenly his mind began to bubble with phrases. The plump woman stood at the top of the steps that led up to the inn door, to greet him.

"Law!" she cried, as he drew near, "'asn't 'e killed you?"

"Do I look it?" said Mr. Polly.

"But where's Jim?"

"Gone off."

"'E was mad drunk and dangerous!"

"I put him in the river," said Mr. Polly. "That toned down his alcolaceous frenzy! I gave him a bit of a doing altogether."

"Hain't he 'urt you?"

"Not a bit of it!"

"Then what's all that blood beside your ear?"

Mr. Polly felt. "Quite a cut! Funny how one overlooks things! Heated moments! He must have done that when he jabbed about with those bottles. Hallo, Kiddy! You venturing downstairs again?"

"Ain't he killed you?" asked the little girl.

"Well!"

"I wish I'd seen more of the fighting."

"Didn't you?"

"All I saw was you running round the house, and Uncle Jim after you."

There was a little pause. "I was leading him on," said Mr. Polly.

"Some one's shouting at the ferry," she said.

"Right-o. But you won't see any more of Uncle Jim for a bit. We've been having a conversazione about that."

"I believe it *is* Uncle Jim," said the little girl.

"Then he can wait," said Mr. Polly shortly.

He turned round and listened for the words that

drifted across from the little figure on the opposite bank. So far as he could judge, Uncle Jim was making an appointment for to-morrow. Mr. Polly replied with a defiant movement of the punt pole. The little figure was convulsed for a moment, and then went on its way upstream—fiercely.

So it was the first campaign ended in an insecure victory.

9

The next day was Wednesday, and a slack day for the Potwell Inn. It was a hot, close day, full of the murmuring of bees. One or two people crossed by the ferry; an elaborately-equipped fisherman stopped for cold meat and dry ginger ale in the bar parlour; some haymakers came and drank beer for an hour, and afterwards sent jars and jugs by a boy to be replenished; that was all. Mr. Polly had risen early, and was busy about the place meditating upon the probable tactics of Uncle Jim. He was no longer strung up to the desperate pitch of the first encounter. He was grave and anxious. Uncle Jim had shrunken, as all antagonists that are boldly faced shrink, after the first battle, to the negotiable, the vulnerable. Formidable he was, no doubt, but not invincible. He had, under Providence, been defeated once, and he might be defeated altogether.

Mr. Polly went about the place considering the militant possibilities of pacific things—pokers, copper-sticks, garden implements, kitchen knives, garden nets, barbed wire, oars, clothes' lines, blankets, pewter pots, stockings, and broken bottles. He prepared a club with a stocking and a bottle inside, upon the best East End model. He swung it round his head once, broke an outhouse window with a flying fragment of glass, and ruined the stocking beyond all darning. He

developed a subtle scheme, with the cellar flap as a
sort of pitfall; but he rejected it finally because (*a*) it
might entrap the plump woman, and (*b*) he had no
use whatever for Uncle Jim in the cellar. He determined to wire the garden that evening, burglar fashion,
against the possibilities of a night attack.

Towards two o'clock in the afternoon three young
men arrived in a capacious boat from the direction of
Lammam, and asked permission to camp in the
paddock. It was given all the more readily by Mr.
Polly because he perceived in their proximity a possible
check upon the self-expression of Uncle Jim. But he
did not foresee, and no one could have foreseen, that
Uncle Jim, stealing craftily upon the Potwell Inn in
the late afternoon, armed with a large rough-hewn
stake, would have mistaken the bending form of one
of those campers—who was pulling a few onions by
permission in the garden—for Mr. Polly's, and crept
upon it swiftly and silently, and smitten its wide
invitation unforgettably and unforgivably. It was an
error impossible to explain; the resounding whack
went up to heaven, the cry of amazement, and Mr.
Polly emerged from the inn, armed with the frying pan
he was cleaning, to take this reckless assailant in the
rear. Uncle Jim, realising his error, fled blaspheming
into the arms of the other two campers, who were
returning from the village with butcher's meat and
groceries. They caught him, they smacked his face
with steak and punched him with a bursting parcel
of lump sugar, they held him though he bit them,
and their idea of punishment was to duck him. They
were hilarious, strong young stockbrokers' clerks,
Territorials, and seasoned boating men; they ducked
him as though it was romping, and all that Mr. Polly
had to do was to pick up lumps of sugar for them and
wipe them on his sleeve and put them on a plate, and

explain that Uncle Jim was a notorious bad character, and not quite right in his head.

"Got a regular Obsession the Missis is his Aunt," said Mr. Polly, expanding it. "Perfect noosance he is."

But he caught a glance of Uncle Jim's eye as he receded before the campers' urgency that boded ill for him, and in the night he had a disagreeable idea that perhaps his luck might not hold for the third occasion.

That came soon enough. So soon, indeed, as the campers had gone.

Thursday was the early closing day at Lammam, and, next to Sunday, the busiest part of the week at the Potwell Inn. Sometimes as many as six boats all at once would be moored against the ferry punt, and hiring row-boats. People could either have a complete tea, a complete tea with jam, cake, and eggs, a kettle of boiling water and find the rest, or Refreshments *à la carte* as they chose. They sat about, but usually the boiling water-ers had a delicacy about using the tables, and grouped themselves humbly on the ground. The complete tea-ers with jam and eggs got the best tablecloth, on the table nearest the steps that led up to the glass-panelled door.

The groups about the lawn were very satisfying to Mr. Polly's sense of amenity. To the right were the complete tea-ers, with everything heart could desire; then a small group of three young men in remarkable green and violet and pale blue shirts, and two girls in mauve and yellow blouses, with common teas and gooseberry jam, at the green clothless table; then, on the grass down by the pollard willow, a small family of hot-water-ers with a hamper, a little troubled by wasps in their jam from the nest in the tree, and all in mourning, but happy otherwise; and on the lawn to the right a ginger beer lot of 'prentices without their collars, and very jocular and happy. The young people in the rainbow shirts and blouses formed the centre of interest; they were under the leadership of a gold-spectacled senior with a fluting voice and an air of mystery; he ordered everything, and showed a peculiar knowledge of the qualities of the Potwell jams, preferring gooseberry with much insistence.   Mr. Polly watched him, christened him the " benifluous influence," glanced at the 'prentices and went inside and down into the cellar in order to replenish the stock of stone ginger beer, which the plump woman had allowed to run low during the preoccupations of the campaign. It was in the cellar that he first became aware of the return of Uncle Jim.   He became aware of him as a voice, a voice not only hoarse but thick, as voices thicken under the influence of alcohol.

" Where's that muddy-faced mongrel? " cried Uncle Jim. " Let 'im come out to me!   Where's that blighted whisp with the punt pole—I got a word to say to 'im. Come out of it, you pot-bellied chunk of dirtiness, you! Come out and 'ave your dirty face wiped.   I got a Thing for you . . . 'Ear me?

" 'E's 'iding, that's what 'E's doing," said the voice of Uncle Jim, dropping for a moment to sorrow, and then with a great increment of wrathfulness: " Come out of my nest, you blinking cuckoo, you, or I'll cut your silly insides out! Come out of it, you pockmarked Rat!   Stealing another man's 'ome away from 'im! Come out and look me in the face, you squinting son of a Skunk! . . . ."

Mr. Polly took the ginger beer and went thoughtfully upstairs to the bar.

" 'E's back," said the plump woman as he appeared. " I knew 'e'd come back."

" I heard him," said Mr. Polly, and looked about. " Just gimme the old poker handle that's under the beer-engine."

The door opened softly, and Mr. Polly turned quickly. But it was only the pointed nose and intelligent face of the young man with the gilt spectacles and the discreet manner. He coughed, and the spectacles fixed Mr. Polly.

" I say," he said with quiet earnestness, " there's a chap out here seems to *want* some one."

" Why don't he come in? " said Mr. Polly.

" He seems to want you out there."

" What's he want? "

" I *think*," said the spectacled young man, after a thoughtful moment, " he appears to have brought you a present of fish."

" Isn't he shouting? "

" He *is* a little boisterous."

" He'd better come in."

The manner of the spectacled young man intensified. " I wish you'd come out and persuade him to go away," he said. " His language—isn't quite the thing —ladies."

" It never was," said the plump woman, her voice charged with sorrow.

Mr. Polly moved towards the door and stood with his hand on the handle. The gold-spectacled face disappeared.

" Now, my man," came his voice from outside, " be careful what your saying——"

" OO in all the World and Hereafter are you to call me man? " cried Uncle Jim, in a voice of one astonished and pained beyond endurance, and added scornfully, " You gold-eyed Geezer, you! "

" Tut, tut! " said the gentleman in gilt glasses. " Restrain yourself! "

Mr. Polly emerged, poker in hand, just in time to see what followed. Uncle Jim in his shirtsleeves, and a state of ferocious decolletage, was holding something —yes!—a dead eel by means of a piece of newspaper about its tail, holding it down and back and a little sideways in such a way as to smite with it upward and hard. It struck the spectacled gentleman under the jaw with a peculiar dead thud, and a cry of horror came from the two seated parties at the sight. One of the girls shrieked piercingly, " Horace! " and every one sprang up. The sense of helping numbers came to Mr. Polly's aid.

" Drop it! " he cried, and came down the steps waving his poker and thrusting the spectacled gentleman before him, as heretofore great heroes were wont to wield the ox-hide shield.

Uncle Jim gave ground suddenly, and trod upon the foot of a young man in a blue shirt, who immediately thrust at him violently with both hands.

" Lea go! " howled Uncle Jim. " That's the Chap I'm looking for! " and pressing the head of the spectacled gentleman aside, smote hard at Mr. Polly.

But at the sight of this indignity inflicted upon the spectacled gentleman a woman's heart was stirred, a pink parasol drove hard and true at Uncle Jim's wiry neck, and at the same moment the young man in the blue shirt sought to collar him, and lost his grip again.

" Suffragettes! " gasped Uncle Jim, with the ferrule at his throat. " Everywhere! " and aimed a second more successful blow at Mr. Polly.

" Wup! " said Mr. Polly.

But now the jam and egg party was joining in the fray. A stout, yet still fairly able-bodied gentleman in white and black checks inquired: " What's the fellow up to? Ain't there no police here? " And it was evident that once more public opinion was rallying to the support of Mr. Polly.

" Oh, come on then, all the LOT of you," cried Uncle Jim, and backing dexterously, whirled the eel round in a destructive circle. The pink sunshade was torn from the hand that gripped it, and whirled athwart the complete but unadorned tea-things on the green table.

" Collar him! Some one get hold of his collar! " cried the gold-spectacled gentleman, retreating up the steps to the inn door as if to rally his forces.

" Stand clear, you blessed mantel ornaments! " cried Uncle Jim. " Stand clear! " and retired backing, staving off attack by means of the whirling eel.

Mr. Polly, undeterred by a sense of grave damage done to his nose, pressed the attack in front, the two young men in violet and blue skirmished on Uncle Jim's flanks, the man in white and black checks sought still further outflanking possibilities, and two of the apprentice boys ran for oars. The gold-spectacled gentleman, as if inspired, came down the wooden steps again, seized the tablecloth of the jam and egg party, lugged it from under the crockery with adequate precautions against breakage, and advanced with compressed lips, curious lateral crouching movements, swift flashings of his glasses, and a general suggestion of bull-fighting in his pose and gestures. Uncle Jim was kept busy, and unable to plan his retreat with any strategic soundness. He was, moreover, manifestly a little nervous about the river in his rear. He gave ground in a curve, and so came right across the rapidly abandoned camp of the family in mourning, crunching teacups under his heel, oversetting the teapot, and finally tripping backwards over the hamper. The eel flew out at a tangent from his hand, and became a mere looping relic on the sward.

" Hold him! " cried the gentleman in spectacles. " Collar him! " and, moving forward with extraordinary promptitude, wrapped the best tablecloth about Uncle Jim's arms and head. Mr. Polly grasped his purpose instantly, the man in checks was scarcely slower, and in another moment Uncle Jim was no more than a bundle of smothered blasphemy, and a pair of wildly active legs.

"Duck him!" panted Mr. Polly, holding on to the earthquake. "Bes' thing—duck him."

The bundle was convulsed by paroxysms of anger and protest. One boot got the hamper and sent it ten yards.

"Go into the house for a clothes'-line, some one." said the gentleman in gold spectacles. "He'll get out of this in a moment."

One of the apprentices ran.

"Bird-nets in the garden," shouted Mr. Polly. "In the garden."

The apprentice was divided in his purpose.

And then suddenly Uncle Jim collapsed, and became a limp, dead-seeming thing under their hands. His arms were drawn inward, his legs bent up under his person, and so he lay.

"Fainted!" said the man in checks, relaxing his grip.

"A fit, perhaps," said the man in spectacles.

"Keep hold!" said Mr. Polly, too late.

For suddenly Uncle Jim's arms and legs flew out like springs released. Mr. Polly was tumbled backwards, and fell over the broken teapot, and into the arms of the father in mourning. Something struck his head—dazingly. In another second Uncle Jim was on his feet, and the tablecloth enshrouded the head of the man in checks. Uncle Jim manifestly considered he had done all that honour required of him; and against overwhelming numbers, and the possibility of reiterated duckings, flight is no disgrace.

Uncle Jim fled.

Mr. Polly sat up, after an interval of indeterminate length, among the ruins of an idyllic afternoon. Quite a lot of things seemed scattered and broken, but it was difficult to grasp it all at once. He stared between the legs of people. He became aware of a voice speaking slowly and complainingly.

" Some one ought to pay for those tea-things," said the father of mourning. " We didn't bring them 'ere to be danced on, not by no manner of means."

10

There followed an anxious peace for three days, and then a rough man in a blue jersey, in the intervals of trying to choke himself with bread and cheese and pickled onions, broke abruptly into information.

" Jim's lagged again, Missus," he said.

" What! " said the landlady. " Our Jim? "

" Your Jim," said the man; and after an absolutely necessary pause for swallowing, added, " Stealing a 'atchet."

He did not speak for some moments, and then he replied to Mr. Polly's inquiries: " Yes, a 'atchet. Down Lammam way—night before last."

" What'd 'e steal a 'atchet for? " asked the plump woman.

" 'E said 'e wanted a 'atchet."

" I wonder what he wanted a hatchet for," said Mr. Polly thoughtfully.

" I dessay 'e 'ad a use for it," said the gentleman in the blue jersey, and he took a mouthful that amounted to conversational suicide. There was a prolonged pause in the little bar, and Mr. Polly did some rapid thinking.

He went to the window and whistled. " I shall stick it," he whispered at last. " 'Atchets or no 'atchets."

He turned to the man with the blue jersey, when he thought him clear for speech again. " How much did you say they'd given him? " he asked.

" Three munce," said the man in the blue jersey, and refilled anxiously, as if alarmed at the momentary clearness of his voice.

I I

Those three months passed all too quickly—months of sunshine and warmth, of varied novel exertion in the open air, of congenial experiences, of interest and wholesome food and successful digestion; months that browned Mr. Polly and hardened him, and saw the beginnings of his beard; months marred only by one anxiety, an anxiety Mr. Polly did his utmost to suppress. The day of reckoning was never mentioned, it is true, by either the plump woman or himself, but the name of Uncle Jim was written in letters of glaring silence across their intercourse. As the term of that respite drew to an end, his anxiety increased, until at last it trenched upon his well-earned sleep. He had some idea of buying a revolver. He compromised upon a small and very foul and dirty rook rifle, which he purchased in Lammam under a pretext of bird scaring, and loaded carefully and concealed under his bed from the plump woman's eye.

September passed away, October came.

And at last came that night in October whose happenings it is so difficult for a sympathetic historian to drag out of their proper nocturnal indistinctness into the clear, hard light of positive statement. A novelist should present characters, not vivisect them publicly. . . .

The best, the kindliest, if not the justest course, is surely to leave untold such things as Mr. Polly would manifestly have preferred untold.

Mr. Polly has declared that when the cyclist discovered him he was seeking a weapon that should make a conclusive end to Uncle Jim. That declaration is placed before the reader without comment.

The gun was certainly in the possession of Uncle Jim at that time, and no human being but Mr. Polly knows how he got hold of it.

The cyclist was a literary man named Warspite, who suffered from insomnia; he had risen and come out of his house near Lammam just before the dawn, and he discovered Mr. Polly partially concealed in the ditch by the Potwell churchyard wall. It is an ordinary dry ditch full of nettles, and overgrown with elder and dog-rose, and in no way suggestive of an arsenal. It is the last place in which a sensible man would look for a gun. And he says that when he dismounted to see why Mr. Polly was allowing only the latter part of his person to show (and that, it would seem, by inadvertency), Mr. Polly merely raised his head and advised him to " Look out! " and added, " He's let fly at me twice already."

He came out under persuasion, and with gestures of extreme caution. He was wearing a white cotton nightgown of the type that has now been so extensively superseded by pyjama sleeping suits, and his legs and feet were bare, and much scratched and torn, and very muddy.

Mr. Warspite takes that exceptionally lively interest in his fellow-creatures which constitutes so much of the distinctive and complex charm of your novelist all the world over, and he at once involved himself generously in the case. The two men returned at Mr. Polly's initiative across the churchyard to the Potwell Inn, and came upon the burst and damaged rook rifle near the new monument to Sir Samuel Harpon at the corner by the yew.

" That must have been his third go," said Mr. Polly. " It sounded a bit funny."

The sight inspirited him greatly, and he explained further that he had fled to the churchyard on account of the cover afforded by tombstones from the flight of small shot. He expressed anxiety for the fate of the landlady of the Potwell Inn and her grandchild, and led the way with enhanced alacrity along the lane to that establishment.

They found the doors of the house standing open, the bar in some disorder—several bottles of whisky were afterwards found to be missing—and Blake, the village policeman, rapping patiently at the open door. He entered with them. The glass in the bar had suffered severely, and one of the mirrors was starred from a blow from a pewter pot. The till had been forced and ransacked, and so had the bureau in the minute room behind the bar.

An upper window was opened, and the voice of the landlady became audible making inquiries. They went out and parleyed with her. She had locked herself upstairs with the little girl, she said, and refused to descend until she was assured that neither Uncle Jim nor Mr. Polly's gun was anywhere on the premises. Mr. Blake and Mr. Warspite proceeded to satisfy themselves with regard to the former condition, and Mr. Polly went to his room in search of garments more suited to the brightening dawn. He returned immediately with a request that Blake and Mr. Warspite would " just come and look." They found the apartment in a state of extraordinary confusion, the bedclothes in a ball in the corner, the drawers all open, and ransacked, the chair broken, the lock of the door forced and broken, one door panel slightly scorched and perforated by shot, and the window wide open. None of Mr. Polly's clothes were to be seen, but some garments which had apparently once formed part of a stoker's workaday outfit, two brownish-yellow halves of a shirt, and an unsound pair of boots, were scattered on the floor. A faint smell of gunpowder still hung in the air, and two or three books Mr. Polly had recently acquired had been shied with some violence under the bed. Mr. Warspite looked at Mr. Blake, and then both men looked at Mr. Polly. " That's *his* boots," said Mr. Polly.

Blake turned his eyes to the window. " Some of these tiles 'ave just got broken," he observed.

" I got out of the window and slid down the scullery tiles," Mr. Polly answered, omitting much, they both felt, from his explanation. . . .

" Well, we better find 'im and 'ave a word with 'im," said Blake. " That's about my business now."

12

But Uncle Jim had gone altogether. . . .

He did not return for some days. That, perhaps, was not very wonderful. But the days lengthened to weeks, and the weeks to months, and still Uncle Jim did not recur. A year passed, and the anxiety of him became less acute; a second healing year followed the first. One afternoon about thirty months after the Night Surprise the plump woman spoke of him.

" I wonder what's become of Jim," she said.

" *I* wonder sometimes," said Mr. Polly.

CHAPTER TEN

Miriam Revisited

I

ONE summer afternoon, about five years after his first coming to the Potwell Inn, Mr. Polly found himself sitting under the pollard willow, fishing for dace. It was a plumper, browner, and healthier Mr. Polly altogether than the miserable bankrupt with whose dyspeptic portrait our novel opened. He was fat, but with a fatness more generally diffused, and the lower part of his face was touched to gravity by a small, square beard. Also he was balder.

It was the first time he had found leisure to fish, though from the very outset of his Potwell career he had promised himself abundant indulgence in the pleasure of fishing. Fishing, as the golden page of English literature testifies, is a meditative and retrospective pursuit, and the varied page of memory, disregarded so long for sake of the teeming duties I have already enumerated, began to unfold itself to Mr. Polly's consideration. A speculation about Uncle Jim died for want of material, and gave place to a reckoning of the years and months that had passed since his coming to Potwell, and that to a philosophical review of his life. He began to think about Miriam, remotely and impersonally. He remembered many things that had been neglected by his conscience during the busier times, as, for example, that he had committed arson and deserted a wife. For the first time he looked these long-neglected facts in the face.

It is disagreeable to think one has committed arson, because it is an action that leads to jail. Otherwise

I do not think there was a grain of regret for that in Mr. Polly's composition. But deserting Miriam was in a different category. Deserting Miriam was mean.

This is a history, and not a glorification of Mr. Polly, and I tell of things as they were with him. Apart from the disagreeable twinge arising from the thought of what might happen if he was found out, he had not the slightest remorse about that fire. Arson, after all, is an artificial crime. Some crimes are crimes in themselves, would be crimes without any law, the cruelties, mockeries, the breaches of faith that astonish and wound, but the burning of things is in itself neither good nor bad. A large number of houses deserve to be burnt, most modern furniture, an overwhelming majority of pictures and books—one might go on for some time with the list. If our community was collectively anything more than a feeble idiot, it would burn most of London and Chicago, for example, and build sane and beautiful cities in the place of these pestilential heaps of rotten private property. I have failed in presenting Mr. Polly altogether if I have not made you see that he was in many respects an artless child of Nature, far more untrained, undisciplined, and spontaneous, than an ordinary savage. And he was really glad, for all that little drawback of fear, that he had had the courage to set fire to his house, and fly, and come to the Potwell Inn.

But he was not glad he had left Miriam. He had seen Miriam cry once or twice in his life, and it had always reduced him to abject commiseration. He now imagined her crying. He perceived in a perplexed way that he had made himself responsible for her life. He forgot how she had spoiled his own. He had hitherto rested in the faith that she had over a hundred pounds of insurance money, but now, with his eye meditatively upon his float, he realised a hundred pounds does not last for ever. His conviction of her incompetence was unflinching; she was bound to have fooled it away somehow by this time. And then!

He saw her humping her shoulders, and sniffing in a manner he had always regarded as destestable at close quarters, but which now became harrowingly pitiful.

"Damn!" said Mr. Polly, and down went his float, and he flicked a victim to destruction, and took it off the hook.

He compared his own comfort and health with Miriam's imagined distress.

"Ought to have done something for herself," said Mr. Polly, re-baiting his hook. "She was always talking of doing things. Why couldn't she?"

He watched the float oscillating gently towards quiescence.

"Silly to begin thinking about her," he said. "Damn silly!"

But once he had begun thinking about her, he had to go on.

"Oh, blow!" cried Mr. Polly presently, and pulled up his hook, to find another fish had just snatched at it in the last instant. His handling must have made the poor thing feel itself unwelcome.

He gathered his things together and turned towards the house.

All the Potwell Inn betrayed his influence now, for here, indeed, he had found his place in the world. It looked brighter, so bright, indeed, as to be almost skittish, with the white and green paint he had lavished upon it. Even the garden palings were striped white and green, and so were the boats; for Mr. Polly was one of those who find a positive sensuous pleasure in the laying on of paint. Left and right were two large boards, which had done much to enhance the inn's popularity with the lighter-minded variety of pleasure seekers. Both marked innovations. One bore in large letters the single word " Museum," the other was as plain and laconic with " Omlets." The spelling of the latter word was Mr. Polly's own; but when he had seen a whole boat-load of men, intent on Lammam for lunch, stop open-mouthed, and stare, and grin, and come in and ask in a marked sarcastic manner for " omlets," he perceived that his inaccuracy had done more for the place than his utmost cunning could have contrived. In a year or so the inn was known both up and down the river by its new name of " Omlets," and Mr. Polly, after some secret irritation, smiled, and was content. And the fat woman's omelettes were things to remember.

(You will note I have changed her epithet. Time works upon us all.)

She stood upon the steps as he came towards the house, and smiled at him richly.

" Caught many? " she asked.

" Got an idea," said Mr. Polly. " Would it put you out very much if I went off for a day or two for a bit of a holiday? There won't be much doing now until Thursday."

2

Feeling recklessly secure behind his beard, Mr. Polly surveyed the Fishbourne High Street once again. The north side was much as he had known it, except that the name of Rusper had vanished. A row of new shops replaced the destruction of the great fire. Mantell and Throbsons' had risen again upon a more flamboyant pattern, and the new fire station was in the Swiss Teutonic style, with much red paint; next door, in the place of Rumbold's, was a branch of the Colonial Tea Company, and then a Salmon and Gluckstein Tobacco shop, and then a little shop that displayed sweets, and professed a "Tea Room Upstairs." He considered this as a possible place in which to prosecute inquiries about his lost wife, wavering a little between it and the God's Providence Inn down the street. Then his eye caught the name over the window. "Polly," he read, " & Larkins! Well, I'm—astonished!"

A momentary faintness came upon him. He walked past and down the street, returned, and surveyed the shop again.

He saw a middle-aged, rather untidy woman standing behind the counter, who for an instant he thought might be Miriam terribly changed, and then recognised as his sister-in-law Annie, filled out, and no longer hilarious. She stared at him without a sign of recognition as he entered the shop.

"Can I have tea?" said Mr. Polly.

"Well," said Annie, "you *can*. But our Tea Room's upstairs. . . . My sister's been cleaning it out—and it's a bit upset."

"It *would* be," said Mr. Polly softly.

"I beg your pardon," said Annie.

"I said *I* didn't mind. Up here?"

"I dare say there'll be a table," said Annie, and followed him up to a room whose conscientious disorder was intensely reminiscent of Miriam.

"Nothing like turning everything upside down when you're cleaning," said Mr. Polly cheerfully.

"It's my sister's way," said Annie impartially. "She's gone out for a bit of air, but I daresay she'll be back soon to finish. It's a nice light room when it's tidy. Can I put you a table over there?"

"Let *me*," said Mr. Polly, and assisted.

He sat down by the open window and drummed on the table and meditated on his next step, while Annie vanished to get his tea. After all, things didn't seem so bad with Miriam. He tried over several gambits in imagination.

" Unusual name," he said, as Annie laid the cloth before him.

Annie looked interrogation.

" Polly. Polly and Larkins. Real, I suppose? "

" Polly's my sister's name. She married a Mr. Polly."

" Widow, I presume? " said Mr. Polly.

" Yes. This five years—come October."

" Lord! " said Mr. Polly, in unfeigned surprise.

" Found drowned he was. There was a lot of talk in the place."

" Never heard of it," said Mr. Polly. " I'm a stranger—rather."

" In the Medway near Maidstone it was. He must have been in the water for days. Wouldn't have known him, my sister wouldn't, if it hadn't been for the name sewn in his clothes. All whitey and eat away he was."

" Bless my heart! Must have been rather a shock for her."

" It *was* a shock," said Annie, and added darkly, " But sometimes a shock's better than a long agony."

" No doubt," said Mr. Polly.

He gazed with a rapt expression at the preparations before him. " So I'm drowned? " something was saying inside him. " Life insured? " he asked.

" We started the tea-rooms with it," said Annie.

Why, if things were like this, had remorse and anxiety for Miriam been implanted in his soul? No shadow of an answer appeared.

" Marriage is a lottery," said Mr. Polly.

" *She* found it so," said Annie. " Would you like some jam? "

" I'd like an egg," said Mr. Polly. " I'll have two. I've got a sort of feeling—— As though I wanted keeping up. . . . Wasn't particularly good sort, this Mr. Polly? "

"He was a *wearing* husband," said Annie. "I've often pitied my sister. He was one of that sort——"

"Dissolute?" suggested Mr. Polly faintly.

"No," said Annie judiciously, "not exactly dissolute. Feeble's more the word. Weak, 'E was. Weak as water. 'Ow long do you like your eggs boiled?"

"Four minutes exactly," said Mr. Polly.

"One gets talking," said Annie.

"One does," said Mr. Polly, and she left him to his thoughts.

What perplexed him was his recent remorse and tenderness for Miriam. Now he was back in her atmosphere, all that had vanished, and the old feeling of helpless antagonism returned. He surveyed the piled furniture, the economically managed carpet, the un-pleasant pictures on the wall. Why had he felt remorse? Why had he entertained this illusion of a helpless woman crying aloud in the pitiless darkness for him? He peered into the unfathomable mysteries of the heart, and ducked back to a smaller issue. *Was* he feeble? Hang it! He'd known feebler people by far!

The eggs came up. Nothing in Annie's manner invited a resumption of the discussion.

"Business brisk?" he ventured to ask.

Annie reflected. "It is," she said, "and it isn't. It's like that."

"Ah!" said Mr. Polly, and squared himself to his egg. "Was there an inquest on that chap?"

"What chap?"

"What was his name?—Polly!"

"Of course."

"You're sure it was him?"

"What you mean?"

Annie looked at him hard, and suddenly his soul was black with terror.

" Who else could it have been—in the very clo'es 'E wore? "

" Of course," said Mr. Polly, and began his egg. He was so agitated that he only realised its condition when he was half-way through it, and Annie safely downstairs.

" Lord ! " he said, reaching out hastily for the pepper. " One of Miriam's ! Management ! I haven't tasted such an egg for five years. . . . Wonder where she gets them ! Picks them out, I suppose."

He abandoned it for its fellow.

Except for a slight mustiness, the second egg was very palatable indeed. He was getting to the bottom of it as Miriam came in. He looked up. " Nice afternoon," he said, at her stare, and perceived she knew him at once by the gesture and the voice. She went white, and shut the door behind her. She looked as though she was going to faint. Mr. Polly sprang up quickly, and handed her a chair. " My God ! " she whispered, and crumpled up, rather than sat down.

" It's *you*," she said.

" No," said Mr. Polly very earnestly, " it isn't. It just looks like me. That's all."

" I *knew* that man wasn't you—all along. I tried to think it was. I tried to think perhaps the water had altered your wrists and feet, and the colour of your hair."

" Ah ! "

" I'd always feared you'd come back."

Mr. Polly sat down by his egg. " I haven't come back," he said very earnestly. " Don't you think it."

" 'Ow we'll pay back the Insurance now, I *don't* know."

She was weeping. She produced a handkerchief, and covered her face.

" Look here, Miriam," said Mr. Polly. " I haven't come back, and I'm not coming back. I'm—I'm a

Visitant from Another World. You shut up about me, and I'll shut up about myself. I came back because I thought you might he hard up, or in trouble or some silly thing like that. Now I see you again—I'm satisfied. I'm satisfied completely. See? I'm going to absquatulate, see? Hey Presto, right away."

He turned to his tea for a moment, finished his cup noisily, stood up.

" Don't you think you're going to see me again," he said, " for you ain't."

He moved to the door.

" That *was* a tasty egg," he said, hovered for a second, and vanished. . . .

Annie was in the shop.

" The missus has had a bit of a shock," he remarked. " Got some sort of a fancy about a ghost. Can't make it out quite. So long! "

And he had gone.

3

Mr. Polly sat beside the fat woman at one of the little green tables at the back of the Potwell Inn, and struggled with the mystery of life. It was one of those evenings serenely luminous, amply and atmospherically still, when the river bend was at its best. A swan floated against the dark green masses of the farther bank, the stream flowed broad and shining to its destiny, with scarce a ripple—except where the reeds came out from the headland, and the three poplars rose clear and harmonious against the sky of green and yellow. It was as if everything lay securely within a great, warm, friendly globe of crystal sky. It was as safe and enclosed and fearless as a child that has still to be born. It was an evening full of quality of tranquil, unqualified assurance. Mr. Polly's mind was filled with the persuasion that indeed all things whatsoever must needs be satisfying and complete. It was incredible that life had ever done more than seemed to jar, and there could be any shadow in life save such velvet softnesses as made the setting for that silent swan, or any murmur but the ripple of the water as it swirled round the chained and gently swaying punt. And the mind of Mr. Polly, exalted and made tender by this atmosphere, sought gently, but sought, to draw together the varied memories that came drifting, half submerged, across the circle of his mind.

He spoke in words that seemed like a bent and broken stick thrust suddenly into water, destroying the mirror of the shapes they sought. " Jim's not coming back again ever," he said. " He got drowned five years ago."

" Where? " asked the fat woman, surprised.

" Miles from here. In the Medway. Away in Kent."

" Lor! " said the fat woman.

" It's right enough," said Mr. Polly.

" How d'you know? "

" I went to my home."

" Where? "

" Don't matter. I went and found out. He'd been in the water some days. He'd got my clothes, and they'd said it was me."

" They? "

" It don't matter. I'm not going back to them."

The fat woman regarded him silently for some time. Her expression of scrutiny gave way to a quiet satisfaction. Then her brown eyes went to the river.

" Poor Jim," she said. " 'E 'adn't much Tact— ever."

She added mildly, " I can't 'ardly say I'm sorry."

" Nor me," said Mr. Polly, and got a step nearer the thought in him. " But it don't seem much good his having been alive, does it? "

" 'E wasn't much good," the fat woman admitted. " Ever."

" I suppose there were things that were good to him," Mr. Polly speculated. " They weren't *our* things."

His hold slipped again. " I often wonder about life," he said weakly.

He tried again. " One seems to start in life," he said, " expecting something. And it doesn't happen. And it doesn't matter. One starts with ideas that things are good and things are bad—and it hasn't much relation to what *is* good and what *is* bad. I've always been the skeptaceous sort, and it's always seemed rot to me to pretend men know good from evil. It's just what I've *never* done. No Adam's apple stuck in *my* throat, M'am. I don't own to it."

He reflected.

" I set fire to a house—once."

The fat woman started.

" I don't feel sorry for it. I don't believe it was a bad thing to do—any more than burning a toy, like I did once when I was a baby. I nearly killed myself with a razor. Who hasn't?—anyhow gone as far as thinking of it? Most of my time I've been half dreaming. I married like a dream almost. I've never really planned my life, or set out to live. I happened; things happened to me. It's so with every one. Jim couldn't help himself. I shot at him, and tried to kill him. I dropped the gun and he got it. He very nearly had me. I wasn't a second too soon—ducking. . . . Awkward—that night was. . . . M'am. . . . But I don't blame him—come to that. Only I don't see what it's all up to. . . .

" Like children playing about in a nursery. Hurt themselves at times. . . .

" There's something that doesn't mind us," he resumed presently. " It isn't what we try to get that we get, it isn't the good we think we do is good. What makes us happy isn't our trying, what makes others happy isn't our trying. There's a sort of character people like, and stand up for, and a sort they won't. You got to work it out, and take the consequences. . . . Miriam was always trying."

" Who was Miriam? " asked the fat woman.

" No one you know. But she used to go about with her brows knit, trying not to do whatever she wanted to do—if ever she did want to do anything——"

He lost himself.

" You can't help being fat," said the fat woman, after a pause, trying to get up to his thoughts.

" *You* can't," said Mr. Polly.

" It helps, and it hinders."

" Like my upside down way of talking."

" The magistrates wouldn't 'ave kept on the licence to me if I 'adn't been fat. . . ."

" Then what have we done," said Mr. Polly, " to get an evening like this? Lord! Look at it! " He sent his arm round the great curve of the sky.

" If I was a nigger or an Italian I should come out here and sing. I whistle sometimes, but, bless you, it's singing I've got on my mind. Sometimes I think I live for sunsets."

" I don't see that it does you any good always looking at sunsets, like you do," said the fat woman.

" Nor me. But I do. Sunsets and things I was made to like."

" They don't help you," said the fat woman thoughtfully.

" Who cares? " said Mr. Polly.

A deeper strain had come to the fat woman. " You got to die some day," she said.

" Some things I can't believe," said Mr. Polly suddenly, " and one is your being a skeleton. . . ." He pointed his hand towards the neighbour's hedge.

" Look at 'em—against the yellow—and they're just stingin' nettles. Nasty weeds—if you count things by their uses. And no help in the life hereafter. But just look at the look of them! "

" It isn't only looks," said the fat woman.

" Whenever there's signs of a good sunset, and I'm not too busy," said Mr. Polly, " I'll come and sit out here."

The fat woman looked at him with eyes in which contentment struggled with some obscure reluctant protest, and at last turned them slowly to the black nettle pagodas against the golden sky.

" I wish we could," she said.

" I will."

The fat woman's voice sank nearly to the inaudible.

" Not always," she said.

Mr. Polly was some time before he replied. " Come here always, when I'm a ghost," he replied.

" Spoil the place for others," said the fat woman, abandoning her moral solicitudes for a more congenial point of view.

" Not my sort of ghost wouldn't," said Mr. Polly, emerging from another long pause. " I'd be a sort of diaphalous feeling—just mellowish and warmish like. . . ."

They said no more, but sat on in the warm twilight, until at last they could scarcely distinguish each other's faces. They were not so much thinking, as lost in a smooth, still quiet of the mind. A bat flitted by.

" Time we was going in, O' Party," said Mr. Polly, standing up. " Supper to get. It's as you say, we can't sit here for ever."

THE END

BIBLIOGRAPHY

1893   *Text-Book of Biology* (2 vols.).
        Honours Physiography (with R. A. Gregory).
1895   *Select Conversations with an Uncle.*
        The Time Machine.
        The Wonderful Visit.
        The Stolen Bacillus and Other Incidents.
1896   *The Island of Dr. Moreau.*
        The Wheels of Chance.
1897   *The Plattner Story and Others.*
        The Invisible Man.
        Certain Personal Matters.
        Thirty Strange Stories.
1898   *The War of the Worlds.*
1899   *When the Sleeper Awakes.*
        Tales of Space and Time.
1900   *Love and Mr. Lewisham.*
1901   *The First Men in the Moon.*
        Anticipations.
1902   *The Sea Lady.*
1903   *Mankind in the Making.*
        Twelve Stories and a Dream.
1904   *The Food of the Gods.*
1905   *A Modern Utopia.*
        Kipps.
1906   *In the Days of the Comet.*
        The Future in America.
1908   *New Worlds for Old.*
        The War in the Air.
        First and Last Things.
1909   *Tono Bungay.*
        Anne Veronica.
1910   *The History of Mr. Polly.*

1911   *The New Machiavelli.*
    The Country of the Blind, and Other Stories.
    Floor Games.

1912   *The Great State.* (Essays by Wells and 12 others).
    Marriage.

1913   *Little Wars.*
    The Passionate Friends.

1914   *An Englishman Looks at the World.*
    The World Set Free.
    The Wife of Sir Isaac Harman.

1915   *Boon . . . Being a first selection from the literary remains of George Boon . . . with an ambiguous introduction by H. G. Wells.*
    Bealby.
    The Research Mangificent.

1916   *What is Coming?*
    Mr. Britling Sees It Through.

1917   *War and the Future.*
    God the Invisible King.
    The Soul of a Bishop.

1918   *In the Fourth Year.*
    Joan and Peter.

1919   *The Undying Fire.*

1920   *The Outline of History* (2 vols.).
    Russia in the Shadows.

1921   *The Salvaging of Civilization.*

1922   *Washington and the Hope of Peace.*
    The Secret Places of the Heart.
    A Short History of the World.

1923   *Men Like Gods.*
    The Story of a Great Schoolmaster.

1924   *The Dream.*
    A Year of Prophesying.
    Atlantic Edition of the Works of H. G. Wells (28 vols.).

1925   *A Forecast of the World's Affairs.*
    Christina Alberta's Father.

1926 *The World of William Clissold* (3 vols.).
1927 *Meanwhile.*
The Short Stories of H. G. Wells (Benn. Contains a few not previously published).
1928 *The Way the World is Going.*
The Open Conspiracy.
Mr. Blessworthy on Rampole Island.
1929 *The King Who Was a King.*
The Adventures of Tommy.
1930 *The Autocracy of Mr. Parham.*
1931 *What are We to Do With Our Lives* (Revised Edition of The Open Conspiracy).
1932 *The Work, Wealth and Happiness of Mankind.*
1933 *The Shape of Things to Come.*
1934 *Experiment in Autobiography.*
1935 *The New America: the New World.*
Science of Life Series with G. P. Wells and Julian Huxley.
> *Biology of the Human Race.*
> *Drama of Life.*
> *Evolution: Fact and Theory.*
> *History and Advent of Life.*
> *How Animals Behave.*
> *Living Body.*
> *Man's Mind and Behaviour.*
> *Patterns of Life.*
> *Reproduction, Heredity and Development of Sex.*
1936 *The Anatomy of Frustration: a Modern Synthesis.*
The Man who could Work Miracles (Film Story).
1937 *Science of Life.*
1938 *World Brain* (Lectures).
Apropos of Dolores.
The Brothers.
1939 *The Fate of Homo Sapiens.*
Brynhild.
Holy Terror.
1940 *The New World Order.*

All Aboard for Ararat.
Babes in the Darkling Wood.
Film Stories.
Star Begotten.
Common Sense of War and Peace (Penguin Special).

1941   *Guide to the New World.*
A Handbook of Constructive World Revolution.
You Can't Be Too Careful.

1942   *The Conquest of Time* (Written to replace First and Last Things).
The Outlook of Homo Sapiens (Amalgamation and modernization of The Fate of Homo Sapiens, and The New World Order).
Phoenix. A Summary of the inescapable conditions of World Reorganisation.
Science and the World Mind.

1944   *A Contemporary Memoir* (1942-44).

1945   *Mind at the End of its Tether.*
The Happy Turning.

BOOKS ABOUT H. G. WELLS:

The World of H. G. Wells by Van Wyck Brooks.
Supers and Supermen by Philip Guedalla.
H. G. Wells : Educationist by F. H. Doughty.
H. G. Wells : a sketch for a portrait by Geoffrey West.
H. G. Wells : Prophet of Our Day by Antonina Vallentin (1950).
H. G. Wells : a biography by Vincent Brome (1951).
H. G. Wells : by Norman Nicholson (1951).
H. G. Wells and His Family by M. M. Meyer (1956).
Henry James and H. G. Wells by Leon Edel and Gordon N. Ray (1958).